PRAISE FOR THE CRUSH NOVELS

Kirkus 2016 & 2015 Best Mysteries/Thrillers
Milwaukee Journal-Sentinel 10 Best Mysteries of 2016
A *Los Angeles Times* "Summer Reading Page Turner"

"As slick as a switchblade with a pearl handle."
— Lee Child, *New York Times*–bestselling
author of the Jack Reacher novels

"There's magic in this book."
— Carole Barrowman,
Milwaukee Journal-Sentinel

"Studios, please option this immediately. With its nonstop
action, snappy dialogue, and wisecracking characters, this
send-up of Hollywood is a surefire winner."
— Denise Hamilton, bestselling author of the Eve
Diamond crime novels and editor of *Los Angeles Noir*

"Nonstop action and variations on the man-with- a-gun
distraction that go Chandler one better.... Like [Elmore]
Leonard, Sutton writes great dialogue and lavishes almost as
much care and attention on his villains as he does his heroes."
— *Los Angeles Times*

"Don't wait for the movie. Buy the book."
— *Kirkus Reviews* (starred review)

"A swagger of a book."
— *Booklist*

ADVANCE PRAISE

"Welcome to the Pasadena you won't find in the guidebooks as Phoef Sutton puts you in the shotgun seat with the tough and terse Crush in the cold-eyed *Colorado Boulevard*."

— Gary Phillips, editor of *The Obama Inheritance: 15 Stories of Conspiracy Noir*

"Caleb Rush, AKA Crush, has a history riveted with dangerous living: soldier, drifter, bodyguard, recovering alcoholic, and "friend bro" to his hapless stepbrother, K.C. Zerbe. When K.C. is kidnapped, Crush sets off on a madcap ride through Pasadena and environs to rescue him. Car crashes, concussions, nail-biting suspense, and a cast of quirky characters...*Colorado Boulevard* has it all. But it's Crush's humor and humanity that highlight the resilience of the human spirit and make this story soar."

— Patricia Smiley, *Los Angeles Times*– bestselling author of *Pacific Homicide*

"Family saga meets thriller on the streets of Pasadena—*Colorado Boulevard* is the best Crush book yet."

— Naomi Hirahara, Edgar-winning author of the Mas Arai and Ellie Rush mystery series

"Man, these Crush novels just keep getting better and better. Crush is like Jack Reacher with a hair up his ass. And the Los Angeles that Sutton writes about is the secret Los Angeles that nobody knows and everybody wants to know. Sutton answers questions about the city that I didn't even know I had."

— Hart Hanson, author of *The Driver* and creator of *Bones*

COLORADO BOULEVARD

A CRUSH NOVEL

BY PHOEF SUTTON

Also by Phoef Sutton

Heart Attack & Vine
Crush
15 Minutes to Live

with Janet Evanovich

Curious Minds
Wicked Charms

COLORADO BOULEVARD

A CRUSH NOVEL

BY PHOEF SUTTON

Published by Prospect Park Books
2359 Lincoln Avenue
Altadena, California 91001
PROSPECT
·PARK· www.prospectparkbooks.com
BOOKS

Distributed by Consortium Book Sales & Distribution
www.cbsd.com

Library of Congress Cataloging-in-Publication Data is on file with the
Library of Congress. The following is for reference only:

Names: Sutton, Phoef, author.
Title: Colorado boulevard : a Crush novel / by Phoef Sutton.
Description: Altadena : Prospect Park Books, [2017]
Identifiers: ISBN 9781945551147 (hardback) | ISBN 9781945551154
(paperback) | ISBN 9781945551161 (e-book)
Subjects: | GSAFD: Mystery fiction. | Suspense fiction.

Cover design by Howard Grossman
Book layout and design by Amy Inouye
Printed in the United States of America

To my friend Mark Jordan Legan;
remembering The Dew Drop Inn,
endless movie nights, and hard-boiled eggs and nuts

PROLOGUE

JANUARY 1, 2001

The dinosaurs were causing a traffic jam in downtown Pasadena. The Brontosaurus's tail had stopped wagging and the Stegosaurus was blocking the progress of a giant bald eagle flying over an enormous American flag. The 112th Annual Tournament of Roses Parade was not going well.

The White Suits (the old-money Pasadena volunteers who were supposed to keep the street clear and make the parade run on time) were milling about and starting to panic. Fortunately, this was happening far down Colorado Boulevard, near the end of the parade route. If they could get things moving soon they would be saved the embarrassment of a televised delay back by the Norton Simon Museum where Bob Eubanks and Stephanie Edwards hosted the Tournament on KTLA Channel 5 with their usual disdain for each other.

Ray Dorsey, in his white Armani suit and red tie, made his way to the well-hidden back cockpit of the Zerbe Enterprises float named, oddly, The Age of Fossil Fuel. He wanted to see what the holdup was. Inside the rump of the Brontosaurus was a tiny command post where the man in charge of working the tail was seated. That man was actually a seventeen-year-old boy named Caleb Rush, and he was beginning to regret volunteering for Dinosaur Tail-Wagging Duty. As a matter of fact, he was beginning to regret everything he'd done for the last six months.

Sitting on a small plastic chair, encased in a claustrophobic little cell, surrounded by the deafening sounds of twenty-two high school marching bands, Caleb couldn't see anything of the outside world but a tiny patch of pavement beneath the float as it traveled down the street. A line of pink paint marked the middle of the road and was supposed to show him that they were going the right way.

The line of pink was nowhere to be seen.

Tournament rules forbade anything as high-tech as a video feed of the parade inside the float itself, so Caleb had no idea of the ruckus the stalled dinosaurs were causing. He had a radio monitor in his ear, but since they'd made the turn from Orange Grove to Colorado it had been blasting nothing but static, so he'd plucked it out. The instructions he'd been given were pretty simple anyway. Wag the damn Brontosaurus's tail at regular intervals until the float stopped moving.

Caleb had a big, muscular frame and looked much older than his seventeen years, which was why he had been selected for this job. It took strength to keep pulling the lever that operated the huge tail. It was reasoned that he could handle a prehistoric monster's rear end. There were other considerations, of course. Family considerations.

Caleb's mother had recently married the head of the Zerbe family, Emil Zerbe. Caleb thought that Emil giving his new stepson the job of piloting the hind part of the Brontosaurus was either an honor or a humiliation, depending on how one chose to look at it.

Caleb knew how he chose to look at it. Especially since the tail had stopped working halfway down Colorado Boulevard and he knew who would be blamed for this malfunction. Not the designers or the builders of this monstrosity. No, it would go down as pilot error, and Caleb was the pilot.

As it was, he was almost relieved when the bigger fuckup occurred and the float drifted off the pink line and came to a stop far from the parade's finish line. He sat calmly in the cockpit and waited for someone to tell him what had gone wrong.

Instead he heard a hammering on the hatch and someone on the street asking him what the hell was going on, as if he knew anything about it. He raised the hatch (a definite breach of parade protocol) partly to talk with the White Suit who was bothering him and partly because the claustrophobia was beginning to get to him. He had been trapped inside that dinosaur for the better part of an hour and a half.

"What's going on?" the White Suit asked him. Caleb recognized him as Mr. Dorsey, the vice principal of his school. This New Year's Day was getting more nightmarish by the minute.

"How should I know?" Caleb asked. "I just run the tail."

"Well, where's the goddamned driver?" Dorsey asked.

"At the base of the volcano." To show him, Caleb climbed out of the dinosaur's ass, which was an absolute violation of all that the Rose Parade held holy. No one was allowed to emerge from the floats except in a dire emergency. Caleb didn't know if this was dire, but as he looked back at all the floats bottling up behind them (the spaceships and Tom Sawyers and cute enormous panda bears), he guessed this at least qualified as an emergency.

Looking at The Age of Fossil Fuel float, Caleb saw that it had driven partway onto the curb, forcing the onlookers to the sides and driving the head of the Brontosaurus inappropriately close to the window of the last remaining adult bookstore in Old Town Pasadena. It seemed to leer at a mannequin dressed in a lacy bra and panties.

Caleb led Dorsey up around to the front of the daisy-and-marigold-covered volcano, which spewed smoke out of the crater on top. He hesitated before tapping on the well-camouflaged hatchway, and speaking to the driver, Victor Zerbe. Victor was Emil Zerbe's brother and his partner in industry and, in general, tearing this city down and building it back up again.

"Mr. Zerbe? Is something wrong?" Caleb asked. He couldn't quite bring himself to call the man Uncle Victor, not after four short months of being his stepnephew. There was no answer from the volcano, so Caleb rapped harder and called louder. Finally, he lifted the hatch and looked inside. Victor sat there, head tilted back, staring blankly. And not blinking. Or breathing. With a little red hole in the middle of his forehead.

Dorsey crowded against Caleb, trying to see in. "What's wrong with him?" he asked.

"I think he's dead," Caleb said.

Dorsey was silent for a moment. Then his true White Suit-ness came to the fore. "Well, can you get in there and drive the float?"

The parade must go on, after all.

CHAPTER ONE

DECEMBER 30, 2017

K.C. Zerbe opened his eyes and saw the barrel of a gun pointed at his face. "Move and I'll kill you," whispered a hoarse voice.

In a skittering heartbeat Zerbe was awake, alert and terrified.

"Do you understand?" the man with the gun said.

Zerbe nodded mechanically. He understood. The years he spent in prison had taught him to be agreeable to men who woke him up holding weapons.

Over the gunman's shoulder Zerbe could see through the picture windows. It was dark and Christmas lights were flickering through the glass. He must have fallen asleep on the sofa. It must be somewhere between one and three o'clock in the morning but he didn't have the nerve to shift his eyes to the clock and make sure. He just kept looking down, submissively. He knew not to look his assailant in the eyes. Not to challenge him. Better to do exactly as he was told.

Then another voice commanded, "Get up." Zerbe turned his head and saw another man in a ski mask holding another gun.

Zerbe hesitated, his heart pounding in his chest. "Okay," he said, hoping he didn't sound like a smart-ass, "I need you to clarify something for me. If I get up I'll have to move, but if I move he says he'll kill me. Which do you want me to do?" No doubt about it, he sounded like a smart-ass. His smart-ass-ness always got him into trouble.

The first gunman kicked Zerbe in the stomach. The impact of the blow to his gut, the rush of air out of his lungs, and the taste of bile in his mouth were all familiar to him, and he felt something like nostalgia flow over him. The nights of prison beatings came back to him and he felt that the two years of relative freedom he'd enjoyed had been just a dream. This was reality. Being beaten and pissed on in a prison cot. This was real life.

"Get up!" the second gunman said. Zerbe tried to suppress his panic, but that only made the adrenaline rush stronger. He was a thirty-two-year-old ex-convict who'd never harmed anyone. What could these men want from him?

"Where are you taking me?" Zerbe asked.

"Out."

"You can't."

The second gunman slapped Zerbe in the face. He was short and round. The first gunman was tall and thin. They were like a brutal Bert and Ernie, Zerbe thought. *Why did he always think things like that at times like this?* he wondered.

"Really, I can't," Zerbe said. "Look." He pulled the right leg of his sweatpants up to reveal the plastic electronic device strapped to his ankle. "That's an ankle monitor. I'm on probation. House arrest, you know? If I leave, they'll know."

The shorter man, whom Zerbe named "Ernie" in his mind, hauled him roughly to his feet and said, "Let's go."

"No, really," Zerbe protested. "If I leave I'll be violating probation. They'll send me back to prison."

"Do we sound like we care?"

"What do you want with me?" Zerbe knew he should shut up. He knew it, but he couldn't. That was his curse. "Do you want a ransom? You won't get anything. My folks have cut me off."

Ernie slapped Zerbe again, harder this time. "Move!" He shoved Zerbe, who took a stumbling step toward the door. They were on the twelfth floor of the American Cement Building on Wilshire Boulevard, with floor-to-ceiling windows overlooking MacArthur Park and the Los Angeles skyline. How the hell did these thugs get in here?

"I need to put on some shoes," Zerbe said, knowing that he was stalling, just trying to put some time between now and the great unknown outside world. He'd dreamed of walking out of here many times over the past two years, but in his dreams he'd always walked into the elevator and onto the street of his own volition. *His own volition.* The phrase struck him as odd and he almost laughed. Could he leave by someone else's volition? Wasn't that the definition of kidnapping?

"What are you laughing at?" It was "Bert" who asked this, and Zerbe detected some fear in the man's voice. A lack of confidence. That worried Zerbe. He wanted his kidnappers to have the assurance of professionals. Better to be in the hands of competent, experienced hoodlums than bumbling amateurs.

"Get your shoes," Ernie said, as if to cover his friend's mistake.

Zerbe slipped into his Merrell Chameleons. He took his time tying the laces and stood up, adjusting his T-shirt with the Captain America shield on it, sneaking a glance at the clock. It was 4:11 in the morning. His stepbrother should be home by now. Or had these gunmen taken care of him down in the garage? Zerbe doubted that. His brother could take care of himself. They didn't call him Crush for nothing.

Ernie pulled him up again. "Come on, are we gonna do this or not?" Zerbe thought it was odd that the hoodlum was asking him, but the time for delaying the inevitable was past.

"Where are you taking me?" Zerbe asked.

"Move or I'll put a bullet in your brain."

That remark was a little melodramatic, but it got Zerbe's attention. He moved past the shiny silver Christmas tree, stepped over the discarded, crinkled wrapping paper, and made his way to the loft's big metal front door. It stood open. Bert and Ernie had let themselves in. They must have had a key to the place, Zerbe realized. How in the hell had they gotten a key? Was this an inside job? It had taken real planning on someone's part. Zerbe's panic grew.

He walked to the door and out into the hall. Zerbe hadn't been out in the hall for over a year. When his probation began, when they attached the monitor to his ankle and left him here at his brother's place, he was overjoyed. As Zerbe often said, not being in prison is something you really don't appreciate until you've been in prison. Even on your worst day, when you have a disgusting stomach virus, when your best friends are annoying the hell out of you, and your future seems bleaker than bleak, you can think to yourself, *At least I'm not still in prison*, and things don't seem so bad.

In those first heady months he had often tried to see what the limits of his freedom were, how far he could go until his ankle monitor told him to stop. And it did speak to him, in an electronic voice, like a computer-taking-over-the-world from a sixties' sci-fi movie. The voice told him when he was moving outside his "home zone." It told him when he needed to plug it in and charge it up. It told him when he had to call in and check with his probation officer. Even with its limited vocabulary, the voice had become one of his closest friends.

With the ankle monitor as his guide, he had discovered how far he could go in his house arrest. And the limit of the electronic leash wasn't the door to his brother's loft. No, it was in the hallway, just by the elevator. So he could stand next to the gateway to the outer world and watch people come and go. He was like Moses, he sometimes thought. He could see the Promised Elevator, but he could not enter it.

After about six months, he stopped going out into the hall. His brother's loft, which at first had felt so spacious, had shrunk down from its actual size of two thousand square feet, which was a hell of a lot larger than his cell in Lancaster State Prison but a hell of a lot smaller than the whole wide world. The world he could see through the big windows of his brother's loft. The world he could not enter for almost another year.

And as time passed, the loft got smaller and smaller, so to stand by the elevator seemed less like freedom and more like torment. So he passed his sentence locked behind the safety of his brother's metal door and waited it out.

Until now, when Zerbe was again thrust out into the whitewashed industrial hallway. The building looked deliberately unfinished, in order to appeal to the hipster urban dwellers who shunned the idea of living in an "apartment" for "rent" and craved the "loft" experience. Out here Zerbe felt vulnerable and exposed and he longed for the walls of the loft, like a tortoise ripped from its cozy shell.

Bert pressed the button for the elevator while Ernie thrust his gun barrel into Zerbe's ribs. "Don't even think about yelling for help," he said.

"Why are you doing this?" Zerbe whispered. "Is someone paying you?"

"Shut up," Ernie said, and Zerbe got the feeling he was

talking to both of them.

"If it's money you want," Zerbe said, "you can have it. I have money. How much is he paying you?"

"Enough," Ernie hissed and gave Zerbe a shove.

As he stumbled toward the elevator doors, the computerized voice spoke up from Zerbe's ankle. "You are moving outside your home zone."

"What the hell is that?" Ernie asked.

"I told you," Zerbe said. "It's my monitor."

"Well, shut it up."

"I can't. Please, don't make me go out there."

As he said this, Zerbe wasn't sure if it was fear of what they were going to do to him, fear of breaking probation, or simply fear of going out into the world that scared him more.

"You are moving outside your home zone," the monitor repeated. It would not be denied.

"Shut that thing the fuck up!" Bert said.

"I tell you, I can't," Zerbe said.

"Does it have a GPS monitor?" Ernie asked, sounding worried. "Can it tell where you are?"

"Yes!" Zerbe seized at this way out. "So there's no point in kidnapping me. They'll find me in no time. They'll catch you."

Ernie thought for a moment. "Take it off," he said.

"I can't. It has fiber optics. It can tell if it gets cut off. It sends an alarm."

"How long have you had to wear that?"

"Two years."

"You have to take it off. Do it. Now."

"Listen to me. On my mother's grave, I swear, I can't. I don't know how to take it off."

Zerbe's mother was alive and he knew how to take the device off.

⌘

Crush, the man whom Zerbe called his brother, was taking the twelve flights of stairs up to the loft because if there was a hard way of doing something, Crush would do it.

"Showing off for me?" Catherine Gail asked with a sly smile.

"Nope," Crush said as he bounded up the stairs. "But you can take the elevator if you'd like."

"No way," she said, keeping right up with him. "The student will not outpace the teacher."

Taking this many stairs after a long day's work might have been too much for most people, but Crush and Gail prided themselves on their stamina and physical conditioning. It wasn't easy for them. They were both recovering from serious injuries, so they had a lot to prove, if not to each other, at least to themselves. She had been beaten nearly to death by Russian mobsters two years earlier; last February Crush had been shot in the stomach by an aging movie director. Trouble seemed to follow them like an old friend. Or maybe a stalker.

Gail was a lithe and lovely forty. Her raven-black hair had a shock of white running through it, just like Lily Munster, as Zerbe used to say. She was Crush's tae kwon do master. At the moment she was without a dojo to teach in or a home to rest her head. The landlord of her downtown storefront school had decided he could make a bigger profit from selling the building to a developer than renting it. This was the inevitable result of DTLA revitalization, Zerbe said. The residents were getting thrown out and the millennials were moving in.

Crush said she could stay with him for the time being. Nobody was surprised. They not only worked out together in the dojo, they worked together in a nightclub, the Nocturne, where Gail was the bartender and Crush was the bouncer. This was that odd time between Christmas and New Year's, that week of extended holiday that never seems real and that is best forgotten in the coming year. Christmas was five days ago, but the Nocturne was still open long hours, and the clientele still acted as though what happened this week, stayed in this week.

Crush and Gail spent so much time together that many people assumed that they were a couple and that living together was the natural next step. The fact that they weren't lovers, despite being two reasonably attractive people of the opposite sex, was something most people just couldn't accept. For them it was natural. It wasn't that Gail didn't find Crush appealing. It wasn't that Crush didn't think Gail was beautiful. It wasn't even that their roles as student and master made it inappropriate. Gail, the more spiritual of the two, said it was because they had been brother and sister in an earlier life. Crush, the earthier of the two, said it was because they knew each other too well to allow sex to complicate things.

Crush wasn't his real name, of course. It was just his street name. He was born Caleb Rush, and the fact that he had a different last name than Zerbe was just one reason Crush objected to being called his brother.

Crush and Zerbe were roughly the same age, both of them in their early thirties, but there the resemblance ended. Zerbe was a doughy computer nerd of average height; Crush topped out at six-foot-five and was 230 pounds of pure muscle. His head was shaved bald, and an old scar ran from his left eye across his face, like an angry exclamation mark. Zerbe's head was covered with a wild mop of curly hair that always made him look like he had just gotten out of bed.

Gail was, to her surprise, having trouble keeping up with Crush. "In a hurry, Grasshopper?" she asked him. She hadn't actually ever seen the TV show *Kung Fu*, but Zerbe had told her about it. Zerbe was their curator of popular culture.

"Not really," Crush said. "I just don't like leaving Zerbe alone any more than necessary these days. He's getting weird."

"Weirder than usual?"

"It's hard to explain."

The whole relationship between Crush and Zerbe was hard to explain. Zerbe came from an old-money Pasadena family. Crush came from Brooklyn, by way of the Russian mob. Their families had intersected briefly when Zerbe's father married Crush's mother. It had been a short, eventful, and horrendous relationship that had occurred when Zerbe and Crush were both in their teens. It hadn't made them friends exactly, but it had made them allies.

If there had been an informal poll among their acquaintances at Pasadena Prep as to which one of them would be sent to prison, Crush would have won hands down. Instead it was Zerbe who was locked up and Crush who got a Purple Heart in Iraq. When Zerbe got the opportunity to finish his prison sentence under house arrest, he agreed to it on the condition that he live with his "brother," the decorated war hero Caleb Rush, rather than with his mother or father. The state, in a hurry to make room for more dangerous criminals than Zerbe, agreed.

So they lived together. Crush liked having Zerbe there. It was nice to know someone was always looking after the place during his frequent absences. Zerbe liked living vicariously through Crush's unorthodox life. It was nice for both of them to have company. It was a win-win situation.

But lately Zerbe had been moody and depressed. He

hadn't showered or changed his clothes for days now and, what was more alarming, Zerbe's frequent masturbation rate had dipped drastically.

"Are you losing interesting in yourself?" Crush asked him last night.

Zerbe shrugged. "It just doesn't seem worth the trouble."

This made Crush really concerned. Zerbe had only eight months to go on his sentence, and Crush prayed he could do the time and stay relatively sane. Sane for Zerbe, anyway.

Crush passed the eleventh floor and put on a burst of speed. Gail kept up right beside him. Competition was part of their relationship. Crush smiled as he reached the twelfth floor and pushed open the door to the hallway.

To his surprise, he saw Zerbe stepping into the elevator with a man standing close to him and another, taller man behind them, as if standing guard.

Most people would have been puzzled. Most people would have paused to react. Most people would have taken the time to figure out what was going on. But not Crush. By the time the doors had started to close Crush had stepped forward, grabbed the tall guard by the shoulder and yanked him from the elevator, throwing him back against the wall. Sensing the movement, the doors slid open again and Zerbe almost broke loose. The shorter man seized Zerbe by the throat and pulled him back.

Crush blocked the door with his foot. "What the hell's going on?" he asked.

Zerbe croaked an unintelligible reply. The short man used Zerbe as a shield and pointed a gun at Crush. "Don't," he said.

Meanwhile, the tall guard had pushed away from the wall and tried to run past Crush into the elevator. Crush blocked his way and shoved him off, but the man was clutching at

Crush's arm, pulling him off balance.

Zerbe broke free, stumbled out of the elevator, and fell against the wall. By then, Gail was in the hallway, throwing herself at the shorter man, who brandished a gun. He didn't fire it, rather, he swung it at her jaw. She arched her back and the pistol sailed past it. She brought her knee up to her chest and kicked out, the ball of her foot colliding with his chin.

The short man fell backward and Crush was on him, driving his fist toward the man's face, knuckles crunching his cheekbone and propelling him to the ground, like a hammer pounding in a nail.

The tall man grabbed Zerbe and dragged him into the elevator. The doors were closing. Crush dove for them but they slid shut before he could reach them. Gail hit the button but the elevator had already started its descent.

Crush ran for the stairs. Could he outrun the elevator? Maybe, if it stopped on one of the other floors. But at four o'clock in the morning? Not likely.

"Shit!" he said, slamming his fist into the door.

"What's going on?" Gail asked.

Crush tromped toward the short man who lay crumpled on the floor. "Let's find out," he said, reaching down and dragging the man by his arm into the loft. Crush flung him against the sofa.

The short man bounded up and ran. Crush's big body was blocking the exit, so the only place he could run was into the bedroom. A dead end with no way out. He slammed the door, but that wouldn't do him any good. The short man was trapped in there.

Something on the sofa caught Crush's eye. He reached for it and picked it up.

"Is that what I think it is?" Gail asked.

"Zerbe's ankle monitor."

"Why's it so shiny?"

"It's covered with this," he said, pointing to an open bottle on the coffee table. One hundred percent virgin olive oil.

"He slid it off?"

"I guess."

"Is it still working?" Gail asked.

"Oh, yeah," Crush said, observing the steady blue light on the monitor. "And it doesn't know he's gone."

"We better call the police," she said.

"Wait." He crossed to the bedroom door. "Let's get some answers first." Crush flung open the door. The short man was cowering in the corner, breathing heavily through his ski mask. Crush grabbed him and threw him to the floor. Grabbing a Christmas garland that was hanging over his bed, Crush wrapped it around the man's throat, choking him. "Where is he going?" Crush asked. "Where's your friend taking him?"

The man's answer was muffled by the ski mask. Crush yanked it off his head. He was just a kid. Asian, hair dyed blond with blue highlights. He couldn't have been more that twenty-two.

"Who sent you here?" Crush asked. "Who hired you to do this?"

"Him!"

"Who do you mean?"

"The guy we kidnapped. He hired us! He hired us to kidnap him!"

CHAPTER TWO

Crush was kneeling on the gunman's chest, putting his full 230 pounds on him. "What are you talking about?"

"He did! I swear!"

Gail entered the bedroom, tossing the ankle monitor on the bed. "Did he?" she asked.

"What are you asking?"

"Maybe he did this," Gail said. "Maybe he got bored. Maybe he thought he could get outside this way and the court wouldn't blame him."

Crush was silent for moment. "You know, that's not a bad idea. I never thought of that."

"He has a lot of time to think of things."

Crush shook his head. "Even if he had, he wouldn't have done this. He'd have to be crazy."

"He's done some pretty crazy things."

"Like what?"

"How 'bout the time he ordered the one-legged stripper to come and sing 'Happy Birthday' to you. And it wasn't even your birthday."

Crush looked down at the frightened kidnapper. "What's your name?"

"I can't breathe," he said.

Crush put more weight onto his chest. "Your name!"

"Donny," the man cried.

"Okay, Donny," Crush lifted his knee from Donny's sternum and unwrapped the garland from around his throat. "Tell me more."

"We were just doing what he told us! He said to break in at four in the morning. He asked us to deliver him to a warehouse in Irwindale. He told us not to be afraid to threaten him and rough him up. We figured it was some kind of sex game."

"A sex game?" Crush asked.

Donny shrugged. "It takes all kinds. I don't judge."

"How did he contact you? Through the internet?"

"No. We met at a bar."

"A bar? What bar?"

"The Abbey, okay?"

Crush knew The Abbey, on Robertson Boulevard in West Hollywood. It was one of the most famous gay bars in the country. A nice place. Crush subbed for the bouncer sometimes. "When was this?" he asked.

"Last night," Donny said. "He was sitting at the bar. He said he'd give us a thousand dollars to kidnap him. Said it was a game. He even gave us the key and a pass card to get in the building."

Crush and Gail exchanged a look. Zerbe hadn't been out in public for four years.

"Fuck me," Gail said.

"Noel," Crush said.

Donny took advantage of their momentary distraction to crawl in the direction of the door. Crush put his big hand on Donny's shoulder. "Stay," Crush said. "Hand over the key. And the pass card."

Donny searched frantically through his pockets and

dropped the key and the pass card into Crush's palm.

"He gave us the gun, too," Donny said. "It isn't loaded. He just told us to make it seem really real. To scare the hell out of him. I should have figured it was a trap. That he'd get off on seeing you beat the crap out of us."

"I didn't beat the crap out of you," Crush said. "When I beat the crap out of you, you'll know it."

Donny's eyes grew wider. "Okay."

"Did he pay you in advance?"

"Half. The other half when we delivered him."

"Let that be a lesson to you. Always get the money up front." Crush stood up. "Come on."

"Where are we going?" Donny asked, trembling.

"Irwindale." Crush grasped Donny by the arm and started pulling him to the door. He stopped to pluck the ankle monitor off the bed. "Take this," he said, handing it to Gail. "Walk it around."

"Why?" she asked.

"Make it look like he's still here."

"You don't want me to call the cops?"

Crush shook his head. "I'll bring him back. Donny had Zerbe's keys. What if he *was* in on this? What if he's violated his probation? He'll go back to prison."

"Noel's the crazy one."

"Noel may be crazy, but he's still Zerbe's brother. What if they cooked this up together?"

"I don't like this."

"Look, if you don't hear from me by eight o'clock, you can call the police."

"And tell them what?" Gail asked.

"That's up to you."

⌘

Crush floored his 1967 Chevrolet Camaro ZL1 down Rampart to the 101. He figured it should take about a half-hour to get to Irwindale at this time of night. Zerbe and his abductor had about a fifteen-minute head start on him. But then, they were probably stopping at red lights. Crush wasn't doing that. He would catch up with them.

While he sped through the darkened city streets, he thought about Noel Zerbe. Noel was K.C. Zerbe's twin brother. Born five minutes before Zerbe, he always looked to the future. Though the twins were identical in appearance, they took very different paths in life. Zerbe was the practical one, the one who went to Harvard Business School, the one who made a fortune on Wall Street before he was thirty. The one who went to prison.

Noel was the artistic one. He went to Rhode Island School of Design, majoring in scenography. He graduated and went on to design Las Vegas shows for the likes of Céline Dion and Cirque du Soleil. He did the sets for numerous Broadway productions, including the wildly successful revival of *A Little Night Music*, for which he became the youngest winner of a Tony for Scenic Design.

The only prison Noel went to was a metaphorical one.

Noel was described by those who liked him as bipolar. He was described by those who didn't like him as bat-shit crazy. The bat-shit crazy ones far outnumbered the bipolar ones.

K.C. and Noel made quite a pair in their high school days. Identical twins, one who dressed like Jerry Maguire and the other who dressed like Neo in *The Matrix*. They had different friends and different goals. And they had a very different relationship with their new stepbrother, Caleb Rush. To Zerbe, he was an ally. To Noel, he was a rival.

But why would Noel have his brother abducted? It didn't

make any sense. Crush thought of calling him on his cell phone and demanding to know what the hell was going on, but then he remembered that Noel didn't own a cell phone. According to Noel, they caused brain cancer and, more to the point, they let them track you. Who was "them?" According to Noel, "they" were everyone from the government to the Russians to aliens to the lizard people who secretly ruled the world. Noel's paranoia was inclusive.

"Where in Irwindale?" Crush asked Donny.

"What?"

"Where were you supposed to deliver him?"

"Oh, I don't know."

"Don't make me mad."

"Really, Jack had the address. He was the one in charge. I was just going along with it. I always go along with him. He always gets me in trouble. This is the last time, I'm telling you."

Crush thought. Where would Noel be in Irwindale? Where would anyone be in Irwindale?

"Cool car," Donny said.

"What?"

"This is a cool car."

"It is," Crush agreed, heading down the 101 to the 10.

"You fixed it up yourself?" Donny asked.

"Why are you asking that? What are you doing? Are you trying to bond with me?"

"That's what you're supposed to do, isn't it? When you're abducted?"

"You haven't been abducted. You were the one doing the abducting."

"Was," Donny said. "I was abducting. Now I'm abducted."

Crush shrugged. He could see the man's point. You never know when you get up in the morning how the day's going to end.

"So where are you from?" Donny went on.

"This isn't going to work."

"I'm from Long Beach."

"Shut up."

"Where'd you go to school?"

Crush turned on the radio. Tory Lanez sang "Luv." Crush hated that song. He turned it up louder. Donny was still talking, but Crush wasn't listening. He was thinking about where he was from, damn it.

⌘

In Brooklyn, on a bright spring morning near the end of the last century, Crush and a woman stole a car and started driving as far west as they could go. He targeted a 1990 Nissan 300ZX that he'd seen parked along Second Street Park in Brighton Beach for a few days. He picked it partly because he thought it had already been stolen and dumped there, so it would be harder to trace to them, but mainly because he had always wanted to drive cool cars. Crush was only fifteen and he didn't have a driver's license, but he'd already done a lot of driving and he was in kind of a hurry to get away.

Blaz Kusinko, kingpin of the Russian mob on Ocean Parkway, would be waking up soon and he would be looking for them. Toni, the woman with Crush, had been one of Kusinko's "wives" until he grew tired of her, beat her up, and threw her out onto the street.

Crush was one of Kusinko's many sons and in spite of his treatment of Toni, Blaz expected Crush to retain allegiance to the mob and to Kusinko himself. After all, Crush was advanced for his age, both in size and in intellect, and Kusinko already had plans for him in the Organization. Not just as a driver but as a soldier and an enforcer. Kusinko was a powerful man and Toni was just one of his whores. Crush would be smart enough to know where his better interests lay.

Unfortunately for Kusinko, Crush didn't see it that way. Toni, the woman Kusinko had left in the gutter, was also Crush's mother. As a teenage runaway, Toni had been adopted by various members of the Russian mob until she was finally claimed by Kusinko as his own. And, as far as Kusinko was concerned, he could do whatever he wished with those who belonged to him.

Crush didn't agree. And when Crush found his mother discarded like so much trash in the alley behind Kusinko's house, he decided it was time to make his feelings known. With a baseball bat.

By the time Kusinko's bodyguard burst in and pulled Crush off him, the mobster was a bloody mess, but he was still breathing. Crush didn't much like being interrupted, so he pounded a few line drives off the bodyguard's head before he fled the scene.

Then Crush and his mother drove away, as far and fast as they could. They stopped in Philadelphia, where Crush stole another car, then they kept on driving. They did this, hopscotching across the country, doing odd jobs and getting enough money to keep moving, all that summer. They reached Los Angeles in the blazing hot autumn that only Angelenos know. They couldn't go any farther west, so they got a fleabag apartment in Koreatown and settled down. Crush was still underage but he didn't look it, so he got jobs bagging groceries, doing construction, gardening, anything that didn't require any paperwork.

Toni did other kinds of jobs. She was somewhere in her thirties, but she still looked twenty-five and with her dyed-blond locks and the wild look in her eye, she was appealing to the kind of man who liked to live dangerously.

Crush never knew what her jobs were. He didn't want to know. She was the "girlfriend" of quite a few men who gave her gifts and paid their rent. She liked to go to fancy restaurants and buy nice clothes when times were good. When times were bad, she took that in stride and did just what was necessary.

If Crush learned one lesson from his mother, it was this: never expect a run of luck to last.

During one of those bad-luck periods, Toni ended up working as a stripper in a club in the Valley called Menage. Crush was seventeen by then, a high-school dropout, and she got him a job as the doorman there. Of course, he was still too young to be legal, but with his straggly black beard and already-receding hairline, he looked at least five years older. The managers were too busy making sure their strippers weren't jailbait to worry about whether or not their bouncer was old enough to vote.

Toni was a bit more mature than most of the other girls there, so she became the den mother, giving them advice, telling them how to make the best profits in the VIP room by giving the customers just enough to keep them coming back for more, but not so much that they felt satisfied.

Then one day Emil Zerbe walked into the club and Toni's and Crush's lives took another turn. That was another thing Crush's mother taught him: there is nothing as consistent in this life as inconsistency.

⌘

"What kind of music do you like?" Zerbe asked.

Zerbe was bonding with his abductor. For instance, he had learned that his name was Jack, though he couldn't help but think of him as "Bert." And when Jack had taken his ski mask off, Zerbe had seen that he was a pleasant-looking young Filipino kid with a buzz cut at his temples and longish hair on the top of his head, flopping down over his eyes. A very likable young man, all things considered.

"I like all kinds," Jack said. "Except country music. Can't stand that shit."

"I hear you. But have you ever listened to Johnny Cash? Or Merle Haggard? Or Hank Williams? They'll change your mind, man. They're the greatest."

"I'll have to give them a try."

Zerbe had a shoe in his hand, his right leg was still glistening with olive oil and his foot was still raw and scraped. Getting the ankle monitor off hadn't been easy.

Jack turned his Nissan Versa into an industrial area full of warehouses and anonymous offices. He pulled up to the elephant doors of a large warehouse and stopped, the motor still running. The big doors were open but only slightly.

"Get out," Jack said.

Zerbe looked around. There was no one in sight. Nothing but the dark parking lot, the dark warehouse, and its darker interior. "There's nobody here," Zerbe said.

"Not my problem. Get out."

"You kidnap me and then you just let me go? In Irwindale? That doesn't make sense."

"I don't care if it makes sense. He'll probably be here soon."

"Probably? Who will?"

"Whoever you're meeting here."

Zerbe shook his head. "This doesn't make sense."

"You said that. It doesn't." Jack gripped the wheel. "I want to get paid."

"I'm sure you do."

"No. I want to get paid now. This is weird and I want to get paid."

"Take it up with whoever hired you."

"Cut it out."

"I want the five hundred dollars. Now."

"You want me to pay you? For kidnapping me?"

"That's right."

Zerbe stared at him. "Who hired you?"

"Stop it. You did, man. You know that."

Zerbe blinked a few times. "Oh, fuck me."

"Now give me the goddamned money."

"Take me back home."

"Fuck that. Give me the goddamned money or I'll leave you here."

"Isn't that what I paid you to do?"

"Damn straight."

"How much did I pay you?"

"You fucking know how much you paid me."

"I don't. 'Cause it wasn't me. How much did the other me pay you?"

"Are you crazy?"

"Yes, I'm crazy. How much?"

Jack paused, then said, "Fifteen hundred." Jack had been paid a thousand for this job, but he figured he'd pad it. "To drop you off here and let somebody pick you up."

"Who?"

"I don't know."

"Fine. I'll pay you twice that to take me back home. That's three thousand, if you can't do the math."

"Do you have it?"

"Sure."

"I mean do you have it on you?"

"Of course not."

"Then get out. Leave. This whole thing is more trouble than it's worth. I should never have let Donny talk me into this. He's always talking me into crazy things."

"I don't want to get between you and Donny...."

Jack pointed his gun at Zerbe. "Get out."

"I don't think that gun is even loaded," Zerbe said.

"Are you sure?"

Swearing under his breath, Zerbe opened the door and got out of the Nissan just before it screeched out of the parking lot, leaving rubber on the asphalt.

Zerbe stood alone under the night sky of Irwindale, thinking this was partly good and partly bad. He was free. He was outdoors. He was at large. That was the good thing. But he was at large in violation of his probation. If they caught him he'd get sent back to prison. That was the bad thing. And the story he'd have to tell his probation officer (that he'd been kidnapped by people who thought he paid them to do it) was suspect, at best.

But his ankle monitor was back at the loft, still registering his presence. If he could get back to it, without anyone knowing any of this, all would be well.

Now, how to cross the twenty-five miles to home without being seen? If he had his cell phone he could call Crush. But his cell phone was sitting back on the coffee table in the loft. So he had to get to a landline to call Crush. That was the only option. Other than walking home.

He sat down to put his shoe on and a car's headlights washed over him. It drove on by, but it made him feel vulnerable. What if it was a cop or a night watchman? What excuse could he give for being here? He looked over to the elephant doors in front of him. Darkness seemed to flow out from the opening, like dirty water from a hose. Inside, there might be a phone. And inside he wouldn't be so visible to passing watchmen.

Getting up to his feet, Zerbe crossed to the dark void. He stepped over the threshold and stood still, waiting for his pupils to dilate so that he could see. It took a long time, and when they did he thought he was going mad.

The warehouse was filled with dragons. And spaceships. And dinosaurs.

They stared down at him from platforms, atop giant wheeled vehicles. He blinked. He could just make out a sign, high up on the wall, and he knew where he was. Carnivàle Parade Floats. Jesus. His fucking brother.

"Noel!" he called out. "Where are you?"

His voice echoed through the black emptiness of the warehouse. No answer.

His brother Noel had been designing floats and driving for the Rose Parade in Pasadena since he got out of college. It wasn't his most lucrative job, but it was the one in which he took the most pride. Sitting in the living room of their mansion on the Arroyo Seco in Pasadena every New Year's, his father beamed with happiness as Noel piloted one of his great flowered creations down Colorado Boulevard, broadcast to the whole world in that mad orgy of Middle American floral celebration that was the Tournament of Roses Parade. It was rather unusual for a designer to also be the driver of a float, but Noel was a most unusual man. He felt that, as the designer, he knew how the float should roll down the parade route. Besides, it was a tradition for a member of the Zerbe family to drive their company's floral monstrosity and had been for many years. Tragedy and bloodshed notwithstanding.

So when Noel's float took home the Grand Marshal's Trophy, as it inevitably did every year, his father reacted with more delight than when he had won that Tony Award.

Certainly with more delight than for anything that K.C. Zerbe had ever done. For longtime residents of Pasadena, first prize in the parade was more important than the Oscars or Emmys or the Nobel Prize. It was the ultimate accolade.

The parade was fast approaching. One more day and it would wind its way triumphantly down Colorado Boulevard. The workers must have just quit for the day even though it was the middle of the night. Zerbe recalled that this year's theme was Transportation: Past and Future. Hence the space-ships and the dragons with children riding them, and the dinosaurs pulling wagons full of cavemen. The Rose Parade was nothing if not historically accurate.

In a few hours this place would again be teeming with volunteers, gluing flowers and seeds and bark onto the bi-planes and steam locomotives and Conestoga wagons, to give them color and life. The warehouse was empty and silent now except for his footsteps echoing off the walls.

Zerbe felt like he was inside a dark cavern, deep in the bowels of the earth, where otherworldly creatures dwelled. His high school years, spent engrossed in reading H.P. Love-craft and J.R.R. Tolkien, came back to him in a rush. Then he heard wailing on the wind and thought he was going mad.

The wailing grew nearer and he recognized it. Police si-rens. Approaching. He began to panic. They'd find him in here. He'd be sent back to that awful place. He couldn't go back there.

He stifled a scream and looked around for a place to hide. If only this really were a cavern, he could crawl deeper into the darkness and disappear. Into the eldritch, hoary depths of the earth, Zerbe thought, his mind going full-on-Lovecraft. If only one of the ancient legendary monsters that surrounded him was real and could reach down with its long neck and swallow him whole.

He heard cars pull up outside. Heard their tires squealing on the asphalt. They were coming for him. He headed deeper into the darkness. He took a left at a giant Santa's sleigh. Then he stopped as a light fell across his face and he saw something that made his blood run cold.

CHAPTER THREE

Crush saw the huge, rugged, empty industrial pits just off the freeway, looking like ancient volcanic craters, and knew he was approaching Irwindale. To most people, Irwindale was just an underpopulated suburb of Los Angeles, far out in the San Gabriel Valley, notable mostly as the site of the Renaissance Pleasure Faire once a year. To Crush it was more personal than that. To Crush it was the place he had been chosen to run the rear end of a dinosaur.

When Crush spotted the flashing lights to his right, he had to look twice before he was sure they weren't a Christmas decoration. Then he recognized it as a cop car. He took a turn toward it, into an industrial complex. He pulled the Camaro up across from a warehouse, watching the patrol car as it idled next to a bright red Porsche. The patrol car siren was off but its visibar lights were flashing like a strobe light on a dance floor. He cursed under his breath. Strobe lights always gave Crush a headache, even in the nightclub.

In the flashing light, Crush could see a policeman standing beside the Porsche, talking to someone through the window. The driver got out and walked with the patrolman toward the warehouse, and Crush thought he recognized her as she walked through the big doors. This was getting all too familiar.

He turned to Donny and said, "You can go."

"Here?"

"Yes, here."

"How do I get home?"

"Hitchhike. Walk. I don't care."

"Where the fuck is Irwindale?"

"It's where you are."

"Thanks a lot."

"Hey, I'm letting you go. You should thank me."

"I did thank you."

"You were being sarcastic. Next time, try meaning what you say. It makes a nice change."

"Fuck you. And Merry Christmas."

"That's sarcasm again. Don't you even know when you're using it?"

Donny threw open the door, got out of the car, and walked off toward the freeway.

The sun was just peeking over the horizon in front of him but Crush didn't give it a glance. He kept his eyes on the warehouse and when he saw lights come on inside, he got out of the Camaro.

Walking toward the elephant doors, Crush felt a sense of nostalgia flowing over him. He had come here once, years ago, with Zerbe and the rest of his high school class, to help pin flowers on the Rose Parade floats. It was fun at first, being out of class and all, but after a while it got pretty tedious. In fact, he had volunteered for tail-duty just because he thought it would be more exciting. That's how naïve he had been at seventeen.

Crush entered the warehouse and tried to cast aside thoughts of the past. As if bidden by his attempt to deny them, images of Angela, Noel, and Renee Zerbe and the

Devil's Gate itself all crowded around in his mind. He tried to brush them aside. He was mostly successful. Inside the warehouse, Crush saw what he had expected to see. A bunch of goddamned floats with a bunch of goddamned freaky animals and monsters and rocket ships. The Rose Parade Floats. Happy New Year.

Over the years, Crush had developed a love/hate relationship with the Rose Parade, and not just because of his own bad experience with it. On the one hand, he loved that for one day everyone in the wintery, snowbound US got to envy warm, sunny Southern California and resent it even more than they did the rest of the year. On the other hand, he hated that most of the floats were sponsored by corporate monoliths and government agencies. It was basically a two-hour commercial for the powers that be.

For instance, next to him was an enormous float, fully thirty-five feet in length, featuring an Art Deco–Futurama-style locomotive taking off from its track and soaring into the air. On its top was a throne for a celebrity to ride, and on the base of the float was the legend: California High-Speed Rail—The Future Is Now.

Even the nonexistent bullet train from Los Angeles to San Francisco had an advertisement here.

Crush remembered that Zerbe's father had been spearheading that endless, mythical project that Angelenos had been reading about, and paying for, for years, but which never seemed to quite get started. If it involved graft, corruption, and wasteful spending in LA, Emil Zerbe was probably behind it. Now Noel was making a tribute to it in steel and roses. It was all too typical.

The policeman came out from under the arching neck of a dragon, looking around, not finding anything. A woman stepped out from behind a space station, calling out to the empty void, "Hey! The cops are here! You better come out!"

Crush had been right. It was Angela, Zerbe and Noel's sister and, for a brief, uncomfortable time, Crush's own step-sister. Her tawny hair still fell over her shoulders, damn it. From what he could see, her eyes were still that wicked, haunting green. Crush had seen her a few times over the past few years, but he always saw her through 2000 eyes and she always looked eighteen to him. And she always made him feel eighteen himself.

"Must have been a crank call," the policeman said.

"Bullshit," she said. "The door was opened. Somebody was here."

The policeman shrugged. "There's nobody here now."

Crush stepped forward. "There's me," he said.

She looked over at him, sternly at first, then with a bright smile blossoming across her face. "Caleb Rush! What the hell are you doing here? Don't tell me you're taking up breaking and entering?" Her green eyes were still startling and her lips were still lush with that damn tilt to the left that always made him wonder.

"Just entering," he replied. "You left the door open."

"So you know this man?" the cop asked Angela.

"Yeah, I know him."

"What's he doing here?"

She squinted at him. "What are you doing here, Crush?"

"You first," Crush said.

"Well, I got an anonymous call that there was a break-in here. So I called the police and we came out. We've been having problems with protestors."

"Oh," Crush said. "Same here."

"You're having problems with protestors?"

"No, I got a call about a break-in. Anonymously."

"Why would they call you?" the cop asked.

"I'm in security." Crush pulled out his wallet and handed over one of his old business cards from when he worked at Tigon Security.

The cop looked at it and was impressed. More impressed than Crush had expected, in fact.

"Sorry," the policeman said, handing it back. "I didn't know. Do you think it's SAGMA?"

Crush had no idea what SAGMA was, but there were times when he'd learned to just not answer. Instead he looked the cop dead in the eye and asked, "What do you think?"

"I don't know," the cop said. "Probably?"

Crush smiled at the cop sagely. "Very good. Why don't we leave it at that, Officer...?"

"Zelazny," the cop said. "Should we search the place? They could have left a...device of some kind?" It shouldn't have sounded like a question.

"We'll take care of the search, Officer Zelazny. We have the equipment."

The cop nodded. Then he looked around. "Where?"

"It's on its way. I came on ahead."

"As reconnaissance?"

"That's right, as reconnaissance. We'll take it from here."

The cop looked uncertain. He turned to Angela. "Miss?"

"I think the Tigon boys can handle it from here."

"All right then," the cop said, kicking a loose pebble down the sewer grate. "I'll say goodnight."

Zelazny hurried off, glad to hand the matter over to someone else. Angela looked at Crush, amused. "I thought Tigon Security fired you?" she asked, once Zelazny had driven off in his patrol car.

"Let's say we had a mutual parting of the ways. You hired them?"

"I remembered you said they were the best."

"They are. Why do you need them?"

She shrugged. "Family business."

"Your family owns this place, too?"

"Daddy bought it for Noel a couple of years ago. As a toy."

"What's SAGMA?"

"A bunch of crazies." She sighed. "Society Against Genetically Modified Agriculture. One of Dad's companies is Angel Foods."

"The organic produce company?"

"Well, organic-*ish*. So we sell Genetically Modified food? People have been modifying food since the Stone Age. It doesn't hurt anybody."

"But the crazies don't like it?"

"No, they insist that their food be 'pure.' Whatever that means. Why are *you* here, Caleb?"

"I'm looking for your brother."

"Noel's back at the house. We flipped a coin to see who would come out. I lost."

So, Crush thought, she still lives with her brother. Did that mean they still lived at the house on the Arroyo. Crush hoped not. "Not that brother," he said.

"Kendrick?" Kendrick was what the "K" in K.C. Zerbe stood for. Crush could never think of Zerbe as a "Kendrick." "I thought he was with you."

"He's supposed to be."

"Did he make a break for it? I was afraid he'd do that."

Crush shook his head. "No. He was kidnapped."

"Kidnapped? Seriously?"

"Not particularly seriously, but yes, he was kidnapped. I think they brought him here."

"Why?"

"Because Noel arranged the kidnapping."

She sat down at the foot of the dragon. "Oh, my fucking family," she sighed. She was wearing black jeans and a designer T-shirt that she must have just thrown on when she got the call. She hadn't had time to brush her hair or put on any makeup. She looked beautiful when she wasn't even trying. "Just when I think they're crazy as they can be, they get crazier."

"You've been pretty crazy in your day."

"That just proves my point." She ran her fingers through her hair. "Do you really think Noel is behind this?"

"Evidence seems to point in that direction. Do you think it's possible?"

"Noel is capable of almost anything." She looked around. "So you think Kendrick is here someplace?"

"He's either hiding here or Noel already picked him up."

"Or?"

"Who said there was another 'or'?"

"There's always another 'or,' Crush. You know that."

They heard the tires of a car rolling in on the asphalt out front. There was no sound of an engine purring, so they knew it must be an electric vehicle. Looking out through the elephant doors, they could see a dark blue Tesla, powering down. The gull wing doors rose and a man got out. The man was K.C. Zerbe.

Except he wasn't. He wasn't dressed in Zerbe's usual uniform of superhero T-shirt and jeans. This Zerbe wore a russet-colored Henley shirt and an unstructured linen sports coat that had been washed within an inch of its life over a pair of green cargo pants, the kind with lots of pockets, all of which were full of unidentified objects. He looked just like K.C., but something about the way he carried himself made him look older. As if maybe he had taken on some actual responsibility. As if he had grown up and didn't like it. The man walked across the asphalt, looking around, as if he expected to see something and was disappointed that it wasn't there.

Angela stepped out of the warehouse and greeted him. "What are you doing here? I thought I won the toss?"

This Zerbe was Noel, K.C.'s older brother by five minutes. "Where are the police?"

Crush stepped out of the warehouse. "They left."

Noel hadn't seen Crush in years. He looked at him in mild surprise. "Caleb Rush. It's you."

"It is," Crush replied.

Those pleasantries taken care of, Noel looked around him. He seemed to choose his words very carefully. "They didn't find anything?"

"No," Angela said.

"What did you think they'd find?" Crush asked.

"Just...something. Somebody called about something, didn't they?"

"Yes, let's go over that call," Crush said. "They called the house, right? Who answered?"

"I did," Angela said.

"And the call was blocked?"

"Yeah, there was no incoming number on my phone."

"Your phone? I thought you got the call at the house."

"I did," she said. "I was at home. What, do you think they called the landline? Like they were selling solar panels? Nobody uses the landline, Crush."

"All right then, you got a blocked call. Where were you?"

"Asleep. It was almost five in the morning."

"But your phone was on?"

"Well, sure. Don't you leave yours on?"

"I don't turn mine on unless I'm at work."

"What if you miss an important call?"

"If it's important, they'll call back. So, the phone rang. You picked it up. The incoming number was blocked. Why did you answer it?"

"The most important people have blocked numbers, don't you know that? Also, Noel told me to."

"Wait, what was Noel doing in your bedroom at five in the morning?"

"Just basking in the postcoital afterglow," she said sarcastically. "No, stupid. I didn't say I was in my bedroom, did I? We fell asleep in the den, watching *Interstellar* on HBO. Man, that movie makes no sense."

"I didn't see it. Go on."

"Anyway, I got the call and I wasn't going to answer it, but Noel said...."

Crush looked at Noel. "You told her to answer it?"

Noel looked wildly guilty. "Yes, I told her to answer it. Why wouldn't I tell her to answer it? What are you getting at?"

"We're not getting at anything," Angela said.

"Oh, we're getting at something," Crush said. "What did you expect to find when you got here? Did you expect the cops to have K.C. under arrest? Did you think they'd be carting him away?"

"No! Why are you saying that? Why would I want that?"

"I have no fucking idea."

Noel looked around, confused. "But nothing is here? Something must be here," he said, walking toward the warehouse.

Crush walked alongside him. "He's not here."

"Who's not here? I don't know what you're talking about." Noel was a very bad liar. He stepped inside and looked around the vast warehouse. "But something must be here...."

"What must be here?"

He wandered among the floats, searching. "Something. You're sure the police didn't find anything?"

"They didn't find anything."

"They must have!" He was starting to sound a little desperate.

"They didn't."

"But that's not right. They must have found something!" Noel had a way of getting stuck on an idea. Crush remembered how, in high school, he'd stayed in his room for a month, trying to make a miniature solar-powered aircraft to fly over the Arroyo and take pictures. A drone before drones, Crush now realized. Noel was always years ahead of his time but three steps behind everyone else in the room. "He must be here!" Noel said, in anguish.

"K.C. isn't here," Crush told him. "The police didn't find him. We didn't find him."

"But what if he's hiding?" With that, Noel gave up the pretense that he didn't know what was going on.

"Why would he be hiding from us?" Angela asked.

"I don't know. Maybe he doesn't know it's us." Noel called out. "K.C.! It's okay! It's Noel. And Angela! And Caleb! It's okay! You can come out now!"

No answer came from the dragons or dinosaurs or ocean liners. Noel looked bereft. "But...I don't understand. I arranged everything."

"You did, huh?" Crush said. "Why don't you call Donny and ask him what went wrong?"

Noel shook his head, dismissive. "Donny's an idiot. I should call Jack." He pulled his mobile phone out of his pocket, punched in a number, and after a minute he started to speak. "Jack. Zerbe here. What went wrong?"

Noel was silent while Jack explained. Angela stood by

Crush's side, silently judgmental.

"I don't know if I believe you, Jack," Noel said after a few moments. "I don't know if you've behaved ethically. I don't think you've earned your money. Do you understand? Hello...hello...." Noel looked at Crush and Angela, affronted. "He hung up on me. That's no way to do business."

"You should give him a bad Yelp review under 'Kidnappers,' " Angela said.

"I wish I could."

"What did he say?" Crush asked.

"He said he dropped K.C. off here, as according to plan. Of course, I don't know if he's telling the truth. I'm afraid I didn't vet him very well."

"Live and learn," Crush said. "Why don't you tell us all about it, Noel? Why did you think kidnapping K.C. was a good idea?"

Noel paced back and forth in front of the bullet train float. "It's hard to make an outsider understand. There's so much to explain."

"Try," Crush said.

"Suffice it to say that I, and my entire family, are in grave danger. "

"Noel..." Angela started to interrupt.

"Let him finish," Crush said.

"I know you don't believe me, Angela. I know everybody thinks I'm crazy. That's how I know they'll win. They convince the world that the ones who know about them are crazy."

So Noel hadn't left his paranoia behind. "Who are 'they'?" Crush asked. "SAGMA?"

"Oh, please," Noel said, rolling his eyes. "SAGMA doesn't have a clue as to what's really going on. They're nothing but pawns in the game. Like everybody else."

"So you're a pawn in the game?"

"No. I've been enlightened. That's why I'm dangerous to them. That's why they have to destroy me."

"But I'm a pawn?"

Noel nodded sadly. "Yes."

"I don't feel like a pawn," Crush said.

"If you're not actively fighting them, you're playing into their hands."

"I see. And what is their goal, exactly?"

"Oh, God," Noel shook his head sadly. Noel spent a lot of time shaking his head. "Don't you see? The mere fact that you ask that question, in that mocking tone? It means they've already won."

"I didn't mean to mock. I'm trying to understand. What are they after?"

Noel shook his head again, as if helpless in the face of such massive ignorance. "The world."

"They want to take over the world?" Crush asked, and though he tried his utmost not to, he sounded like The Brain talking to Pinky in the old cartoon.

"They want to change it. To bend it to their will. Oh, God, it's like talking to someone in a different language." Noel was literally pulling his hair. "Let's just say someone is trying to destroy me. And my whole family. And I'm desperately trying to keep them safe. That includes you, Angela. I'm afraid it even includes you now, Caleb."

Crush thought it was nice to be included in the family. "How does kidnapping K.C. keep him safe?"

Noel smiled. "He was the easiest one to protect. Everybody else is out in the world, where anything can happen. But with K.C., all I had to do was make him break his probation and then I'd know he'd be in prison, safe. Where they couldn't get at him."

"So you arranged for him to be kidnapped and dropped off here? Then you arranged for an anonymous call to bring the police here and find him? So they'd arrest him?"

"Yes, isn't that simple but brilliant?"

Crush was silent for a moment. "Let me get this straight. This Great Whatever, they can reach out to anyone, at any time, in any place? They are everywhere, am I right?"

"Absolutely," Noel said, "at least you understand that much."

"Then why can't they reach out to K.C. in prison?"

Noel looked as if he'd swallowed a brick. "I hadn't thought of that. Oh, my God. He'd be trapped. They could do whatever they wanted to him."

"Fortunately, it hasn't come to that. He hasn't been arrested."

"But where is he?" Angela asked. "That's the first order of business, isn't it?"

"Not the first," said Crush, looking at his watch. It was 6:14. He pulled out his cell phone and pressed a speed-dial number. "Gail," he said when she answered, "it's all right. We found him."

Angela looked at Crush in mild surprise.

"Thank God," Gail said on the other end of the line. "Where was he?"

"It's a long story. But you don't have to call the police, understand? Just keep walking that ankle monitor around. I'll bring him back this afternoon."

"This afternoon? Why?"

"We have to take care of a few things. I'll explain when we get back."

"That won't be soon enough. Frida just called." Frida Morales was Zerbe's probation officer. "She said his monitor went out of bounds last night. She wanted to talk to him."

This was bad news. But Gail had always taught him that, during a match, it was a waste of time to resist an attack. The thing to do was to react to it. "Okay. What did you do?"

"I told her he was asleep. She said fine, she'd call back."

"Okay." Frida had been Gail's student in the dojo for some time now. "You know her. What did she mean?"

"She meant she'll be dropping by for an unscheduled visit this morning."

"All right. We'll be there." He ended the call and slipped his phone back in his pants pocket.

"You're still a good liar, Crush," Angela said.

"Not good enough. She knew I was bullshitting her."

"Is she used to you lying to her then?"

Crush shook his head. He was distracted. Trying to think of a way out of this. "It's not like that. She's a friend. I don't lie to friends."

"Only to lovers?"

"Maybe that's why I don't have many of those."

"Really? You've changed since I knew you."

"It's been fifteen years. I hope so."

"I don't think I've changed much. But then I was pretty much perfect from the get-go."

Crush wasn't listening. He headed out. "We don't have much time. Come on, Noel."

"What? Where are we going?"

"We have to keep K.C. out of prison."

"But we don't even know where he is."

"First things first," Crush said, getting into his car.

CHAPTER FOUR

Frida Morales had been a parole officer for the County of Los Angeles for five years, nine months, and two weeks. *That*, she thought as she rode up in the elevator, *should just about complete my sentence.*

She had become a PO for all the right reasons. She wanted to make a difference. She wanted to give the downtrodden a second chance. She wanted to prove that the system could work. That idealism stayed with her for approximately ten months. The reams of paperwork, the maze of red tape, and the grinding cynicism of her fellow officers were all factors in her growing disillusionment. But the real cause of her burnout was simple. She spent all her time with ex-convicts.

All of them were guilty, of course. They had done either really stupid or really terrible things, and most of them had done both.

That was why she liked coming here, she thought, as she stepped out of the elevator and walked to K.C. Zerbe's door. Not that Zerbe was an innocent man. He hadn't been railroaded or anything like that. It was just that he was less dangerous than her average offender. He'd read the occasional book and was a good conversationalist. She liked him.

Also, she felt sorry for him. She had read his case-file

and it was clear he had been set up to take the fall for wealthier, more culpable higher-ups. Zerbe wasn't blameless; he was simply less guilty than the people who sent him to prison. He deserved to have someone cut him some slack.

Cutting slack was Frida's favorite thing. She did it whenever possible, whenever she felt someone deserved it. She didn't get the chance to do it very often. When she did, it made her feel like she was on the side of mercy, and it felt good. For a few minutes.

If she could have become one of those right-wing, "lock 'em up and throw away the key" types, she would at least have had a gang to side with. But most cops she knew, though nice enough in civilian life, were bullies on the street. Too quick to look at a parolee and just see a potential threat. Too fast with their fists and their clubs and their guns. Too ready to meet any form of resistance with brutal force.

So that left her living with the volatile combination of a group of stupid, impulsive people with little or no self-control opposite a bunch of aggressive, suspicious, well-armed people who were spoiling for a fight. All Frida could do was wait for something truly terrible to happen.

It happened yesterday.

Afterward, she went home and fell into bed but she couldn't sleep. She just lay awake and stared at the ceiling and wished to God she could drink. She was over being a P. O., she knew that. All her life she had wanted to be involved in the criminal justice system, but now she wished she'd gone into teaching or accounting or comedy improv or anything else. Her life had reached a turning point but she was too exhausted to take the wheel.

That was when she got the alert from Zerbe's location monitor. It was just the distraction she needed. An excuse to visit a relatively benign offender and remind herself that not everyone in this bleak world was a piece of shit.

Not that Zerbe hadn't caused her a fair amount of grief. She had gone out on a limb for him when he had requested that he serve out his sentence with Caleb Rush rather than with his wealthy parents. She looked the other way when it became obvious that he had internet access, in violation of the terms of his probation. She argued for the continuation of the probation arrangement with Mr. Rush, despite that fact that Crush (as Mr. Rush was called on the street) was repeatedly in trouble with the law, though never officially charged with anything.

She didn't know exactly why she put herself on the line for Zerbe so often. She knew Zerbe was in love with her, but offenders falling for their probation officers was fairly common. Not as common as offenders hating their probation officer's guts and wanting to kill them, but common all the same. Her roommate joked that Frida had a crush on Zerbe, but that was ridiculous. Just ridiculous.

Frida brushed her dark hair over her forehead to cover the bruise she'd tried to conceal with makeup this morning and took a breath before she knocked on the steel door of Crush's loft. Zerbe hadn't committed a location violation since he learned how to operate the ankle monitor. With only eight months and change to go on his sentence, this seemed like a crazy time for him to go AWOL. But Frida had known felons to act a little crazy at times. Most of the time, actually. She felt a wave of weariness wash over her.

Frida steeled herself and recalled that she was an authority figure and a representative of the State of California. She closed her fist and knocked on the door. There was no answer. This was not a good sign. Had Zerbe really bolted? Run off to Mexico? True, his monitor said he was in the apartment but, although the State of California did not want this to be widely known, monitors could be beaten.

The door swung open and Catherine Gail stood inside. Gail had answered the phone when Frida had called this morning, so she had expected her to be there, of course. But seeing her like this took all the resolve out of Frida's spirit. She blinked, like a twelve-year-old girl who was caught by the Mother Superior smoking in the bathroom. "Master Gail," she said, her voice breaking.

"I'm just Catherine Gail here," Gail said. "We're not in the dojo."

"Of course," Frida said. She had been studying tae kwon do with Master Gail for a year now, ever since one of her "clients" had taken a swing at her with a bottle of Royal Crown Cola and she'd decided she needed to learn to defend herself. Zerbe had recommended her highly, so Frida thought she would give Gail a try. She hadn't realized until just now how much she had come to depend on Gail's firm and steady influence. She was the mentor Frida had been searching for all her life.

It was all she could do to stop herself from letting the events of yesterday spill out of her in a long, plaintive monologue. But this was not the time. Their roles were reversed now. Frida was the authority figure and Gail was the civilian. "I need to talk to Zerbe."

Gail hesitated. Not a good sign. "He's sick. Can he call you later?"

"I need to see him. Now." Frida used her most authoritative voice. The one her grade school teachers told her to never use. Her bossy voice.

"All right," Gail said. "Give me a minute." She stepped aside and let Frida in.

"Are you staying here, Gail?"

"What makes you ask?"

"It's a little early for a social call."

"Gail's staying with me." Crush was speaking up from the kitchenette, sipping from a coffee mug. He was dressed in a white T-shirt and sweatpants with a five o'clock shadow shading his bald head. She knew a lot of people found Crush thug-ishly sexy, but he didn't ring Frida's bell. She preferred the more bookish, nerdy, less-threatening type.

"As Zerbe's P. O., I should have been informed of any changes in the living arrangements," Frida said, as Gail climbed the homemade stairs to the upper loft-within-the-loft.

Frida had always liked Crush's place. Its odd decor of mounted auto parts hanging next to Japanese samurai movie posters gave the place an unmistakably masculine feeling, but that was belied by its uncharacteristic neatness. It was as if she'd found the mythical beast—the manly man who could do housekeeping.

She walked past the view of MacArthur Park in the early morning, over to the kitchenette where Crush was eating from a steaming bowl of oatmeal. "It's only for a few days," he said. "You know she got kicked out of her place."

"Nevertheless," Frida said. "I should have been told."

Gail came down the stairs. "He's coming but I warn you, he might be contagious."

"I'll chance it," Frida said, beginning to lose patience.

Gail stopped and looked at her. "What happened yesterday?"

"What makes you think anything happened yesterday?"

"It's too early for anything to have happened today and something's got you on edge." Gail peered more closely at Frida's face. "Is that a bruise over your right eye?"

Frida brushed her hair back down. "It's not appropriate for me to talk about it now."

"You want me to leave?" asked Crush.

"I'm fine," Frida said.

"Really?" Gail asked.

"It's nothing that won't keep till our next lesson. Have you found a new dojo?" Frida asked, trying to change the subject.

"I'm still looking. We can do our lessons here until I find a place."

"Here?"

"Why not?"

"It might conflict with my professional..." Frida faltered. "Oh, what the hell, by next week I'll be a substitute teacher anyway."

"Are you sure you don't want to talk?"

Frida was about to let it all come out when, to her immense relief, Zerbe came shuffling down the stairs, a blanket wrapped around his shoulders and a mug of steaming something in his hand. He looked like someone playing "sick man" in a community theater production.

"How are you feeling, Zerbe?" Frida asked.

"Not so well," he whispered in a strained voice as he walked to the sofa. He folded his feet, covered in red striped fuzzy socks, underneath him and wrapped the blanket around his head, as if were trying to disappear into his own shell.

"We think it's either stomach flu or something he ate," Crush said. "It's been pretty nasty in here the past few hours."

"Pretty nasty," Zerbe muttered.

"We're going to need to do some laundry," another woman said, coming down the stairs with a bundle of sheets in her hand. "Or you're going to have to buy some new sheets. I recommend buying new sheets." The new woman dropped the bedding into the trash and crossed to the sink to wash her hands. "Have you had your flu shot?" she asked Frida. " 'Cause you don't want to get what he has."

The woman was almost a redhead and was quite a bit younger than Frida or Gail. She had a trim figure and was wearing expensive but casual clothing that said, "I make more money than you but I don't have to show it off." Frida took an immediate dislike to her.

"I've had my flu shot," Frida said.

"Good for you." The woman extended her freshly toweled hand to Frida. Her nails were manicured and painted with clear nail polish, in a "humble-brag" style of beauty treatment Frida found very annoying. "I'm Angela Zerbe, K.C.'s sister."

Frida took Angela's hand. It was soft and surprisingly firm. Damn her. "Pleased to meet you. But I thought Zerbe wasn't on speaking terms with his family."

"Yeah, but that's me," Angela said, "always the peacemaker!"

Crush choked back a laugh as he spooned more oatmeal into his mouth. Frida got the feeling that she was losing control of this situation.

"Zerbe, there's a question I need answered," Frida said, in her most businesslike manner. "Where were you at 4:13 this morning?"

Zerbe looked at her with an expression that said that either he had been caught or he was about to throw up. Or both. "I was here. Where else would I be?"

"Where, here?"

"He was either on that sofa or in the toilet," Crush said. "Take your pick."

Frida kept her eyes on Zerbe. "At 4:13 your monitor said that you left this apartment." She bent down to take a look at the device on his leg. Zerbe jerked his feet back.

"Oh, that," Angela said, quickly. "I can explain that. You see, he was alone in the apartment, feeling sick. Very sick. He tried to call Crush and Gail but he couldn't reach them. So he called me. I came right over."

"And?"

"Well, I don't know the building very well. I got off the elevator, but I took a wrong turn. K.C. came out to get me. That must have been when it registered that he went out of bounds."

Frida considered. "Okay," she said. "But I still need to examine the monitor."

The three of them exchanged a look. No doubt about it, Frida thought, they were definitely exchanging a look.

"Let me see it," she said.

"But...."

"Zerbe, look at me," Frida said. Zerbe pulled the blanket off his head and looked at her. "I'm on your side. You know that, right?"

Zerbe looked uncertain, but nodded.

"Now I need to check your monitor to see if it's operating correctly. Just like I always do. Why are you resisting me?"

Zerbe slowly slid his right leg out from under the sofa. He lifted the leg of his sweatpants to reveal the ankle monitor.

"All right," she said. "That's more like it." Frida reached out to touch the monitor. It was wet with oil. "What's this?"

"What?" Zerbe asked innocently.

"It's all slimy."

"Oh, that..." Angela said.

"Take off your socks," Frida demanded.

"My feet are cold," Zerbe said.

"Take them off."

Zerbe bent over and pulled off his left sock.

"Now the right one," Frida said.

Zerbe looked to Angela and to Crush. Receiving no help from either of them, he pulled off the right sock.

Frida looked at Zerbe's naked foot. "All right, I want an explanation."

"For what?" Zerbe asked.

"Why is your foot raw and scraped and covered in olive oil?"

"Is it?"

Frida stood up, trying to make her five-foot-four frame appear as imposing as was humanly possible. "Were you trying to take the monitor off?"

"No!"

"It was me," Angela said. "I did it. While he was asleep."

Frida turned to Zerbe's sister, relieved that she didn't have to hide her dislike for the woman now. "Why?"

"It was hurting him. Can't you see how swollen his leg is? I thought if I took it off, he could rest."

"You said he was asleep."

"He *was* asleep. But not resting. He was restless."

"Didn't it occur to you that taking the ankle monitor off him would get him sent back to prison?"

"Yeah, that's why I stopped. I almost had it off when I came to my senses."

Frida considered. "Okay. I guess that answers all my questions." She headed for the door.

"I'm here if you need me, Frida," Gail said.

"I'll take you up on that some time. See you later, Crush. Nice to meet you, Angela." Then she added, just as she opened the door, "Goodbye, Noel."

"Goodbye," said the sick man on the sofa. Then he looked a lot sicker.

CHAPTER FIVE

Frida stepped back inside. "Okay, who wants to tell me what's going on?"

"What do you mean?" Angela asked.

"He just answered to Noel," Frida said, pointing at Noel.

"He thought you said *Noël*," Crush volunteered. "He thought you were wishing him Merry Christmas."

"Is that what you thought, Noel?" Frida said.

"Yes. I mean, no. I mean..." Noel lapsed into quiet muttering.

Frida stepped forward and offered her hand. "We haven't been formally introduced. I'm Frida Morales and I believe you're K.C.'s twin brother, aren't you?"

Noel looked up at Frida. Then he looked over to the others.

"Give it up, Noel," Crush said.

"I can't believe you'd do this," Frida said. "All of you." She turned to Gail. "Especially you. Why?"

So Gail told her why and when she was done Frida stared long and hard out the window at the traffic that was creeping along on Wilshire Boulevard. "Now tell me the real reason," she said.

"That's the truth," Gail said.

"Come off it," Frida said. "Zerbe just flaked, didn't he? He ran off. And you brought Noel over to cover for him? That's it, isn't it?"

"Frida..." Crush started.

"Tell me you didn't plan this so he could go on a trip to Vegas or something."

"What I told you was the truth."

"If you want to make up a story," Frida said, exasperated, "at least tell me one that makes sense. Don't tell me Noel arranged for him to be kidnapped and then you lost him. Don't tell me that."

"We'd rather not tell you that, but it's the truth," Crush said.

"Where is K.C. now?" Frida demanded.

"I don't know," Crush said.

"Gail?"

"We really don't know," Gail said.

"For God's sake don't *lie* to me. Don't you lie to me." Frida was shocked to feel a rush of sorrow and frustration. *Calm down*, she told herself. *Don't let them see how fragile you are right now*. She turned to the sink and gripped the counter.

Gail walked up to her and placed her hand on Frida's back. "Do you want to talk about it?"

"No, I don't want to talk about it!" She spun around to face Gail. "You know what I'm going to have to do, don't you? I'm going to have to call this in. They're going to put a BOLO out on him. He's going back to prison."

"That's right," Gail said calmly. "That's what will happen. If you do that."

"What do you mean, *if* I do that?" Frida asked, affronted. "That's what's going to happen."

"Are you on the clock?" Crush asked.

"Pardon?"

"Have you reported in? Or did you stop by on the way

to work?"

Frida stared at him. "You're not really suggesting what I think you're suggesting."

"I'm suggesting it," Crush said.

Angela spoke up. "If you haven't reported in, then this really hasn't happened. Professionally speaking, I mean."

"Don't you talk to me." Frida turned to Gail. "Tell her not to talk to me."

"Don't talk to her, Angela," Gail said.

Frida pulled out her cell phone.

"Frida, wait," Crush said. "At least hear us out."

Noel shook his head. "It's useless, can't you see? She's working for *them*."

"For who?" Frida asked.

"You're not helping, Noel," Crush said. Noel huffed and shuffled back upstairs to the bedroom.

Frida's thumb was poised over the keypad on her phone.

"Tell me one thing before you call," Gail said. "How did you know?"

"How did I know what?" Frida replied.

"How did you know it wasn't K.C.?" Gail asked.

Frida paused. "I could just tell. It was obvious."

"Not from the first. If you knew from the first you would have called him out. When did you know?"

Frida thought. "I guess...when he looked at me. It wasn't the same."

"What wasn't the same?" Gail asked.

"It wasn't the same feeling. When he looked at me." Frida struggled to put it into words. "It just wasn't...there."

"What wasn't there?"

"The feeling. The familiarity." Frida shook her head in frustration. "Why am I even talking to you about this?"

"The familiarity. The friendship, you mean?" Gail asked.

"This is just wasting time."

"He's your *friend*, Frida. Whether you want to admit that or not," Gail said. "He's your friend and you deserve to hear him out."

"All right. Fine. You win. And I will hear him out. As soon as I can talk to him. Which means, as soon as they bring him in."

"You can hear from him before that," Gail said.

"What are you talking about?" Frida asked.

Gail looked to Angela who pulled out her cell phone. "Somebody texted me," Angela said. "They said to FaceTime this number at eight-thirty."

"And you think it was him?" Frida asked.

"Or the people who *have* him," Gail said. "There's only one way to find out. Just wait five minutes. You can be here when we call."

Frida did a turn around the kitchen table. "This is stupid."

"But you'll wait?" Gail asked.

Frida sat. "What the hell, I'll wait."

"You want some coffee?" Crush asked.

"What the hell, I'll have some coffee," Frida said.

Crush poured her a cup and Gail pulled up a chair to sit next to her. Crush poured Gail a cup, too. Gail gestured for Crush and Angela to leave them alone. Crush took Angela into the bedroom.

"That was subtle," Frida said.

"I wasn't trying to be subtle," Gail said. "I was trying to give you some space. What happened yesterday?"

Frida sipped her coffee. "I don't know whether you're my sensei, my therapist, or an accomplice to an offender."

"Well, I'm not your therapist. But I can listen."

Frida put her cup down. "Remember that INKY I told you about?"

"Inky?"

"Sorry, P. O. talk. Incorrigible Juvenile Offender. Aaron Reddick and his family. The usual Friday night routine. Dad comes home, beats on Mom, the kid tries to break it up, the parents gang up on the kid, the kid fights back, and the parents call me. To put the fear of God and the law into him."

"That sounds pretty bad."

"Yeah, it's what we call an F.U.F.U.—A Fucked Up Family Unit. They have a choice. They could work on their problems or they could blame the kid. They blame the kid. Of course Aaron acts out, just to give them something to complain about. Vandalism, tagging, shoplifting. He's been in amd out of Juvie and on probation since he was thirteen. A problem child, they say. With an alcoholic, abusive father and an enabling mother. This is the stuff I have to deal with, day in, day out."

"But this time it was different?"

Frida ran her fingers through her hair, put her hands on the table, and looked at her nails. "This time it was different. I should have sensed that, but it started just the same as always. Mom and Dad had been wailing on each other and Aaron started breaking up the place, just to distract them. By the time I got there, he was busting up the kitchen with a broom handle and they were yelling at him. I tried to get Aaron to stop, to calm everybody down. You can guess how well that went. By the time I got the kid to put down the broom, his father was picking up an old stainless-steel meat tenderizer and bringing it down on Aaron's head. So Aaron picked up a cast-iron skillet and started swinging at his father while his mother was screaming like a scalded cat.

"I don't think the dad meant to hit me with the mallet. I just got caught in the back swing. I fell back against the counter and the mother decided to help me by screaming in my face. Aaron dropped the skillet and ran to me, but his dad kept pounding at him with the mallet.

"I don't know who called the police. I guess one of the neighbors finally ran out of patience, or maybe somebody new had moved in, somebody who wasn't used to the mother's screeching. The cops burst in just as Aaron grabbed a butcher's knife off the counter. They took one look at the scene and decided that the young guy with the knife was the aggressor."

Frida paused and took a sip of coffee.

"Well, they didn't shoot him, I'll give them that much credit. But Aaron wouldn't drop the knife—not as long as his dad still held that mallet. So they tased him. Aaron fell to his knees, but he still didn't drop the knife. One of the cops put him in a choke hold. Flipped him over and put his knee on his chest and his hand on his throat. Until he stopped struggling."

Frida stared into the murky depths of her coffee cup for a long moment.

"*Positional asphyxia* they call it. Not intentional, of course. But the position made it hard—impossible really—for Aaron to breathe. So what they thought was him resisting them was actually him struggling to breathe. And when he stopped struggling, that didn't mean he was subdued, it meant he was dead.

"The mother screamed louder then. And the father, when he saw what they'd done to his precious boy, he started to swing the mallet at the cops. Beat one of them bloody. And the other one, seeing his partner getting clubbed senseless, hollered for Aaron's father to stop. He didn't. So the cop shot him."

Frida looked out the window.

"It wasn't your fault," Gail said.

"No, it wasn't. But I didn't do anything to stop it. And that's what I'm supposed to do, isn't it? To help...I don't know what I'm going to do now."

Gail put her hand on top of Frida's. "You're going to hurt for a while."

Frida gave a wry smile. "Is that the best you can give me?"

"Yeah."

"I need a better therapist."

"Maybe."

"I keep hearing this voice in my head saying I blew it. That I should have done something."

"Fuck the voice in your head. I have the same voice. Everybody does. Trust me, it doesn't know everything."

"But it does, doesn't it? I mean, it was there. It's *me*, isn't it?"

Gail shook her head. "The voice in your head is never you."

"How can you be sure?"

"Simple. You're the one who says fuck the voice in your head."

⌘

Crush and Angela waited in Crush's bedroom, which he hadn't put back together after the altercation with Donny last night and which was pretty small. Angela had to sit on the bed and Crush had to pace about in the tiny space.

"You look like a caged tiger, Crush," Angela said. "Why don't you sit down next to me?"

"No thanks."

"Speaking of animals," she said, "how 'bout that elephant in the room?"

Crush stopped and looked at Angela on his bed. "The whole point of having an elephant in the room is to ignore it. However big it is."

She lay back, stretched out on the bed. "What if I don't want to ignore it?"

"That's your choice. Me, I'm going to keep acting like it's not there."

"That might not be so easy."

"I've tackled worse."

She sat up and pouted. "All right. What time is it?"

He checked his phone. "Eight twenty-eight."

"Two minutes till the phone call. Do you think it was Zerbe who texted me?"

"It didn't sound like him. There was nothing funny in it."

"Maybe he didn't feel like being funny."

"Zerbe always feels like being funny."

"Can we trace the number?"

"We can try, but it's probably a burner. They'll use it and throw it away."

"Who will?"

"Whoever has him."

"It doesn't make any sense. Noel arranged for K.C. to be kidnapped. He didn't arrange for anybody to keep him."

"You sure about that?"

"Noel's crazy but he's harmless. He wouldn't trap somebody against their will."

"Not even to save them from the Great Whatever?"

She shook her head. "Noel's not lying. He's a terrible liar."

Crush walked to the door. "I guess we'll find out what we'll find out."

They walked out to find Gail and Frida sitting silently at

the kitchen table. "It's time," Crush said.

Gail took out her iPhone, dialed the number, and waited.

CHAPTER SIX

Zerbe dreamed of being beaten.

The dream had the feeling of being a memory, but a memory from when Zerbe wasn't sure. Was he recalling one of his many prison beat-downs? Was it a playground altercation in grade school? Or one of the nasty scenes that played out in his high school locker room? Zerbe had to admit he'd been beaten up with regrettable frequency throughout his life.

He hoped he was reliving one particular Pasadena Prep locker room beating. The one that seemed to change his life for the better. It was after the usual painful game of dodgeball, when Zerbe had to endure the daily humiliation of the communal shower. What could be worse than having to march, naked, into a cold, tiled room and lather up with a bunch of pubescent but still immature and confused males? Zerbe darted in and out of the shower, just long enough to get his hair wet to prove he'd washed, then dashed back to his locker to get dressed.

Then the gang of blond, blue-eyed Aryans came up to Zerbe and called him a Jew-fag, though in truth he was neither. When he didn't answer to their satisfaction, they slammed his locker shut on his hand and let loose with their fists and their knees. Zerbe had tried every strategy, from curling up like a possum to ineffectual slapping in resistance, but nothing seemed to make them lose interest in the constantly entertaining sport of beating up K.C. Zerbe at the end of gym class.

And all at once it changed. Zerbe's new stepbrother, Caleb (the one who brooded silently in his room, glared at his new family over the dinner table, and had never seemed to like Zerbe), loomed up from behind his attackers, big and powerful and naked. He grabbed a couple of them by the hair, yanked their heads back, and told them to stop it. When Redmond Hart, the bulliest of the bullies, tried to fight back, Caleb showed him what a street fighter could do to a prep school bully. In short order, Caleb fractured his wrist and smashed his nose without breaking a sweat.

As Hart lay in a heap and his friends cowered, afraid to go near him, Caleb Rush said quietly, "So you won't bother him again, am I right?" They nodded rapidly.

He wasn't called Crush yet, but in his memory Zerbe got the timelines mixed and said, "Thanks, Crush." Crush just nodded and walked on to get dressed. In that moment, Crush became Zerbe's superhero.

However, the beating in his dream continued and Crush didn't show up to save the day, so perhaps this was one of Zerbe's other beatings. Which one? It was more methodical than the playground scuffles he'd gotten into in grade school. And less sadistic than his prison assaults had been. In fact, the blows seemed...softer. As if the fists that were striking him were wearing boxing gloves or at least half-finger mitts, the kind Crush and Gail wore when they sparred. And the blows came at oddly regular intervals, as if there was no passion behind them. As if they were just fulfilling an assignment.

It was then that Zerbe realized he wasn't dreaming. He was being beaten in the here and now. Tied to an upright chair, he was being pummeled like a punching bag.

Oh, yes, Zerbe remembered. He'd been kidnapped. Twice.

The first time was by an incompetent young wannabe. That had been almost funny. The second time, not so much. He had been wandering through the warehouse full of unfinished Rose Parade floats, trying to figure out how to get back home before the police found him, when he saw a figure in a baggy, black hoodie holding a machete in one gloved hand and an iPhone in the other.

The figure held the iPhone out in front of him, like the Ghost of Christmas Past pointing his finger at Scrooge. On the phone's screen were words printed in plain type: BE QUIET. COME WITH ME.

Zerbe thought of running, but the image of that machete slicing at his throat, like Betsy Palmer in *Friday the 13th*, was too much of a deterrent. So he followed the shrouded figure through the maze of parade floats to a door in the back of the warehouse that led to the front office. He heard someone calling his name as the door shut behind him. Was it Angela? Zerbe drew a breath to answer when the shrouded figure raised his finger to point at Zerbe and lifted the machete as if to strike. Zerbe remained silent.

The figure led Zerbe to the street exit, and Zerbe reflected that, whoever the man was, he certainly knew his way around here. This was clearly an inside job. But the shrouded figure was a head taller than Zerbe, so he knew it couldn't be Noel. Who was it?

He led Zerbe across the parking lot to a nondescript white van and, opening the back doors, gestured for Zerbe to get in. Zerbe hesitated. He had seen enough serial killer movies to know that people who got into nondescript white vans seldom made it out alive. He started to run.

The figure chased after him and tackled him to the ground, bringing the machete butt down on his head. That was the last thing he could remember until now.

But he wasn't dead, he felt sure of that. If he was dead, how could he feel so much pain? Unless his Catholic upbringing had turned out to be correct after all, and this was hell. An eternity of being beaten while tied to a chair in the back of a white van. Hardly Dante, but effective.

Then the beating stopped.

The blows were no longer raining down on his face. He caught his breath. *Now what?* he thought. Nothing happened. And nothing happened again. And again. Things were looking up.

All right, he thought, *this gives me a chance to gather myself. To put myself back together again. A chance to see what condition my condition was in*, he thought, and realized he was quoting *The Big Lebowski* quoting The First Edition. He laughed at the absurdity of it and sputtered blood all over his Captain America T-shirt. *Don't get hysterical. Don't lose it. Keep calm and carry on. Just concentrate. How do you feel physically?*

The short answer was he felt bad. His head ached and his face felt like it had been gone over by an industrial sander. There was a pain in the back of his head that was greater still. Had the machete split his skull? He doubted it. He didn't feel any brains dripping down his back. So his attacker had probably been kind enough to use the hilt of the weapon on him, rather than the blade. So he wanted to keep Zerbe alive. For now. That was okay—even a "for now" was comforting under the circumstances.

Now what can you tell about your surroundings, he asked

himself. *The first thing you have to do is look.* He opened his eyes. Well, he opened one eye. His left one was too swollen shut to be of much use. Still one eye was better than none.

Now, what can you see? Not much, at first. It was dark but not completely dark. As his eye adjusted to the murky light, he could see that he had been correct, he was still in the van. He was seated in an upright metal chair that had been bolted to the floor of the van, facing the back doors. Not a factory installation, but one that had been prepared for this express purpose. So this wasn't a spur-of-the-moment "snatch and grab." This had been planned.

That made him feel good, too. The preparation involved meant that the kidnapper wanted something specific from Zerbe or his family. And he would keep him alive, at least until he got what he desired.

Zerbe tried to move his arms and legs but they were bound tightly to the arms and legs of the chair. Probably with those little plastic thingies they used for the purpose nowadays, which was good as well. That was what a professional would do, so Zerbe was definitely in the knowledgeable hands of an expert. One who wouldn't kill him unless it made good business sense to do so.

Things were looking better and better.

He squinted through the darkness to see if he could make out anything. He saw an object in front of him. Was it a table? With something on it? He could vaguely discern three objects but couldn't tell what they were. Torture implements, perhaps? Just because this guy wanted to keep him alive didn't mean he wouldn't make him wish he were dead. Zerbe felt his stomach contract.

All at once, the back doors of the van were flung open and bright light flooded in. Zerbe flinched and shut his eye, then took a deep breath and forced his eyelid to open. *Better to see what's coming than to have it surprise you*, he thought.

The light was blindingly intense at first, but as his pupils contracted he could see, outlined by white glare, the three objects on the table in front of him become clear. An iPhone on a tiny tripod, facing him. An iPad on a slightly larger tripod, also facing him. *That's good*, he thought. *No pliers. No scalpels. No hammers, no saw, no nail gun. This was turning out to be the best day ever.*

Then he noticed movement in the background and the van rocked. A hooded figure was climbing in through the back doors. Zerbe could barely see him, the lights behind him were so bright. *Clever of him to use the light to obscure his identity*, Zerbe thought. The man (Zerbe felt almost sure it was a man) held a small device up to his mouth and spoke. Then a voice that sounded like a schoolgirl on Auto-Tune said, "Hello, Zerbe. If you do what I say I promise you won't be hurt."

It was the hooded man, talking to him through an electronic voice-modification device. This was even better news. This meant he didn't want Zerbe to be able to identify his voice later. This meant there would *be* a later. There would be a time when Zerbe would be telling his story to the police and the man didn't want him to be able to describe his voice. This meant the man didn't mean to kill him after he got what he wanted.

Zerbe felt his heart flutter with hope. This was turning out to be the best New Year's of the young century. "Okay," Zerbe said. "But you know, you *did* hurt me before. With the punching."

"I'm sorry about that. I had to do it." The voice sounded like a teenager apologizing to her father for playing hooky. "I have to make her see I mean business."

"Could you switch to another voice setting? It's hard to

take you seriously when you sound like Miley Cyrus."

"Don't be a smart-ass or I'll cut off one of your fingers."
He still sounded like Miley Cyrus, but a Miley Cyrus who
had taken a very wrong turn in life.

"Sorry," Zerbe said.

"In two minutes you are going to get a phone call. You
will see her. She will see you."

"Who?"

"Shut up. Can you read what's written on the iPad in
front of you?"

Zerbe blinked a few times. There were words there but
he couldn't make them out. "I'm really sorry, but I can't."

"Just a minute." The man stepped forward and plucked
the iPad from its tripod. Zerbe shut his eye. He didn't want
to see any more of the man than the man wanted him to see.
He didn't want to give the man any excuse to kill him.

"Now?" the schoolgirl voice asked. Zerbe opened his eye.
The man had made the font bigger and now Zerbe could read
the words.

"That doesn't make any sense to me," Zerbe said.

"And they won't make sense to her either. But your father,
he'll know what they mean."

"My father?"

"Instruct her to tell your father this. Tell her not to call
the police if she ever wants to see you again."

"Is it my *sister*? Is that who's going to call?"

"Yes."

"You should have done a little more research. My sister
wouldn't mind not seeing me again. We're not a close family."

"Perhaps the tragedy will bring you closer together."

"What tragedy?"

"The one that's going to happen to each and every one
of you."

Zerbe swallowed. The New Year was looking a little bleaker. The phone beeped.

"Are you ready?" the girl's voice asked.

Zerbe nodded.

CHAPTER SEVEN

Angela entered the number in her iPhone and pressed "call." She put the phone down on the kitchen table and Crush and Gail and Frida gathered around to look.

The call was connected and they could see Zerbe on the screen.

"Oh shit," said Angela.

Zerbe did not look good. His cheek was bruised, his lip was split open, and his left eye was swollen completely shut.

"Hey, guys," Zerbe said. He sounded surprised.

"Are you okay?" Frida asked.

"Yeah, I just didn't expect to see all of you there." Zerbe looked "off camera." "I didn't know they'd all be there," he said to someone. "Is it all right that they're there?"

A young woman's voice spoke up. It sounded artificial, like a distorted sample from a hip-hop tune. "Just read the words."

"Are you in danger?" Crush asked.

"Yeah, I think so," Zerbe said. He looked off camera again for confirmation. "I'm in danger, right?"

"Read it," the unknown woman said.

"Yeah, I'm in danger," Zerbe said. "That's why he beat me up, I guess. So you'd see that he means business."

"He sounds kind of like a girl," Angela said.

"Yeah, that's a voice-modification app," Zerbe said. "It's very creepy."

"What does he want?" Frida asked. "Does he want money?"

"He doesn't want money," Zerbe said. "He wants Angela to do something."

"What does he want me to do?" asked Angela.

"He wants you to tell Dad something," Zerbe said.

Angela swallowed. "Okay."

"First of all, he says that you shouldn't go to the police," Zerbe went on. "At the first sign that you've gone to the police, he'll kill me deader than dead. That's what it says here. 'Deader than dead.' So that's pretty serious. Do you hear that Frida?"

Frida nodded. She tried to keep her professional composure. "Where are you?" Frida asked.

"I'm in a van. Parked somewhere. But I don't think I'm supposed to talk about that," Zerbe said. "He just wants me to read this message. And for Angela to deliver it to Dad. Are you ready, Angela?"

"What do you mean?" Angela asked, worried.

"Write this down," Zerbe said. "It's important."

Angela looked around for a pen. Crush handed her a pencil and a napkin. "All right." She took a deep breath. "I'm ready."

"Wait," Crush said. "I want to talk to the other person in the room."

"Oh, I don't think that's a good idea," Zerbe said.

"Are you listening to me, whoever you are?" Crush said. "Answer this question. If Angela delivers this message, will you let Zerbe go free?"

There was an awkward pause.

"Just let me read the message," Zerbe said.

"No. Not until we have an agreement," Crush said.

"This isn't a negotiation, Crush," Zerbe said, plaintively.

"That's exactly what this is," Crush said, and reached down to the phone and ended the call.

The others in the room gasped.

"What did you just do?" Gail said.

"Are you crazy?" Angela asked.

Crush raised one of his big fingers, telling them to wait.

"I hope you know what you're doing, Crush," Frida whispered.

"So do I," Crush said.

"If he thinks he's in control," Frida explained to others, "then he *is* in control. Crush is giving him reason to doubt that."

"Is that a good thing?" Angela asked.

"We'll see," Crush said.

The phone beeped. Crush reached down and connected the call.

Zerbe appeared on the screen. He looked like he'd taken a few more punches to the face. "Don't make him mad, Crush. Really, don't."

"What did he say?" Crush asked. "Did he answer my question?"

"He said it all depends on what my father says," Zerbe said, not even trying to keep the desperation out of his voice. "He says it's all up to him."

Crush nodded. That would have to do. "All right. Go ahead."

"Here goes," Zerbe said and proceeded to read with great deliberation. "*'The GV is dead. The SG is out of the HSR. Remember the seventy-six thousand. The debt is not paid.'*" Zerbe looked quickly toward the camera. "Did you get that?"

Angela wrote feverishly. "I don't think so. Can I read it

back to you?"

The line went dead. Angela panicked. "I don't think I got it. I didn't get it! Call him back."

"We'd better not." Crush took the napkin from Angela and read it over. "That's almost right." He crossed out a few letters and fixed some of the phrasing.

"You're sure you're right?" Angela asked him.

"I'm sure," he said. Running numbers for the Russian mob at age fifteen, Crush had developed a good memory. He'd had to—his life had depended on it. He folded the napkin and put it in his pocket.

"I'm supposed to deliver that," Angela objected.

"And you will," Crush said. "But I'm going with you." He turned to Frida. "What are you going to do, Frida?"

Frida sat at the kitchen table, her face set in concentration. "My next scheduled visit is on January 2nd. I haven't been here this morning. You have three days." She finished the rest of her cold coffee and got up. "Zerbe better be here when I get back, Crush." Her voice cracked a little as she spoke, which made it sound less like a warning and more like a plea.

"He will be," Crush said.

"How do you know?"

"Because I'll bring him back." Crush didn't say dead or alive. He didn't think Frida could handle that.

⌘

They decided to leave Noel in the loft with the ankle monitor on. He said it made him feel safer to know that "they" thought he was someone else. Gail stayed with him, to keep an eye on him and make sure that, if he went totally crazy (always a possibility according to Angela), at least he wouldn't be alone. Crush and Angela went to see her father and deliver the message.

Now Crush was piloting the Camaro through busy downtown traffic. It would still be the morning rush hour for the next three hours, so he knew enough to stay off the 110 and the narrow tunnels that led to the San Gabriel Valley. Instead, he traveled to Pasadena through the surface streets of what was nowadays called DTLA. Through the canyons of old buildings that were used by film crews to double for New York and Boston. Past the gleaming new skyscrapers that were sprouting up like immense, glass Lego kits, changing the face of Los Angeles from the sprawling western burg he knew into a Dubai-like city of the future. For all the years Crush had known it, LA had always been an evolving city. But now it was evolving in ways Crush didn't really understand.

"The skyline's really changing," Angela said, echoing his thoughts.

Crush grunted noncommittally. Then he said. "I guess that's your father's work."

"Not all of it."

"But enough?"

"Enough."

After that, they drove in silence up Broadway until it crossed the concrete ditch that was the LA River and turned into York. In no time at all, Crush felt like he was in another land. A part of the Gilded Age Midwest. *Magnificent Ambersons-land*, Zerbe called it. The fabled land of Pasadena.

Turning left, Crush maneuvered through tree-lined streets and made his way onto San Rafael Avenue, the legendary lane of Tudor mansions that bordered the steep bluff of the dry riverbed called the Arroyo Seco. Hidden from the road by hedges, fences, and long driveways were great imposing houses. Houses that looked like Wayne Manor from the TV show *Batman*. In fact, one of them *was* Wayne Manor, or at least the house they used for the establishing shots back in the sixties. The illusion of great wealth met the reality of great wealth on the Arroyo Seco.

The shadows of tree branches swept over the Camaro's hood and Crush stuck his head out the window and took in a deep breath of cool December air. *What was that smell?* Crush wondered. *Oh that's right. It's the smell of power.*

Fifteen minutes away from downtown LA and it seemed to Crush like another country and another time. A time of western culture and money and white people's rule. *A time a lot like right now*, Crush corrected himself.

As he drove, he thought back to another time. Near the end of the last century, when he first drove down these streets with his mother. On the day they moved in.

⌘

Toni Rush had married Emil Zerbe in Las Vegas just a few days before. Toni had left the one-room apartment she shared with Crush in Koreatown (and this was before Koreatown got all hipster-cool) one day in late June and didn't come back till July. She was gone for two weeks, but Crush didn't worry. She did that from time to time. Went off with men for a week or two. Sometimes she even came back with them. Sometimes she came back with a few trophies. Sometimes she came back with a black eye or a busted lip.

This time she came back with a husband.

Crush hadn't thought that Emil Zerbe would be a keeper. To be honest, he thought Emil Zerbe was out of Toni's league. Crush knew that was kind of a rotten thing for a son to think about his mother, but

Emil was one of the richest men in Southern California and Crush's mother was...Crush's mother. Good for a rich man's fling but not much more. To be honest, Crush was surprised when she was gone with him for more than a weekend. When the weekend stretched to two weeks, he was half afraid that Emil was a rich maniac and that he had buried her somewhere in the desert.

For that reason, Crush was ecstatic to see Toni leaning over his bed one morning, alive and well and looking exceedingly well fed.

"I'm back, Cabe," she said. "Pack your things. We're moving."

He sat up and shook his head to clear it. All right, he thought, we're moving again. What's Toni done this time. Robbery? Blackmail? Something worse? Best not to ask. Just get on the move.

"You pack," he said, jumping out of bed. "I'll get a car. An inconspicuous one. Maybe a Corolla. I saw one parked around the corner last night. I'll be back in five minutes."

Toni laughed. "Slow down, Cabe. We're not on the run. We're just moving."

He sat back down. "Where?"

"To Pasadena."

He blinked and thought. "Where's that?"

She laughed again. "It's just to the east of here. I spent last week out there. It's like another world."

"Okay." Crush tried to adjust to this new change in his always-changing life. "Is this on account of Emil? Is he getting you an apartment?"

"No," Toni said smiling. "A house! A huge fucking house!"

Crush had to ask. "What for?"

She showed Crush her left hand. There was the most spectacular diamond Crush had ever seen, with a gold band nestled beneath it, sitting there on her third finger. Still, Crush couldn't quite put it together. "Why did he give you those?"

"Why do you think? We got married, Cabe."

Crush just stared. Was she kidding? "Why?"

"What kind of question is that? Because he loves me."

Crush nodded. Then he nodded again. Then he thought to ask, "Do you love him?"

Toni looked at him like he'd asked her something that had never occurred to her. Then she answered, "Sure. Of course, I do. Now come on."

So, she wasn't kidding, Crush thought as he drove the Mustang that he'd stolen from somewhere in Bell Gardens last month down San Rafael Avenue. She had really done it. She had landed a big one.

"Here. On the right," Toni said.

"Where?" There was nothing but a large hedge on the right.

"It's there. That's the entrance. You passed it."

He turned the car around, pulled up to the massive greenery, and on closer inspection saw a small metal box inset in the bushes. Toni rolled down the window, stuck out her hand, and pressed a button on the box like she'd been doing it her whole life.

A bored, officious voice came through the little box. "Who's there?"

"Samantha! It's me, Toni."

"And?"

"And let me in."

There was a passive-aggressive pause. "Just a minute."

Toni turned to Crush with a happy smile. "Samantha hates me."

After another pause, the hedge started to open, revealing a long curving driveway. Crush steered the car down the lane and they listened to almost all of "My Favorite Mistake" on the radio before they came upon what Crush thought must have been a four-star hotel. Or perhaps they'd gone through a wormhole and ended up in England in front of a damned castle.

It sure looked like a castle. Massive stone walls overgrown with ivy. What Crush thought were called battlements along the top of the façade. The little windows to shoot arrows out of and the big windows to let light in. A huge front door with enormous iron studs set into it. True, there was no drawbridge, but the large pond in front of the house could serve as a moat in a pinch.

"Is that his house?" Crush asked as he circled the pond and pulled up in front of the stone steps that led to the entryway.

"I told you it was fucking huge," Toni said gleefully as she got out of the Mustang.

"How many people live here?"

"I don't really know. I think four. At least part of the time. When his kids are staying with him."

"And the rest of the time?"

"Emil lives here alone."

Crush got out of the car. One man alone in that gigantic mansion could get pretty lonely. But lonely enough to marry Toni Rush? Crush felt the hairs on his back stand up straight, the way they always did when he sensed danger. Something wasn't right.

Toni raced up the steps, taking them two at a time, and rang the doorbell, which chimed with appropriate solemnity. Crush climbed the stairs with more caution, eyeing the ivy with suspicion. Rats lived in ivy, he'd heard. This damn house could contain hidden dangers.

The huge door swung open and a young woman who had dirty-blond hair swept up on the top of her head with a pencil pushed into it to keep it there greeted them with a stony expression. The woman wore wire-rimmed glasses and a trim little business suit that somehow managed to look disheveled even though it was actually quite tidy. She looked all business. "I didn't expect you," she said to Toni.

"Why not?"

"Because I thought you'd come to your senses. You had a good week. You got a nice ring. Why don't you quit while you're ahead?"

"You think I'm nothing but a gold digger, don't you Samantha?"

"No, I think you're probably a number of things in addition to being a gold digger." Her eyes fell on Crush. "And who's this, if I may ask?"

"This is Caleb. My son."

She couldn't have looked more skeptical. "Your son, huh? How old is he?"

"Seventeen."

"He looks pretty big for seventeen."

"I drank all my milk," Crush said.

"Emil's waiting for you. In the swimming pool," Samantha said, her voice heavy with resentment, and left the room.

"I like her," Crush said. "She doesn't put up with your shit."

"Thanks a lot."

"What does she do around here?" Crush asked as Toni led the way through the maze that was the inside of the house.

"She's Emil's private secretary. I think she was his private secretary, if you know what I mean. She's not too happy about being replaced."

"Do you think she wanted to marry him?"

"Sure, who wouldn't?" Toni grinned. "But she doesn't have my hidden assets!"

Crush didn't know what his mother's hidden assets were and he really didn't want to.

The house on the inside looked about like what you'd expect from the outside. Colossal wooden banisters and balustrades.

Colorful woven antique tapestries hanging from the walls. Big heavy furniture. Even a damn suit of armor in one corner. It looked like the setting for a Vincent Price movie, minus the cobwebs.

Toni led Crush down a tiled corridor. The echoes of water splashing came down the hall. Crush stopped. "Emil's in the pool, right?"

"Yep! You should see it. It's spectacular."

"Mom, I really don't want to see the new dude you're banging in his swimming trunks."

"He's my husband," Toni said, a little offended.

"But you're banging him, right?"

"Well, of course. Come on. You have to see this natatorium!"

"I thought it was a swimming pool."

"It is! That's how rich he is, he can call it whatever he wants."

Reluctantly, Crush followed his mother. And the pool was indeed amazing. Inside a glass-enclosed greenhouse, it was done up with what Crush guessed were Greek- or Roman-style sculptures and tiles. All blue and white. Images of gods holding up the world and statues of fat dolphins and fatter Cupids squirting water out of their mouths. Crush guessed it must have cost a fortune and supposed it was very nice if you liked that sort thing. He preferred the pool at the Y. It was less full of itself.

The pool smelled freshly of chlorine and was at least Olympic size. The tiles or the lighting made the water look blue, like Crush imagined the water looked in the Mediterranean or the Aegean or one of those far-off seas that Crush wasn't sure even existed in real life.

A man was gliding through the water with expert strokes, barely leaving a ripple as he shot across the pool. He came to the edge, grabbed onto the lip, and pulled himself out in one graceful motion. He stood dripping on the deck.

If this was Emil Zerbe, he didn't look anything like Crush had expected. If you'd asked Crush what kind of rich older man would marry Toni, he'd have picked someone with a toupee, or an artificial tan, or a serious case of erectile dysfunction—someone who was short or overweight or both. Someone who was either a nerd or a narcissistic asshole or both. Someone who wanted some thirty-five-year-old eye candy to replace his previous trophy wife who'd aged out. An insecure man with an inferiority complex who used money and sex to make up for it.

This man, on the other hand, was handsome. Movie-star handsome. His body was fit, and Crush could see a lot of it since he was wearing a Speedo. Speedos don't look good on guys unless they have a six-pack and don't have an ounce of body fat. The Speedo looked good on him.

Crush guessed he was in his fifties, but movie-star fifties. The mythical ageless fifties. He didn't look so much like Liam Neeson as he looked like the way Liam Neeson wished he looked. His graying hair was cut long in the European style, and the water glistened from the hair on his chest. This man didn't look like he ever had an insecure moment in his life.

"Emil!" Toni said.

So it was Emil. He walked over to Toni and kissed her comfortably but with great passion, as if they had spent the past week kissing and that's how they would spend the next and the next. She was wearing a Versace outfit that Emil must have bought for her and it was getting all mussed and wet and ruined, but she didn't care.

Crush took this as his cue to leave but Toni came up for air and Emil looked over and noticed him. "Hello. And you are?"

"Emil, I want you to meet my son, Caleb," Toni said, beaming with pride.

Emil eyed him skeptically.

"I know," Crush said. "I'm big for my age."

"Pleased to meet you, Caleb. Your mother's told me a lot about you. She's so proud of you." Emil spoke with a barely noticeable foreign accent. Crush guessed that it was French, or maybe Austrian.

"Well, I'm proud of her."

Toni dropped the bomb as casually as she could. "Could you have Samantha show Caleb to his room?"

After an eloquent pause, Emil asked, "His room?"

"Yes," Toni said, still calm as ever. "Where he's going to live."

"Hmmm. It's odd," Emil said, "but I hadn't really thought about that."

"Why not? You knew I had a son."

"Yes, of course. Tell you what, I could get him an apartment. One of those nice ones on Orange Grove. That's only five minutes away."

Toni tried a different tack. She pouted a little and got just the tiniest crack in her voice. "But he has to live with his mother. He's just a boy. Only seventeen."

Emil cast his eye on Crush. "He doesn't look seventeen."

"I had a growth spurt." He could tell he was going to enjoy needling this man.

Shaking his head, Emil said, "I'd like to accommodate you, but I have my own children to think about. They live here two weeks out of every month."

"Where are they the rest of the time?" Crush asked.

Emil looked askance at Crush. "With their mother, of course."

"I see," Crush said. "How long have you been divorced?"

His steel-gray eyes locked with Crush's. "Three years. Why do you ask?"

"I just wanted to make sure my mother isn't a homewrecker," Crush said, smiling a little half-moon smile.

Emil's lips smiled back at Crush, but his eyes held him in a steady gaze, like a python eyeing its prey. "No. No, the home was well wrecked before I ever met your mother."

"That's a relief," Crush said. The two men kept sizing each other up, two gunfighters in the Old West.

Toni jumped in to cut the tension. "Oh, your kids will love Caleb. He gets along with everybody!"

"Do you?" Emil asked.

"I kind of do," Crush said, dryly.

"Actually, I'm more worried about how they'll treat you," Emil said. "My children are...difficult to get along with."

"I've had worse," Crush said.

"You don't know them."

"Trust me, I've had worse."

"I really don't know...."

"He'll keep to himself," Toni said. "They won't even know he's here."

"That shouldn't be too hard, in this house," Crush added.

Emil frowned. "I suppose he could use the guest room in the East Wing."

Toni smiled. She'd won a victory. Now she had to take care of the details. "Oh, that would be perfect! Thank you so much. Of course, we'll have to enroll him in school. It's very important to us that he finish high school. It's a promise we made to his father just before he...died."

Emil looked too smart to fall for such an obvious scam. Maybe he didn't know yet what a liar Toni was. Or maybe he just didn't care. "They have very nice public schools in Pasadena. So I understand."

"But couldn't he get into that private school that your kids go to? Pasadena Prep? I want him to have every advantage. His life has been so hard up till now. So has mine."

Emil took her in his arms. "That's all over now."

"I know, baby." They were at it again. But was this kiss partially for Crush's benefit? Emil's way of claiming his mother in front of him?

When the kiss ended, Emil whispered, "I'll see what I can do."

"Oh, thank you, darling. You won't regret it."

Crush wasn't sure the same could be said of himself.

Emil extended a hand to him. "I think we'll get along fine. I won't call you 'son.' You're too old for that."

"Just call him Caleb," Toni volunteered.

"All right, Caleb. And you call me Emil." His hand was still extended. Crush took it and they shook. Emil had a firm grip and wanted Crush to know it. Crush could have squeezed his hand to a pulp, but he decided now was not the time to show off. That time would come later.

Turning to no one in particular, Emil said, "Samantha, show Caleb to the East Wing guest room."

A disembodied voice answered, sounding rather bored with the whole thing. "Yes, Emil."

Crush looked around. "Does she listen to everything?"

Emil smiled at Toni. "Not everything."

⌘

Crush was pulled back into the twenty-first century when he hit a speed bump on the road and Angela said, "It's here on the right."

"I know," Crush snapped, although in reality he'd have driven right past that hedge with the hidden voice box. It had been too long.

Angela stuck her hand out the window and pressed the

button. Now the box had a camera in it so it could see who was approaching. A voice spoke up. "Hello?"

"Hi. Let me in."

"Who's with you?"

"I'll explain when I get in."

The hedge slowly started to move. "Who was that?" Crush asked.

"My stepmother. Samantha."

CHAPTER EIGHT

The van's engine started. Zerbe braced himself, still strapped in the chair, as he felt the van begin to move.

So he was being taken somewhere. From a place he didn't know to a destination he didn't know. Was this good or bad? Maybe he was being taken to a spot where he'd be released? Maybe his father had given them what they wanted and they were going to let him go?

Or maybe they weren't? Maybe they were taking him somewhere to kill him and dispose of his body? But why wouldn't they kill him first? Wouldn't that be easier?

Or maybe they were just moving him for the sake of moving him? It didn't really matter. All that mattered was that, for the moment, he was alive and he wasn't being beaten. So he could be happy for now.

⌘

The pond in front of Emil Zerbe's mansion had been filled in and replaced with a rocky lawn of succulents and cactuses, which didn't exactly suit the European-castle theme but was in keeping with the water-conservation movement that was sweeping Southern California. This drought had

lasted for so many years that, when rain did come, the local news affiliates pushed their daily reports of murders
and hit-and-run accidents aside and opened their broad-
casts with correspondents standing under umbrellas at
various points in the city and reporting that, yes, it was
indeed raining.

Emil didn't seem to be the xeriscape type, so this must
have been Samantha's influence. *Well, good for her,* Crush
thought as he parked the car and got out. *At least she's using
her hard-won position to do some good. Even if it was only one
lawn in front of one mansion. What does Gail always say? 'Think
globally, act locally.'*

Crush looked up at the house. Maybe the ivy had been
cut back a bit but other than that, it hadn't changed since
Crush had last seen it some fifteen years before. It was as
if Emil saw this house as an ancestral home, one that the
Zerbes would pass down from generation to generation in
perpetuity. In reality, and knowing Emil's children, Crush
doubted that the house would last a month after the old
man's death. It would be sold, razed, and replaced by somebody else's idea of an ostentatious display of wealth.

Angela and Crush walked up the familiar steps. Crush
felt a chill go down his spine. Angela must have noticed his
shiver, because she asked, "Are you sure you're up for this?"

"No," he said as a preppy-looking young man in his
mid-twenties opened the door. Angela told him they wanted to
see her father and walked past him to the living room.

"A male secretary?" Crush asked Angela.

"Sure. Samantha's no fool."

"She does the hiring?"

"Yeah. Things have changed a bit." Angela threw open
the big double doors and walked into the parlor.

Samantha Adamski, now Samantha Zerbe, turned from

a big flat-screen television. She looked at Angela, then at Crush. Then harder at Crush. Her face blossomed into a broad smile. "Caleb! My God, how are you?" She opened her arms and hurried to Crush, giving him a fond hug. He hugged her back. She pulled away and beamed, "Look at you! You've grown up to be such a man!"

"It's been fifteen years," he said.

"What have you been doing?"

"A little of this, a little of that."

"Mostly that," Angela added.

"Of course Angela and K.C. have kept us informed about you. Your war record. Your work with that security agency. Are you still with them?"

"He just started back this morning," Angela said.

"Oh, I'm so glad. It's nice to know you have a career." Then her face grew sadder. "We were so sorry about what happened to your mother."

Crush nodded. "Thank you, Sam."

Samantha struggled to find words. "I thought of reaching out to you when I heard but...too much had happened by then, hadn't it?"

"A lot happened," Crush said.

Angela ended the awkward moment by saying, "We need to see Daddy. Where is he?"

Samantha hesitated. "He's not doing very well. Why do you need to see him?"

Angela began. "I don't know quite how to say this...."

Crush cut her off. "It's a security matter. About the parade."

"I don't know," Samantha said. "All his energy is going into the HSR. I don't think...."

"The HSR?" Crush asked.

"The high-speed rail. LA to San Francisco. He sees it as

his legacy. It's all he can think about. We're going to start construction next month, God willing. It means the world to him. He wants it to be a monument to Zerbe Enterprises. A tribute to his brother Victor. You can understand that."

"Well, Uncle Victor always did like to go to San Francisco," Angela said.

Samantha ignored Angela's quip. "The float in the Rose Parade this year is a tribute to it. Noel even wants us to ride in it. Me and Emil. Waving to the crowd. Emil says he doesn't want to do it, of course, but I know he does. It will be his victory lap."

"We have to speak with him," Crush said.

"Why don't you give *me* the message?" Samantha asked. "I can tell him when he's rested."

"There's no time," Crush said.

"It really *is* urgent," Angela added. "It'll just take a second."

"All right. He's in the gym. But don't upset him."

"I'll try not to," Crush said.

As soon as they reached the hall, Angela whispered to him, "Why didn't you want me to tell her about the kidnapping?"

"The fewer people who know, the better. Besides, I didn't want to worry her."

"You always had a soft spot for Sam."

Crush grunted. "You didn't tell me your father was sick."

"He had a stroke. Two months ago."

They entered the gym. Emil was hanging onto a metal walker, moving with slow determination across the mat-covered floor. He pulled his right leg behind him slowly, and his right arm looked shrunken and weak under his white T-shirt. He was concentrating so much on the effort of crossing the room that he didn't notice they'd entered until Angela cleared her throat. He looked up. Crush could see that the left side of his face was sunken and expressionless. His bright right eye stared at Crush for a moment. Then he started to cry.

Crush didn't know what to do. Emil approached him slowly, dragging his right foot behind him and weeping silently. When he had made it almost all the way to Crush, his right foot collapsed from the effort. He tried to hold himself up with his left arm but it wasn't strong enough and he started to topple to the floor. Instinctively, Crush reached out to grab him. Emil clutched onto Crush's arms, buried his head in the big man's chest, and sobbed.

Angela brought a wheelchair over from the corner of the room and Crush settled Emil into it. Seeing the great man transformed into a weeping wreck almost brought Crush to tears himself.

"I'm sorry for the display," Emil gasped when he finally stopped crying. "My emotions have become a bit unstable since the stroke." His speech was slightly slurred but perfectly understandable.

"That's okay," Crush said, because he couldn't think of anything else.

"I don't have many regrets in my long life," Emil said. "You are one."

Crush's heart almost went out to him. Then he remembered. "How 'bout my mother?"

Emil hesitated. "Of course, I was sorry when I..."

"Yes," Crush cut him off, "when you heard what happened to her. But you weren't sorry enough to come to her funeral."

"No," Emil said. "Nor was I sorry enough to check to see how you were. That is my regret."

Crush shook his head. "I didn't come here for that. I came here for K.C."

Some of the old disdain came back into Emil's voice. "Kendrick? What has he done now?"

"He hasn't done anything," Angela said.

"He's been kidnapped," Crush said.

Emil didn't sound surprised. "Did you call the police?"

"They say they'll kill him if we involve the police," Angela said.

The old man was dismissive. "Oh, they always say that."

"Have you dealt with kidnappers before?" Crush asked.

"How much do they want?" Emil asked, ignoring Crush's question.

"They don't want money, Daddy," Angela said.

"They always say that, too."

"He wants you to hear something," Crush said, pulling the napkin from his jacket pocket and handing it to Angela.

"We talked to K.C. on the phone," she said. "His face looked horrible. He'd been beaten."

Emil grunted. "Well, what do they want me to hear?"

Angela unfolded the napkin and started to read. " 'The GV is dead. The SG is out of the HSR. Remember the seventy-six thousand. The debt is not paid.' "

Emil listened. The live side of his face was just as expressionless as the dead side.

"Does that make sense to you, Dad?" Angela asked.

Emil made a sound that might have meant he was thinking or might have meant his jaw was hurting him.

"What's your answer?" Crush asked. "What do you want me to tell them?"

"When are you going to talk to them?" Emil asked.

"I don't know. What difference does that make? What's your answer?"

Emil started to turn the wheelchair away. "I'll think about it."

Crush blocked the wheelchair with his foot. "Goddamn it, this is K.C.'s life we're talking about. You didn't care enough to keep him out of prison. Don't you at least want to keep him alive?"

"Please. He only served two years. It probably did him some good."

"Someday I'll have him tell you how much good it did him."

Angela spoke up. "Daddy, this really is serious. They might kill him."

Emil spit. "Oh, they won't kill him. They don't have the guts."

"Who doesn't?" Crush asked.

"Whoever has him."

"Do you know who that is?"

"Stop asking stupid questions."

"What does the message mean?" Crush demanded.

"I have no idea."

"HSR. That stands for high-speed rail, doesn't it?" Crush asked. "What does SG stand for?"

"How should I know?"

"SGCF," Angela said. "Is that it?"

"Could be," Emil said. "Could be a lot of things."

"What's that?" Crush asked Angela.

"It's the French railway company. Daddy's one of the main shareholders. They're the ones who are bidding for the high-speed rail."

"High-speed rail is the future!" Emil burst out with the speech as if it were his mantra. "High-speed rail was the future back in the *nineties,* when my brother and I started *trying* to build it. Every country in the civilized world has an HSR. Most of the countries in the *uncivilized* world have one. But not America. Why? Why does the US lag so far behind?

Why can't we invest in our infrastructure? Well, when we start building the HSR next month, that will make a *statement*. America is *not* in decline. America is the greatest nation on earth!"

"Is that what this is about?" Crush asked. "Is somebody trying to stop you from building your bullet train? Who? A rival company?"

Emil erupted in anger. "Enough! You want my answer? I'll give you my answer. Tell them the debt *has* been paid. In full. They can't threaten me!"

"But what about K.C.?" Angela asked.

Emil brushed her off with his good hand. "Oh, they're bluffing."

"But what if they're not?" Crush asked.

Emil leveled his eye on him. "That's a chance I'm willing to take."

⌘

Zerbe didn't know how long they'd been driving. It was certainly more than an hour and certainly less than a day. Buffeted around in his metal chair, he'd long ago given up counting the number of right turns and left turns, the stops and the starts. All he knew was he had traveled a long way through the heavy traffic of metropolitan LA until they had broken clear of the gravitational pull of the city and were now driving steadily toward destination unknown.

He listened to the steady hum of the wheels on the road and thought about his life. There were a number of things he wanted to do that he hadn't done. Direct a movie for one. Climb Mount Everest for another. Make love with Scarlett Johansson. Why not? "Ah, but a man's reach should exceed his grasp, or what's a heaven for?" as Browning wrote.

Then he heard something and decided he was going crazy. What he heard was the road. The sound of the wheels on the road. A rhythmic sound. Almost musical. And he could make out the tune.

The theme to *The Lone Ranger*. Yes, that was it. The road was playing the *William Tell Overture*. He was definitely going crazy.

Then he thought he'd replay some happy childhood memories to help him hold onto his sanity. The only problem was that he couldn't come up with any. None that didn't turn dark in the end.

⌘

Zerbe thought of the nights he used to spend as a teenager playing Dungeons & Dragons with his brother and sister and her friends. Her friends. Not his friends. And certainly not Noel's friends. Neither of them had many friends. Or any, really.

Still, they were an integral part of what K.C. had named the Colorado Boulevard Irregulars. They played other games, of course. They even did some live-action role-playing and practiced with a bow and arrow at the Arroyo Seco Archery Range with the Roving Archers of Pasadena. But it was at Dungeon & Dragons that they really excelled.

Noel was the Dungeon Master but Angela was the Queen of the Game. The reason everyone came. Her character in the game was a high-ranking elf by the name of Loralana. Her cousin, Renee Zerbe, was the other reason they came. She was a lovely Halfling called Dardrey.

K.C. himself was a gnome named Billin. The other players were mostly male Orcs, Tieflings, half-elves, Dragonborn, even humans, and they all wanted to sleep with Dardrey and Loralana, or both. The real secret of the game was the Power of the Magical Cousins.

Renee was sad, K.C. could see that. There was a troubled look in her eyes and a deep sorrow in the way she gripped her twenty-sided dice. K.C. was two years younger than Renee and had been in love with her for as long as he could remember.

It was, of course, an impossible love. The two of them were first cousins, blood relations. A taboo if ever there was one. But still, she was his ideal. His dream woman. His Guinevere. His Zelda. His Hermione Granger. Only with long black hair, black like the night. Black like a starry sky wrapping around her face, falling upon her dreamed-of milk-white breasts. A girl he could never love, but couldn't help but keep loving.

Renee didn't love him back, of course. How could she? Or if she did love him, she loved him, quite appropriately, like a younger cousin. A friend. A group mascot. It was a role Zerbe grew all too comfortable with as the years passed. The loyal friend who was in love with the beautiful woman who didn't see him as a potential lover. Look at Frida now. The pattern only repeated itself.

It didn't help Zerbe's heartache that Renee was always attracted to alpha males who were total assholes. Football players and rich preppies who used her and tossed her aside. Who even beat her, Zerbe was sure of that. Who left her broken and yearning.

Like tonight. Zerbe could swear he saw tears glittering on her lashes. He cast his eyes around the table to see which of the players was the one who had hurt her. There were Evan Gibbard and Sonny Kraus, both obnoxious rich kids who thought they were born not on third base, but having hit the game-winning home run. Renee, suffering from low self-esteem for no reason Zerbe could think of, had been traded between Evan and Sonny like a joint at a frat party. Zerbe wondered which one had hurt her last?

Of course, it didn't have to be just romantic heartbreak that could be bringing tears to her eyes. Renee, who had always been melancholic for no particular reason, came face to face with real tragedy when her father had died just a few weeks before, on New Year's Day, in a most spectacular suicide that was all over the front pages and had brought the Rose Parade to a sudden halt. He had been in charge of driving the Zerbe Enterprises float that year, a phantasmagoria of happy dinosaurs frolicking at the base of a smoking volcano. The calm before the storm.

Halfway down Colorado Boulevard he had blown his brains out with a Glock 18. They hadn't mentioned that in the television coverage of the parade, of course. It didn't quite match the celebratory mood of the occasion. But afterward, on the evening news, it was all anybody wanted to talk about.

Renee had been very close to her father. The tragedy and the subsequent publicity cut her to the core. Her mother was all but destroyed by it. It had turned what had previously been a Byronic pose into a harsh reality. Renee really was a "sad girl" now.

As Zerbe surveyed this memory, he was a little surprised to see Crush there. Or "Caleb," as they all called him then. Then he realized what night he was remembering and he knew he'd find no comfort there.

Zerbe watched as Renee suddenly pushed away from the table and hurried into the kitchen. He didn't know if he should follow her or not. For some reason he looked to Caleb for reassurance. The big guy just shrugged and looked toward the kitchen door. Was he telling Zerbe to go after her?

Zerbe got up and walked into the kitchen. Renee was standing by the open door to the garden.

"Hi, Billin," she said. He saw that she was holding a large carving knife in her right hand.

"Hi, Dardrey," he said. "What's the knife for?"

"It's for to kill myself, Billin," she said.

Was this the game, or was it reality? Zerbe wondered. "Why do you want to kill yourself?" he asked.

"Because my father didn't," she said. Then she took the knife and slid it over her left wrist. A bright thread of blood followed the knife as she drew it across her flesh. Then she threw it into the sink and ran out the door, dripping blood on the tile as she went.

Zerbe remembered how he stood there in the kitchen, stunned, staring, thinking it must be a joke. A special effect. A magic trick.

But the blood. It looked so real. It looked so final.

⌘

Fuck that memory. This reality—being kidnapped and tied to a chair in the back of a moving van—was better than that recollection. He tried his best to banish it from his mind, but in his mind's eye, all he could see was that open door and the blood trail leading out of it.

So he tried to think of nothing at all. He tried to be grateful he hadn't had to pee all this time, but that seemed a small consolation. After a little while, the van stopped moving. Had they reached their destination? *What now?* he wondered. He heard doors opening and closing from the outside. Was that the driver getting out of the van?

He waited. He waited longer. He waited so long he almost fell asleep. He waited so long that he really had to pee. Then the back door of the van opened. A figure in a hoodie got in and Zerbe shut his eyes. He heard the figure settling in opposite him. Heard the girl's electronically modified voice again.

"Why are your eyes closed?" his kidnapper asked.

"Because I don't want to see you," Zerbe said. "I don't want you to worry about me identifying you. When you let me go."

"What makes you think I'm going to let you go?"

Zerbe's heart sank. "Because you don't want to kill me?" he said. He didn't like that it sounded like a question.

"That's up to your father. Do you want me to tell you why you're here?"

"No. I don't want to know anything."

"Why not?"

"Because I might learn something you don't want me to tell anyone else."

"And then?"

"And then you'll have to kill me."

"And you're worried about that?"

"Yes, I'm worried about that!"

"Worrying won't help, you know. You should relax."

"Really? Relax?" Zerbe asked in disbelief. "I'm tied to a chair and you're telling me to relax?"

"I'm telling you that what you're feeling will have no effect on what happens to you. Or to your family. Or to your city."

"Jesus, shut up!" Zerbe cried.

But his kidnapper kept on talking in that silky, feminine voice. "So you might as well...relax."

"I think I'll panic instead. It just feels right, you know? And I'm going to wet my pants. I hope you don't mind."

"As long as you listen to what I'm going to tell you...."

And Zerbe had no choice but to listen.

⌘

Crush and Angela walked away from the gym, leaving Emil to his physical therapy and his regrets.

"He didn't mean that," Angela said. "He cares about K.C., he really does."

"He hides it well," Crush said. "I want to see Noel's room."

"What for?"

"Whoever kidnapped K.C. knew about Noel's plan to get him arrested. They knew where he'd be. Does Noel confide in anyone?"

"Nobody. Not me. And I'm the closest thing to a friend he has."

She led him upstairs to Noel's room. It was the same room he'd had when they were kids, but now it was transformed into an artist's studio. Scale models of Rose Parade floats and various sets and installations filled the floor so that they had to maneuver around them.

Crush opened the drawers of Noel's desk. He looked for personal papers, bills, anything to show some contact with another person. But there was nothing. No letters, of course; this was the twenty-first century, after all. But no notes. No bills. No receipts. Nothing jotted down. Nothing in his handwriting. No flyers for concerts or clubs. Nothing to show that anyone lived here at all.

The one personal item he found was a small, oblong metal disc, like an oval coin, with the initials TI engraved on one side and the words "one year" engraved on the other. "What's this?"

"I never saw it before," Angela said.

"It looks like a chip from an Anonymous organization."

"Anonymous?"

"You know, Alcoholics Anonymous. Gamblers Anonymous. I have no idea what 'TI' stands for though. Do you know if your brother is an addict?"

"He's got problems. He has OCD. He's paranoid. He may be bipolar. But I don't think he's addicted to anything."

Crush pocketed the token. "Tell me about that French railroad company."

"The SGCF?"

"Yeah. What does that stand for?"

"The Société Générale des Chemins de Fer Français. *'Chemins de fer'* means 'paths of iron.' Isn't that a cool term for 'railroad'? It was founded in 1938."

"Does your father own it?"

"I don't think he owns it. He controls it. It's been in the family for generations."

"But they're French. What are they doing in this country?"

"Oh, they've built a lot of railroads all around the world. In Spain and Israel. South Korea and Taiwan. My father's been trying to get a foothold in America for years."

"And who wants to stop him?"

"Who doesn't? The environmentalists. The California High-Speed Rail Authority. People who don't like the route they're proposing. People who want the train to go along the coast rather than along the 5 and up through the Grapevine. And people who just want the graft for themselves."

"This is personal. Who wants to stop it personally?"

"I don't know. It's a long list. Lots of people hate Daddy. Hank Gibbard for one."

"Is that Evan Gibbard's father?" Crush remembered Evan from Pasadena Prep. Evan was a creepy friend of Noel's. He was usually accompanied by Sonny Kraus, and the two of them were notorious for supplying kids with adequate fake IDs and more-than-adequate pot.

"Yeah. He used to be my dad's partner, remember? Until he got forced out. Now he runs a nonprofit. Save the Ha-hamongna Watershed. That's the big muddy mess between JPL and the Devil's Gate Dam at the foot of the San Gabriel Mountains."

"I know what it is." Crush didn't want to be re-minded of it.

She sighed. "Well, if we build the bullet train on the route Daddy wants, which is up what they call the Grapevine, along the 210, you know? Then it'll plow right through there. They'll have to dig the whole watershed up. And good rid-dance, I say, but a lot of tree huggers want to save it. Some-thing about it being an 'alluvial canyon,' or something. And there's even some fucking endangered bird that lives there, too. The Least Bill whatever.

"Believe it or not, Hank Gibbard was *suing* us to stop the dig. But, if you ask me, he was really doing it to fuck with Daddy. He couldn't care less about some stupid warbler. Well, Daddy got that suit thrown out of court so now noth-ing's stopping him. The bullet train is definitely on. When it's done, we'll be able to get to San Francisco in, like, three hours. Isn't that great?"

"Is it really? I hate the Giants." Crush said as he glanced out the second-story window and saw a brown UPS truck pulling up in front of the house. He sat on the edge of Noel's bed. "Let me get this straight. Your father has the anti-GMO-food folks after him. He has the bullet train haters after him. And he has the wetland lovers after him. Are there any ac-tivist groups he's missing out on?"

"There are a few more I haven't mentioned."

"But none of them sound crazy enough to kidnap K.C."

"You'd be surprised. You don't know what these vegan enviro-nuts can be like."

"Some of my best friends are vegan enviro-nuts," Crush said.

"I bet they are. But I think it has something do with the bullet train. That has the most money surrounding it."

"And you think this is about money?"

"Don't you?"

"Maybe. But like I said, this feels personal. 'The seventy-six thousand. The debt is not paid.' What the hell does that mean?"

"Maybe we *should* go to the police," Angela said.

"Okay. But it's been my experience that the police are not at their best when handling a delicate situation."

"Is that what this situation is? Delicate?"

"What would you call it?"

"I'd call it fucked up," she said. "And you don't have an exactly unbiased opinion of the police, do you? You haven't always been on the right side of the law, remember?"

"That's how I know about them."

"So if we don't call the police, what *do* we do?"

"I have to talk to Noel."

"Oh, he doesn't know anything."

"Well, we can't just wait for them to call back and for your father to tell them to fuck off."

"Oh, he didn't mean that," she said. "That's just the stroke talking. He'll change his mind. I'll work on him."

"You better do it quickly. I don't know how much time we have."

Just then, the door to the bedroom opened. Samantha stood looking at them from the hallway. Her expression was odd. "We just got a UPS delivery," she said. Then nothing.

"Okay," Angela said.

Samantha still stood there.

"What was it?" Crush asked.

"It was a bomb," Samantha said.

"You'd better call the police now," Crush said as he ran to the window, flung it open, and jumped out.

CHAPTER NINE

There were a lot of things Crush could have clarified before he took that jump. He could have found out whether or not the bomb was live. He could have found out how Samantha knew that what had been delivered was a bomb. He could have asked who the bomb was from. He could have found out whether or not they were all in danger of being blown sky high.

But when he glanced out the window and saw the UPS truck driving down the long driveway, his instincts kicked in. He leapt out the second-story window and hit the ground running. Taking off for his Camaro, he flung the door open, climbed in, slid the key into the ignition, heard the engine roar to life, and peeled off down the driveway.

Speeding around the bend, he could see the UPS truck heading out through the gate. The hedge started to slide closed behind it, and Crush floored the ZL1. If he timed it right he could make it through before the gate slid shut. He jammed his foot on the accelerator and shifted gears. Too late. And he was too close to brake. Best to just crash on through.

At the last minute, the gate started to slide open again. It just scraped the side of the door of the Camaro as Crush shot on through it and out onto San Rafael Avenue. But which way did the truck go? He screeched to a halt and looked both ways.

The truck was heading off to the left. Crush spun the wheel and tore off after it. If he'd been wondering whether it was just an innocent delivery truck on its rounds, the way it sped up as he approached told him all he needed to know. As the distance between them diminished, he saw that the truck didn't have a license plate and that the shade of brown was a little off for a UPS truck.

He ran over a speed bump and his head hit the ceiling of the Camaro. The truck hit another one and nearly flew off the road. These wealthy neighborhood streets had speed bumps placed at regular intervals to stop the hoi polloi from racing through them. Another one and Crush felt jarred to the bone.

Even so, he was overtaking the truck easily when it took a hard left and went down a twisting, turning lane that was thankfully free of the asphalt bumps. Crush followed the truck, scraping against the shrubbery that lined the road.

Bouncing off the curb, he came up alongside the truck. Crush didn't want to hurt the paint job on the Camaro—it had been so hard to get just that shade of green—but he did what he had to do. He slammed into the truck, and it ran off the road.

But the driver knew what he was doing. He tore across the front lawn of the next big house and made it back onto the street ahead of Crush. When Crush tried to edge him out, the truck pulled onto a tiny, two-lane bridge that crossed the Arroyo. Crush slammed on the brakes just before he went off into the abyss.

He swerved onto the bridge close behind the truck. The Arroyo opened up beneath them like a river gorge minus the river. The bridge curved until it reached Arroyo Boulevard on the other side.

The neighborhood on this side of the ravine was merely rich instead of super-rich. The faux-UPS truck went barreling onto the lawn of a big house, caromed across it and back onto the street, traveling north. Crush hit the brakes, spinning left. He followed the truck as they raced down the wooded street that wound alongside the Arroyo, taking sharp turns with the unpredictable topography of the landscape. Crush rammed the truck from behind and sent it careening into the guardrail. The truck slid across an intersection and ground to a halt, sparks flying from the guardrail.

Running through a stop sign, Crush was getting ready to close in on the truck when a white SUV suddenly barreled into the intersection. Crush cursed the vehicle, though he had to admit the driver had the right of way, and spun the wheel to the left, hitting the brakes. His car hurtled off the road, colliding with a sweet gum tree.

If the Camaro had had an airbag it would have deployed. As it was, Crush's chin cracked against the steering wheel, causing him to bite down on his cheek, filling his mouth with blood. When he lifted his head off the wheel to look out the windshield, his neck felt sore and tight. He heard a thudding sound and, with some difficulty, he turned and looked to his left. The driver of the SUV, an angry suburban mom with a shag haircut, hammered on his window with her fist.

He cranked down the window. "What the hell did you think you were doing?" she yelled. "Didn't you see that stop sign? I have kids in my car!" Crush opened his mouth to reply and blood flowed out of it down his chin. The mom gasped. "Holy crap! Are you okay? Should I call 911?"

Out of the corner of his eye, Crush saw the brown truck

back off from the guardrail and drive away. "No, I'm fine," he said, spitting blood on the mom's blouse. "I just bit my cheek. No problem." He tried to start the car, but it just growled angrily and then sputtered out.

"Really, you need help," she said, wiping the blood from her arm, "I'm sorry I yelled at you."

"Why should you be sorry? Your car's okay, right? Just go. I'll be fine."

"I should wait. I should call 911."

"Don't you have to be somewhere? With your kids?"

"Hockey practice, but...."

"Hockey practice, very important. Don't want to be late for that. I'll be fine. Look, I'm calling 911 myself." He pulled his phone out of his pocket and made as if to enter a number.

"Well, okay. But I don't feel good about this."

"You should feel good, you should feel great. I'm fine, really. Go, take care of your kids."

She got in her SUV and drove off, looking back at him as she went. Crush took a deep breath, slipped his phone back in his pocket, and tried to start the Camaro again. It didn't even make a grinding noise this time. He opened the door to go take a look, but getting out of the car wasn't as easy as he thought it would be. He was stiff and achy and he almost lost his balance. He had to hang onto the door to keep from falling down.

The Camaro didn't look too bad. The front grill was a little crumpled, but that could easily be fixed. He made his way over to the hood and tried to lift it, but the latch was jammed shut and he didn't feel like he had the strength to wrench it open. Actually, he really didn't feel very good at all. *Maybe I should call 911*, he thought with a laugh. Then he wondered if he should be joking about it.

Well, he wasn't very far from the Zerbe house. He could

walk back there and call a tow truck. And maybe take a couple of aspirin. His head really was hurting.

He stumbled once on a root, caught himself, and then walked back to the bridge. He stopped to read the sign and learned that it was called the La Loma Bridge. He thought that was a very pretty name for a bridge. He paused in the middle to look down at the Arroyo. It was really quite a view. The steep slopes covered with brush and trees; a wilderness carved into the middle of a suburban neighborhood. Not too far away, he could see the magnificent Colorado Street Bridge and beyond that the 134 heavy with traffic. It was framed so perfectly by the valley that it looked like a viewfinder card clicking into place. He sat down on the bridge to take it in.

Then he thought he'd sleep for a little bit. Why not? Just for a little bit. He could use it. He'd feel better afterward.

⌘

Caleb Rush Zerbe. Was that his name now, he wondered? It was a simple question but he hated to have to ask anyone. Why wouldn't somebody just tell him?

He hated his new bed, too. This was his first night in the East Wing and it was too damned quiet here and the mattress was too damned soft. There were too many blankets and sheets and quilts and who-knew-what-they-were-called. The pillows were also too soft. He checked his watch and saw that it was one-thirty. Fuck, the night was barely started. He threw off the covers, grabbed one pillow, and curled up on the floor. That was better. The carpet was as soft as most beds he'd slept on.

After a few hours of restless sleep, he woke up when he felt his internal warning system go off. He rolled onto his knees, ready to spring up and attack. He was all too used to late-night intrusions. They came with his mother's lifestyle.

He peered over the bed. There were two boys standing in the doorway. They looked to be about sixteen or so and they also looked just alike. A pair of twins in identical powder-blue pajamas standing there, backlit in the hallway light. He'd seen enough horror movies to know this wasn't a good sign.

"He's not there," said one twin.

"Where did he go?" asked the other.

"Maybe he's robbing the house," the first one said.

Behind them, two taller girls, maybe a year or two older than the boys, came into view. A blonde and a brunette. "He's there," the blonde said. She was wearing a Sleater-Kinney T-shirt and a pair of leggings that showed off her curves.

"Look," said the brunette, who was dressed in an oversize T-shirt with a reproduction of an old French poster with a black cat on it. "He's on the floor behind the bed."

Crush took that as his cue to stand up.

"What were you doing on the floor?" the brunette asked.

"Maybe he likes to sleep that way," the blonde said. "Like an animal. That's why he likes to sleep naked, too."

Crush wasn't embarrassed by his nudity. If somebody broke into your room, they deserved what they got. "You want something?" he asked.

"Hi," the second twin said. "We just wanted to meet you."

"Okay, you've met me."

"I'm K.C.," the second twin continued. "This is Noel, my brother, and this is Angela, my sister," he said, pointing to the blonde.

"All right," Crush said.

"And I'm Renee," the brunette said.

Crush looked at Renee. He liked looking at her. "A sleepover friend?"

Renee smirked. "Sort of. I'm their cousin."

"Which makes her your cousin, I guess," said K.C.

"Hello, Cousin," Renee said to Crush with a sly smile.

Angela noticed the interaction between Crush and Renee. She didn't seem to like it. "You're Cable, right?" asked Angela.

"Caleb," he corrected her. "But I think you knew that."

"I did," she said with a smirk. "You want to cover up, Caleb?"

"Yeah," Renee said. "There are impressionable boys present."

Crush lifted one of the sheets up to cover his waist. "That better?"

"Yes," Angela said.

"For them," Renee said.

"You didn't join us for dinner," said Noel.

"I didn't want to," Crush said.

"Why didn't you?" said K.C. He seemed like the nice one, Crush thought. Noel seemed like a nosy little kid. And Angela seemed like she wanted him out of there. Renee seemed amused by the whole scene.

"Because I didn't want to meet you," Crush said.

"That's a straightforward answer," Renee said.

"We met your mother," K.C. said.

"That's nice," Crush said.

"Angela thinks she's a prostitute," Noel said.

Crush felt his fingers squeezing to form a fist. "Is that right?" Crush asked.

"It's just a feeling I have," Angela said.

Crush wanted to knock the smirk right off her face. But he knew that was just what Angela wanted him to do. Any excuse to get Crush and his mother thrown out of the house. He wouldn't play her game.

"She's not a prostitute," Crush said, calmly.

"My mistake," Angela said. "Prostitutes fuck for money, don't they? They don't marry for it."

Crush controlled himself. He checked his watch. "Okay, we've met. It's three-thirty in the morning. Can I go back to sleep?"

"We don't like your mother," Noel said. "We don't want her to be married to our father."

"I'll tell her you said that. Now get out of my bedroom."

"It's not your bedroom," Angela said. "It's the guest room. And you're not a guest."

"Then what am I?"

"You're an intruder," Angela said. "And we're going to get rid of you."

"That's nice," Crush replied. "Can I get some sleep?"

"Sure," Angela said. "Get back on the floor like a dog."

"I will," Crush said, dropping the sheet and lying back down on the rug. "Turn out the light in the hallway, will you?"

"Good night, Caleb," he heard K.C. say.

"Don't say that," Noel said. "He's the enemy."

"Sorry," K.C. said.

"'Bye, Caleb," said Renee. "For now."

After the rest of them were gone, Angela walked around the bed and looked down at Crush. "They're stupid. I'm not. You and your mother better clear out of here. If you know what's good for you."

"Well, that's the thing," Crush said, closing his eyes. "We've never known what's good for us."

⌘

"Caleb?" Angela was saying. But it wasn't the Angela of his memories, this was the grown-up Angela in her thirties. She was standing on the La Loma Bridge calling his name. It was kind of annoying.

"What do you want?" Crush asked.

"Are you all right?"

"Sure. Why wouldn't I be?"

"You're passed out in the middle of the road. In the middle of a bridge."

"I'm just napping."

"In the middle of the road. In the middle of a bridge. Come on, get up." She helped him to his feet and led him to a Bentley Mulsanne that was parked on the bridge.

"Nice car," he said.

"Yeah, it's Dad's. Where's your car?"

"I had a little accident."

"I thought so."

"How come?"

"You're covered in blood."

"Oh, that. That's nothing. I just bit my cheek. You gotta help me get the car towed."

She put him in the passenger seat and got behind the wheel.

"Where are we going?" he asked.

"Back to the house," she said as she turned the sedan around.

Crush sat forward suddenly, remembering. "The bomb. What did you do about the bomb?"

"It's being taken care of. Look, I think you've got a concussion. I think we ought to get you to a doctor."

"A concussion?" He touched his head. "Yeah, it could be. It feels like that."

"Have you had concussions before?"

Crush laughed. "Yes." That was a really funny question. He laughed harder.

"Okay, you're freaking me out, Crush," she said.

"It's just that I was a Marine. In Iraq. Concussions kind of go with the territory."

"How many?"

"How many what?"

"How many concussions have you had?"

"Oh." He tried to tally them up on his fingers but he lost count. "A lot," he said.

"They're not good for the brain," she said. "There've been studies."

"I don't read studies. And I don't need a doctor. I'll be fine."

"Are you sure? Do you suffer from depression?"

"Only when people ask me questions like that."

They'd reached the house. Angela rolled down the window and pressed the magic button in the hedge. The gate began to roll aside.

"Open sesame," Crush said, and he laughed again.

"See?" she said. "That's not a normal laugh."

"At least I'm not depressed."

They'd pulled halfway up the drive when Angela stopped the car and placed a call on her cell phone. "Hey? Is the coast clear?" she asked whoever was on the other end. While she waited for an answer, Crush opened his door and got out. "Wait," she said. "I don't know if it's okay to...."

But Crush didn't need to wait to hear what she had to say. He knew she was going to tell him that the bomb had been defused or it hadn't and either way he was going to find out. He walked around the bend until the house came into view. There was a large plastic bucket in the middle of the cactus garden. A figure in a bomb-disposal outfit was bending over it, looking like an astronaut from a fifties sci-fi movie. The occupant of the heavy suit raised a hand to Crush, telling him to stop.

"Come on, Donleavy," Crush said. "Set that bomb off. I got things to do."

Victoria Donleavy gave Crush the middle finger of her heavily gloved right hand. Donleavy was the founder and CEO of Tigon Security, and Crush's former boss from his days as a bodyguard. A retired lieutenant from the Los Angeles Police Department and a retired MP from the Army, Donleavy knew a thing or two about law enforcement, security, and smart-ass subordinates.

She was appalled to see Crush keep on walking toward her, as if there weren't an unexploded bomb right there in front of her. Crush just kept ignoring her as she waved her arms at him like a crazed grade-school crossing guard. Behind her, he could see a couple of other guys back by the house, watching her. He recognized them as Stegner and Kagan, two of Donleavy's favorite operatives. They were close to danger, but Donleavy was in the middle of it. That was what Crush liked about her.

He just walked up beside her and looked inside the barrel. Yep, there was a bomb there, all right. Red wires, blue wires, blinking red lights. It looked just like a prop bomb from a TV show. Donleavy picked up a pair of wire cutters from a tray on top of the barrel, getting ready to defuse the detonator. She brought the tool close to the wires and hesitated.

"Really?" Crush asked. "The red wire or the blue wire? What is this? Are we watching *Homeland* or *24*?" He didn't know if Donleavy could hear him through the heavy mask, but she gestured to Stegner and Kagan to come drag Crush away. Stegner hesitated, but Kagan was on the move. Crush had always liked Kagan.

"Hey, Kagan!" Crush called out. "Who was this bomb addressed to?"

"What?" He stopped, confused.

"Who was it sent to?"

"Emil Zerbe."

Donleavy gestured impatiently for Kagan to keep coming. Crush looked down. There was another pair of pliers on the barrel's edge. Crush picked them up, bumped Donleavy's heavily gloved hands aside and cut both the red and the blue wire.

He couldn't hear Donleavy's voice through the mask but her body language said something like, "Are you completely insane? You've just killed us!"

The blinking red lights went out on the bomb. There was dead silence for a moment.

"See? Done and done," Crush said.

Then the bomb went off.

It went off with a loud click, then it burst open and a mound of shaving cream flowed out of it. That was all.

Donleavy ripped the mask off her head. Her short-cropped gray 'do' had a bad case of helmet hair. "What the fuck do you think you're doing?"

Stegner got up from the ground where he'd thrown himself when Crush clipped the wires and shouted, "Yeah, what the hell do you think you're doing?" Stegner was always Donleavy's yes-man.

"Relax," Crush said. "It wasn't a real bomb."

"Did you know that? How did you know that?" Donleavy demanded.

"Well, look at it. It looks so fake. And the truck had a bad paint job. It was total amateur-time."

"That's it?"

"And it was addressed to Emil Zerbe. Trust me, they don't want Emil dead."

"Who doesn't?"

"Them."

"Do you know who sent the bomb?"

"No idea."

She stripped the heavy gloves off. "You didn't know that bomb was a dud, did you?"

"I was pretty sure."

"Pretty sure? Pretty sure?!"

"Almost a hundred percent. But I might not be thinking too clearly. I might have a concussion."

"You might, huh?" Donleavy hauled off and slugged him in the jaw. Crush didn't expect it. He shook it off, but staggered. Kagan caught him. "How 'bout now?" Donleavy yelled.

Angela came running up from the Bentley. "What are you doing? He's been hurt."

It was only then that Donleavy noticed the blood all over Crush's dark T-shirt. "What happened?"

"He was in a car wreck."

Crush corrected her. "It was more of a fender bender, really." Then he threw up all over Donleavy's bomb-disposal suit and passed out.

CHAPTER TEN

The first three days Crush spent in the Zerbe castle after his mother moved in, he stuck mainly to his room and to himself. He made occasional forays to the library to find something to look at, but all Emil had was stuff about ancient Rome and that kind of shit. He was forced to read histories by somebody name Tacitus. It was actually pretty good when you got into it.

The reason he stayed in his room was that Emil's kids were in the house, and they'd be staying there for the next two weeks. It wasn't that Crush was afraid of them. He just didn't see the point in getting to know them. Because, though he hated to admit it, Angela was right. It would be better if Toni cleared out soon. This place was nice. This place was money. But come on. This place wasn't for them. It was too dangerous.

He was stretched out in bed—he'd gotten used to the mattress—reading his Loeb Classical when he heard a knock on his bedroom door. He closed the book and told whoever it was to come in. The door opened and Samantha and Angela walked in.

"What do you want?" he asked. "You're interrupting the Year of the Four Emperors."

"This is a serious matter, Caleb," Samantha said.

"Why don't we just forget it?" Angela asked. "It's not important."

"Why are you saying that now?" Samantha said. "You brought me here."

"Anybody want to tell me what's going on?" Crush asked. "Or do I just get to guess?"

"Angela says she's been robbed," Samantha said.

"There was five hundred dollars on my dresser," Angela said.

"And you want me to figure out who took it?" Crush said.

"I want you to give it back."

"You think I have it?"

"Nothing was ever stolen in this house before you came."

"We're not saying you stole it," Samantha said. "We're just concerned."

"We want to search your room," Angela said.

"Go ahead," Crush said. "And take out my dirty laundry while you're at it."

Samantha started going through his chest of drawers, but Angela objected. "I don't know why you're looking in such an obvious place. He's smarter than that."

"It's true," Crush said, opening his book again. "I'm a criminal mastermind."

"Look at him," Angela said. "He's lying on the bed. Why is he lying on the bed?"

Samantha looked at her as if she was waiting for an answer.

"I give up," Crush said. "Why am I lying on the bed?"

"Get up," Angela said. "Let me look under that mattress."

"Really?" he asked.

"See?" Angela turned to Samantha. "He doesn't want to do it. He's hiding something."

"Could you get off the bed?" Samantha asked him, a little

embarrassed.

"All right. I'll do it for you." He got off the bed with a sigh. "Now what?"

"Look under the mattress," Angela said.

Crush looked at Samantha, who reluctantly nodded. Crush shrugged and lifted the mattress up off the bed. Angela pointed at the box spring in triumph. "There! Do you see?"

Samantha looked. "See what?"

There was nothing on the freshly exposed white box spring. Angela moved in on it in disbelief. "It has to be there! I..."

There was a profound silence in the room. "You what, Angela?" Samantha asked her.

"I...I was sure it was there."

"You want to keep looking?" Crush asked.

"Should we keep looking, Angela?" Samantha asked, but in an accusatory tone.

"Well, I don't know. I'm sure he took it, but..." her voice dwindled off.

Samantha turned to Crush. "I'm sorry, Caleb. Truly sorry."

Crush threw the mattress back onto the box spring. "No worries. She probably just misplaced the money."

"Yes," Samantha said. "That's probably what happened, Angela. I'm sure you'll find it."

Angela looked daggers at Crush. "I'll tell Daddy about this."

"Yeah, do that," Crush said, plopping back down on the bed. "I'm sure he'll give you another five hundred."

Angela huffed and stormed out of the room.

Samantha eyed Crush. "What did you do with it after you found it, Caleb?"

"I don't know what you're talking about," he said, turning a page.

"Okay. Just keep it hidden. Angela, she doesn't give up easily," she said as she left the room. Crush grunted a noncommittal grunt, not lifting his eyes from the page. He wasn't worried. If there was one thing that life with his mother had taught him, it was how to hide things well.

⌘

Dr. Milland shined a light in Crush's eyes. "Who is the vice president?"

"Don't remind me," Crush said.

"Knock it off, Crush," Donleavy said. "He's trying to see if you're coherent."

"Then why doesn't he ask me who won the World Series?"

"Because he doesn't know," Donleavy said.

"I resent that," Dr. Milland said. "Just because I'm gay doesn't mean I'm not a baseball fan." Dr. Milland was the physician on call for Tigon Security. He looked like a doctor on a late-night infomercial, all well-coiffed white hair, bronze tan, and deep blue eyes. "Now what's three times twenty-four?"

"Mike Pence," Crush replied.

"Wise-ass," Donleavy said.

"So how long have I got, Doc?" Crush asked. They were in the parlor of Emil Zerbe's mansion and Crush was resting on the sofa where Kagan and Stegner had carried him, with some difficulty, after he'd passed out in the driveway.

"The way you live?" Dr. Milland asked. "I'd give you five years at most."

"What about the concussion?" Donleavy asked. "Does he have one?"

"Hard to say without an MRI."

"I'm fine," Crush said.

"See, he says he's fine," Dr. Milland said. "Think of how much money we'd save on tests if we just took the patient's word for it."

"What should he do for it?" Angela asked.

"Rest," the doctor said.

"Just rest?" Angela said in disbelief.

"Rest is the best treatment for a concussion," Dr. Milland said.

"See, all I have to do is rest." Crush started to get up.

"That's not resting," the doctor said, pushing him back down. "Resting means lying down. Resting means not reading, not listening to music, not watching TV. It means no texting, no email, no cell phone. Resting means physical and cognitive rest."

"Sounds boring."

"It should be. Most people who sustain a concussion are back to normal in a week or two. A few months at most."

"How 'bout an hour?" Crush asked. " 'Cause I feel fine."

"Others can have long-term problems either from the concussion or from injuries to the surrounding soft tissues of the brain. And a word of caution: the injured person may lack clear judgment to make an informed decision regarding what goes on around him."

"Like whether or not to set off a bomb?" Donleavy said.

"That's just a for-instance," Crush said.

"Well, I've given my advice, which will no doubt be ignored. And for which I will be well paid. Take care, Victoria. And tell me where to send the wreath when Mr. Rush's time comes." With that Dr. Milland was gone and Crush started to get up from the sofa.

"What are you doing?" Angela said.

"I'm going to watch TV, listen to music, and read," Crush

said. "Oh, and I'm going to get my car."

"Lie back down."

"Let him go. You can't stop him," Donleavy said.

Crush looked around. "Why aren't the police here?"

"Samantha didn't call the police," Donleavy said. "She called Tigon."

Samantha was sitting by the window. "I only did what Emil told me to do."

Crush turned to Donleavy. "So she called you?"

"That's right," Donleavy said.

"But you didn't call the police either?" Crush asked. "Even though you thought it was a real bomb?"

"Go home," Donleavy said. "Get some rest. Real rest."

"I can't," Crush said. "Didn't you hear? I'm working for you again."

"That's the concussion talking," Donleavy said.

"No, that's Angela Zerbe talking," Crush replied. "She said you hired me again."

"Since when?"

"Since this morning," Angela said. "To protect Noel."

Donleavy looked offended. "Tigon is protecting the entire family."

"I don't like the way you do business," Angela said. "And Crush has better motivation."

"All right," Donleavy said. "Everybody out. I need to talk to Crush. Alone."

"Why?" Angela asked.

"Go," Crush said. "It's all right. I'll fill you in later."

Angela and Samantha left the room. Donleavy looked through the cabinets. "You'd think they'd have something to drink in a house like this."

"It's eleven o'clock in the morning," Crush said with disapproval in his voice.

"Too early for you?"

"It's always too early for me."

"Oh, that's right, I forgot," Donleavy said. "Well, I drink early on days when I defuse bombs." She slammed the last cabinet shut. "Fuck it. I'll have to make do with a stick of gum." She sat down across from Crush and unwrapped a stick of Wrigley's. "Tell me the reason Angela Zerbe hired you."

"I can't."

"Why not?"

" 'Cause you'd be involved then. She doesn't want you involved. I don't either."

"How come? Are you afraid I'd go to the police?"

"Trust me," Crush said. "I'll tell you everything. At the right time."

"Do you know who sent the bomb?"

Crush shook his head. "No. But I think I know why it was sent."

"Why?"

"To get him to stop the train."

"That's what we figured. That it was probably one of the other protest groups that are targeting Emil."

"There are quite a few."

"Tell me about it. I'm thinking of joining one myself." She took the gum out of her mouth and wrapped it up in the crumpled paper. "Yeah, at first I thought this was all about the bullet train. But...."

"But?"

"Now I think it's about you, Crush."

Crush didn't react to that, not much. "Really?"

Donleavy went to the briefcase she always carried with her. Her Little Box of Secrets, she called it. She opened it and took out a piece of paper. "Remember this?" She showed him a copy of a *Los Angeles Times* clipping from December 30, 2000. The banner headline read:

ROSE QUEEN STILL MISSING
THE DEVIL'S GATE DAM MYSTERY

Crush didn't have to read the rest. "Yeah, I remember."

"I thought you would," Donleavy said. "This was found in Emil's mailbox today. Along with this note." She showed him another piece of paper:

REMEMBER THE SEVENTY-SIX THOUSAND

"Do you know what that means?"

"I have no idea," Crush said.

"Neither do I. Tell me about what happened back in 2000."

"Oh, you know all about that."

"Tell me again. Tell me about Renee Zerbe's disappearance."

Just then Crush's cell phone rang. He recognized the tune (the theme from *Enter the Dragon*) as Gail's ringtone. "Hey, what's up?"

"He left," Gail said on the other end of the line.

"Noel?"

"Yes. He said he had to go to a meeting."

"Did he take off the ankle monitor?"

"Yeah, I've got it. I asked where he was going but he wouldn't tell me. He said it was anonymous."

"Thanks." Crush clicked off.

"Something?" Donleavy asked.

"Noel's on the move."

"Where to?"

"I don't know. At some meeting."

The door opened and Samantha came in. "I know where he is."

"You were listening to us?" Donleavy asked.

"Sure," Samantha said. "What did you expect?"

"Where is he?" asked Crush.

"He goes to a meeting at the Grace Brethren Church on Mission Street in South Pasadena at noon every day."

"What kind of meeting?" Crush asked.

"A Targeted Individuals support group," Samantha said.

"What the hell is that?" Donleavy asked.

Samantha shook her head. "I can't explain. You have to see for yourself."

"I will," Crush said, getting up.

"Sit down," Donleavy said. "I'll send Kagan to get Noel. We can protect him better at the house. Besides, you shouldn't be on your feet. You should be resting."

"I'll rest when I'm dead," Crush said.

Donleavy frowned. "I hate it when people say that."

CHAPTER ELEVEN

The van was dark. He had been alone for hours. Or Zerbe thought it had been hours. Since he was tied to this chair, he couldn't check his cell phone's clock, so he didn't really know how much time had passed. That was the hardest part about being tied up. That and the fact that he couldn't get up and take off his wet pants. That and the fact that he couldn't get up at all. That and the fact that he could barely move. Okay, there were a lot of hardest parts about it.

"Hey!" he yelled at the top of his lungs. He had tried hollering that a few times. And what the hell, he tried it again. He'd been glad when his kidnapper left him alone, finally, but now he wanted some company. He wanted to know he wasn't forgotten.

He tried to peer into the darkness of the van. To see if that table with the iPhone and iPad was still there. But it was blacker than black in here. There were gaps around the doors that usually let light in, but there was nothing now. They must be parked in a garage. It was stuffy and hot, and Zerbe felt a little panic well up in his chest. What if they left him here? Forgot him? What if that was how they planned to kill him? To leave him to starve? To leave him almost buried alive?

"Hey!" he yelled again, to give the panic in his gut some outlet. "Hey! I'm here! I'm alive!" He was talking—yelling—to himself now. "I'm alive and I'm getting mad!" Then he started singing the theme to *The Lone Ranger*, the way he used to when he was a kid. "To-the-dump-to-the-dump-to-the-dump-dump-dump." Anything to make himself heard, if only to himself.

⌘

When Crush stepped out of the Zerbe house, he remembered he didn't have a car anymore. It bothered him a little bit that he'd forgotten that, but he shrugged it off and called Gail to take one of his cars and come pick him up. Then he sat on the front step and waited.

By the time she pulled up in a red 1970 Buick GSX, Crush was curled on the step. Donleavy was sitting next to him, watching over him like a border collie tending a sick sheep.

Gail got out, worried. "What's wrong?"

"Concussion," Donleavy said. "He should see a doctor."

"I saw a doctor," Crush said, eyes still closed. "He says I'm fine."

"He didn't say that," Donleavy said. "He said you should get an MRI."

"He says I should rest. I'll rest." Crush got up, all on his own, and walked to the car. "Thanks for worrying about me, Donleavy." He swung open the driver's door.

"No," Donleavy said. "Let Gail drive."

Crush looked at her as if she were a crazy person. "But I always drive."

Gail shoved him over to the passenger side and got behind the wheel. "Just this once."

Crush didn't really fight it. "All right. Just this once."

Gail got in and Crush asked her, "What did you do with the ankle monitor?"

"Don't worry. I took care of it," Gail said as she started the car. "Thanks," she called out the window to Donleavy as she pulled out.

Donleavy waved to her. "Get him to tell you what happened in 2000."

"Mind your own business," Crush shouted back at her. The shouting was a bad idea; it made his head throb.

He rubbed his temple and Gail noticed. "We're getting you to a doctor," she said.

"No," Crush said. "First, we're going to a church."

"Did you get religion, Crush?"

"I'm thinking about it."

Gail followed Crush's directions and drove the Buick down San Rafael. Crush flexed his left foot when she touched the brakes, as if he was driving by remote control. To get his mind off the fact that he wasn't behind the wheel, he caught Gail up to speed. "I have to talk to Noel," he said finally. "He must have told somebody about his plan to get Zerbe arrested. They were waiting for him at the warehouse."

"Okay," Gail said. "What else?"

"What else what?"

"Tell me what happened back in 2000," Gail said.

Crush frowned. "It's only a ten-minute drive. It would take longer."

"Give me the short version."

"The short version isn't possible."

"Sure it is. Come on, now, I know your mother was living with Emil."

"She was married to him. For almost a year."

"When you were sixteen?"

"Seventeen."

She smiled. "I can't picture you at seventeen, Crush."

"I haven't changed much."

"And you lived back there. In that castle?"

"Yep. Just like Downtown Abbey."

"Downton. Tell me about Renee Zerbe."

"She was their...I guess, *my* cousin. Emil's brother's daughter. We went to school together. Emil pulled some strings to get me into Pasadena Prep. I didn't quite fit in."

"I wouldn't think so."

"Noel and Angela hated me at first. Hated me and my mother. K.C. was all right. I think he felt sorry for me. I know I felt sorry for him, growing up in that freak show."

"How did Renee treat you?"

Crush was silent for a moment. "She was all right. But I didn't hang out with them too much. I spent most of my time in my room, reading."

"Reading?"

"Yeah, that'll give you an idea how bored I was. That's why I volunteered to be in the Rose Parade. It gave me something to do."

"You drove a float?"

"I didn't drive it. I was the animator."

"Animator?"

"I operated the animation. The dinosaur's tail. I wagged it."

"Sounds like fun."

"It was. At first."

Gail gripped the wheel uneasily as she asked, "And that's how you found her father's body?"

"Yeah," Crush said, "but everybody knows about that."

"How did Renee handle it?"

"How do you think? I didn't see her for a few weeks. Then..." Crush sighed. "My mom and Emil went out on a date one night and the kids had some friends over. To drink and smoke pot. And to play some stupid game."

"What game?"

"One of those nerdy, geeky games nerdy geeks used to play back in the day. Dungeons & Dragons, I think. They were talking about gnomes and elves and orcs and throwing weird-shaped dice and doing all kinds of math and acting like it was fun. Maybe it was for them. I never really played a lot of games and I never liked math. Unless you count running numbers, which I guess is both."

"Was Renee there?"

"Yes. Along with Evan Gibbard and Sonny Kraus. Those two were sort of interchangeable preppy punks. Evan was the blond Aryan mastermind, while Sonny was his dark-haired lackey. They did everything together. Smoked pot together. Cheated on tests together. They said they fucked girls together, though I don't know why the girls were there, to be honest. Their real love affair seemed to be with each other.

"Anyway, Noel was in charge of the game and he was asking the others if they'd 'taken any damage.' They all said 'no,' and Angela said Noel's dragons were 'asleep on the job' and everybody laughed, like that made sense. Zerbe said he was going to throw an Acid Splash at the dragons, and he rolled his twenty-sided dice a couple of times and Noel added up the totals and said he missed and instead he hit Renee. Everybody found this hilarious too and they laughed and laughed. But Renee started crying and ran into the kitchen. They felt bad about that, but not bad enough to do anything.

"Zerbe was the only one who ran after her. After a while, I went in, too, to see how they were getting along. Zerbe was standing there alone, looking all stunned. I asked what was wrong. He said Renee had cut her wrist and walked out into the yard."

"Whoa," Gail said. "What did you do?"

"I ran after her. She must have moved pretty fast because I couldn't find her. She couldn't have gone out through the gate. It was closed. So she must have headed across the backyard. To the Arroyo.

"Angela ran up behind me and I told her to go back and call the police. She said Renee wouldn't want that. They'd take her to the hospital and put her under observation. For some reason, I agreed that that made sense. I guess when you're a teenager you just don't trust the adult world to know best. Maybe you're right not to.

"I thought I heard footsteps in the distance, so I scrambled along the edge of the Arroyo, leaving Angela behind me. I went through the backyards of a couple of other estates until I made it to the Colorado Street Bridge. Suicide Bridge."

Gail shivered. "That's an ugly nickname for such a pretty bridge."

"I don't know," Crush said. "If I was going to kill myself, I'd like to do it off a bridge like that. You'd have such a nice view all the way down."

"That's not funny."

"It wasn't meant to be."

"Was Renee there?"

Crush nodded. "They'd put high railings up there to discourage jumpers. I guess she just took that as a challenge, because she was climbing up the fence when I got there.

"I ran onto the bridge and I called out to her. I walked up closer to her and I could see that she was bleeding from her wrist, but she hadn't cut herself deep. That made me think that she didn't really want to kill herself. That she wanted help and didn't know how else to ask for it.

"So I climbed outside the railing and held my hand out. She just looked at me and I thought I was supposed to say something, anything. Well, what do you say in a situation like that? I asked her why she was doing this.

"She said, 'Don't you know I have the power of flight?' I thought she was talking crazy. I said she didn't. She said, 'In the game, stupid. In D & D I can fly.'

"I said, 'I don't know how to play that damn game.' She said I should really learn. 'It's so much better than real life.' I said real life wasn't so bad. I said she had a lot to live for. She said, 'Like what?'

"I didn't have an answer for that. So I just said her father would want her to live. She blew up at that. She started crying and screaming that her father didn't kill himself. That the Nazis killed him."

"The Nazis?"

"That's what it sounded like to me. But then she said it was Zerbe's fault. Then she said it was the Jews. She wasn't acting rational."

"But she didn't jump?"

"She didn't jump. She fell. She climbed to the top of the iron fence and let go. I don't know how I caught her. I strained my back and wrenched both my shoulders, but I grabbed her and pulled her into my arms. I held her in my arms till the shaking stopped. Both hers and mine. Then I climbed back onto the bridge and dropped her on the pavement."

"Good for you, Crush."

"Yeah," Crush said bitterly. "Good for me."

"So when did it happen?"

Crush looked over at her, puzzled. "When did what happen?"

"When did you fall in love with her?"

Crush didn't answer. They pulled up to the church and he hurried out of the Buick. He strode to a little outbuilding behind an old adobe church. It was a ramshackle structure that had looked like it was about to collapse for the past century. Sometimes the flimsiest things are the longest lasting.

Gail caught up with him and stopped him at the door. "What are you going to do?" she asked him.

"What do you think? I'm going to grab him and drag him out of there."

"You can't do that," Gail said.

"Why not? I have to get answers from him."

"But this is a support group, Crush. You can't violate that. You know that."

Crush shut his eyes in frustration. "You don't even know what they're supporting."

"Even so," she said. "Wait till it's over. There's only another fifteen minutes."

"You don't know that. It could be a marathon."

"How would you feel if somebody broke into an AA meeting and dragged somebody out?" she asked.

Crush gripped the doorknob. "All right, I'll wait. But I'm going in."

Gail tried to stop him but he pushed the door open and stepped in. The plywood walls of the room were lined with inspirational Christian posters. Underneath them were a number of old worn-out sofas, and the sofas were filled with people. People you might pass on the street and never notice. People of different ages and races and walks of life. The only thing they had in common was that they all called themselves Targeted Individuals. Whatever that meant.

A woman in her mid-twenties was talking as they slipped in and took the last empty seats. Noel was sitting across the room, and he watched without expression as they settled onto the stained cushions. Crush noticed that there were no Big Books or pamphlets on display as was usually the case in twelve-step gatherings.

"Okay," the woman was saying in a faltering tone while brushing her long hair out of her eyes and wrapping her cardigan sweater around her like a security blanket, "my name is Amy and I'm a Targeted Individual."

"Hi, Amy," the crowd said. Crush rolled his eyes and fidgeted impatiently while Gail smiled politely at the questioning gaze of a few other Targeted Individuals.

Amy continued. "Until a couple of years ago, I didn't even realize there was a name for what I am...a Targeted Individual. I didn't know that was a *thing*, until.... Okay, let me start over. About three years ago I started to get these intense feelings of *panic*. It took me a long time to figure what it meant. I got a lot of...not mixed messages but mixed messages. I was new to the whole...not consciousness movement, but consciousness movement. I found that most of the time a Targeted Individual will experience extreme panic or a form of psychic attack. A lot of people in the Targeted Individual Community are convinced that the enemy is using actual *weapons* to do this. Like, they've got microwave *weapons* that they're using. And that is *true*. There are people who've had *documented* experiences where they've come in contact with these weapons and they've seen them and they've experienced them firsthand. They cause extreme heat. You know, it's a wave that's being shot out of these weapons at a targeted person and it's causing that person to, you know, *feel* different things.

"But that's not the only way that they do this. Now this might be extremely left field for most who won't understand anything that I'm fixing to say, but we are more than just human beings. We have abilities that are *encoded* into our DNA. There have been studies throughout time about psychological...not transmutation but transmutation. There's more than you can sense with your quote-unquote five senses. There are more senses in your brain than science or technology can even begin to understand. We are evolving and they want to *stop us*. It all goes along with...now I'm not trying to compare myself with Nicola Tesla, but he was a Targeted Individual. And they would *steal* his stuff. Like he would come up with the *genius* idea and this group of individuals would come in and steal it! And they'd try to destroy him. They didn't want him live up to his full potential. He was trying to give people free electricity and free technology. And radio. I'm pretty sure that he invented radio, right? I don't know, I'm not an expert on Nicola Tesla, but what I'm saying is, there are so many people out there that are being targeted and they don't even *know* that they're being targeted. They just think they're having a *shitty life*. And they don't know why. And it's *not* okay. It's *not* okay for these people to continue to do this. Like me. I would have these instances where they were trying to make me feel like a piece of *shit*. And it wasn't my *fault*.

"Did you know that if you're a Targeted Individual everything you say and do is being recorded? It is. I know that as I am talking to you right now, *in this room*, every word I say is being recorded. I *know* it. I got to the point where I was scared shitless. Then I thought, fuck it, let them record me. They can't hurt me any more than they already have. What can they find out about me? I'm not about to rob and steal. I'm not planning to blow up buildings. I'm not a part of Isis! I have *vans*, literally *white vans* that follow me wherever I go. Like, I'm at the bus stop, taking my kid to school and at the bus stop there's a *van* that parks there every day and has for the last year and a half. With huge antennas on top of it. Can you explain that? Can you? And then it would start happening more and more. Like, I'm at Walmart and I come out and there's a *white fucking van* with fucking *antennas* on top of it.

"Now, I'm not saying that all Masons are bad. But I know that there are Masons who are involved in that practice of targeting these people. And hurting them. Trying to destroy them. I can't post things on the internet without, it's like jet lag, it takes a long time for them to be posted. It's crazy. And a lot of people can't handle it. Remember that lady who drove her fucking kids into the ocean? Remember that? And that lady, she was hearing fucking *voices*. That's another thing they do when it comes to these fucking attacks, they'll make you hear *voices*. I've never heard voices. I've never heard any buga-buga voices, but that's 'cause my brain's too strong to accept those vibrations. Well, I've heard voices sometimes, but just when I'm almost asleep and stuff. But when you hear voices and you go to therapy, some of these doctors are *in* on it! They're in on the *situation*. So they'll diagnose these people as paranoid schizophrenics. And as soon as you're diagnosed as paranoid schizophrenic, your credibility is out the door. And that's part of the way that it works! That's all a part of the Overlords' major plan! To stop evolution from occurring! I'm seeing so many people getting attacked!

"So if you're targeted and you're spreading knowledge, I fucking love you, friend! I fucking *love* you. You're *not* alone. Find groups like this. Don't go shoot up schools for attention. Don't do that. That's bad. It's fucking *sad* that some people feel they have to go to those extremes to make themselves heard. Share the power. They can't shut us up. There are way too many of us. Thanks. Did I go over my time?"

Gail and Crush didn't know how to react. They sat expressionless as everybody else in the room applauded. An African-American man wearing a chambray shirt over an old "Vote for Bernie" T-shirt nodded and said, "You went a little bit over, but that's all right, we needed to hear that. Thank you, Amy." He stood up and gave her a supportive hug. Everybody applauded that, too. This crowd really liked to applaud.

When he was done hugging Amy, he looked around at the others. "Now, we've had some late arrivals. Would you like to introduce yourselves, using your first names only? I'm Will, by the way. I'm a Targeted Individual."

Everyone said, "Hi, Will," in unison.

An old man wearing a red "Make America Great Again" baseball cap spoke up. "My name is Al. I'm a Targeted Individual." *At least the nuts in this crowd are bipartisan,* Crush thought.

Everyone said, "Hi, Al," in unison. Then they turned to Gail and Crush. Crush cleared his throat. "My name is Caleb. I'm a Targeted Individual."

Everyone said, "Hi, Caleb," and then it was Gail's turn. She looked uncertain. "My name is Catherine. I don't know what I am." Everyone in the room looked a little sour but Will smiled at her in an understanding way.

"We don't any of us know who we are," Will said. "Until we do." He walked over and gave Gail a warm hug. Then he hugged Crush, too, just to be fair. "It takes a lot of courage to come here. Let's all greet Catherine."

"Hi, Catherine," they all said, shamed by Will into welcoming her.

"You don't have to testify yet," Will went on. "Just sit and listen. But when you feel the urge, by all means speak up. This a place to be heard. It's a safe place." The room applauded that, too. "Now we open the room for anyone who wants to share for five minutes. No cross talk, please. If anyone feels triggered by the testimony, please signal by raising your hand. Who would like to begin?"

Noel raised his hand. Will nodded to him, giving his assent. "My name is Noel. I'm a Targeted Individual." A man in a suit sitting next to Gail crossed his legs in what seemed to Crush to be a rather annoyed fashion. "Hi, Noel," everyone said.

Noel began. "Some of you have heard this before but I feel the need to share it again." He looked straight at Crush and Gail as he spoke. "This is my story."

The man sitting next to Gail sighed. Crush noticed that he wore a white surgical mask over his face. *This place was full of all kinds of crazy*, Crush thought as Noel opened a worn spiral notebook and prepared to read from it.

Crush frowned and whispered to Gail, "This is going to take some time," and Gail shushed him. She had no idea.

CHAPTER TWELVE

THE STATEMENT OF NOEL ZERBE

First of all, let me state categorically that I do not know what became of Renee Zerbe. I hope she rests in peace, as the saying goes. But I fear her fate is a far, far worse one.

I'm speaking of the first days of the twentieth century. January of the year 2001. (And don't tell me that the century started in the year 2000. I can count. I know there was no year 0 in the Gregorian calendar.) I was enrolled in Pasadena Preparatory School at that time and had no notion of the plans and machinations that the Overlords use in plotting against us. I was more interested in the eldritch secrets of the past: sorcery, wizardry, and necromancy. With some close friends, I played various games in which we took the characters and guises of ancient and powerful characters. Dungeons & Dragons. Call of Cthulhu. Shadowrun. These were called "role-playing games" by amateurs, but for those with more awareness of the arcane past, these "innocent pastimes" provided rituals through which one could gain access to the Ancient Knowledge.

My comrades in this quest for enlightenment were varied and joined me for a variety of reasons. Some, like my twin brother

Kendrick (called K.C.), did so out of a sense of filial responsibility. My sister Angela pursued arcane secrets mainly to make our father angry. Others, like my cousin Renee, did so out of genuine curiosity and desire to know more of the secrets of the past and the present and the future. Some, like my muscle-bound and rather dim-witted half-brother, Caleb, did it out of stupid loyalty. There were others, like Evan Gibbard and Sonny Kraus, who mainly took part in the investigations from a decadent desire to taste taboos of any sort. They were merely placeholders. Spear carriers in the production I was trying to mount. Renee and K.C. were my real coconspirators.

After a time, these store-bought games and rituals became dull and pedestrian to me. I needed to reach deeper into the primordial source of the unknown. I needed to touch the real, antediluvian depths of the forbidden and the fiend-inspired! I needed to find a place where the veil between this world and the other was thin and could be pierced with incantations of proper antiquity.

There was but a single place in all of Los Angeles County that fit my needs. It was, oddly, right in my own backyard. Or near to it. At the northern end of the Arroyo Seco was the aptly named Devil's Gate. From time immemorial there have been hushed whispers of the nature of that unholy landscape. Tales that spoke of it as the very gateway to Hell itself.

The Devil's Gate was an ancient formation on the rock face of the Arroyo Seco that, some said, bore the image of Satan himself. At the very least, the jagged boulders resembled the face of a terrible, demon-like, horned creature, its features contorted in laughter at some unheard, undreamed-of jest. The Tongva Indians, in the time before the Europeans came, told of eerie, nightmarish sounds that the water made as it ran through the gorge. Sounds like the cacophonous laughter of many malignant spirits. The indigenous peoples shunned the place as evil and malevolent.

In the 1920s, the Army Corps of Engineers, in their wisdom, decided to build a dam there to control flooding. And thus they preserved the Devil's Gate and kept it dry. They even built a tunnel through it. Why? No one can say.

In the 1940s, a society of occultists became fascinated with the Devil's Gate Dam. The group was led by esteemed rocket scientist Jack Parsons, one of the founders of the Jet Propulsion Laboratory in Pasadena and a follower of infamous British occultist Aleister Crowley. Rumor has it that they performed rituals that were intended to open a portal to Hell itself.

In the 1950s, Jack Parsons was killed in a mysterious explosion that demolished his mansion on Orange Grove Boulevard.

After that, the strange incidents at Devil's Gate Dam took a more sinister turn. Several children were reported missing in the area. In time a serial killer, Mack Ray Edwards, took credit for the disappearances. Edwards was a highway construction worker, and the children's bodies were found buried in the concrete foundation of the freeway that borders the dam. Before he hung himself in a cell in San Quentin State Prison, Edwards is reported to have said that the devil made him kill the children.

But the disappearances at Devil's Gate did not stop with Edwards's death. Two other children vanished into thin air. One was hiking with his parents; he walked ahead, turned a corner, and simply disappeared. The other, returning to a campsite, was never heard from again.

Some believe that the rituals Jack Parsons and his acolytes performed in the Arroyo had succeeded all too well in opening that portal to Hell and transforming the area into a magnet for some unknown malignant force. Others say that it is merely a coincidence that so many tragedies have occurred in this one spot. No one truly knows. The strange face in the rock refuses to divulge its secrets. Whatever joke it laughs at remains a mystery.

Needless to say, the Devil's Gate Dam offered too tempting a target for our teenage explorations into the unknown to be ignored. On the appointed night, my crew was assembled at the top of the dam, ready to descend. The Colorado Boulevard Irregulars, we called ourselves. Named after the main thoroughfare in Pasadena, Colorado Boulevard, and the juvenile helpers of Sherlock Holmes, the Baker Street Irregulars. K.C. had come up with this rather whimsical name and I let it stand, because it amused me.

It had not been easy to gather the Irregulars. It was just after the New Year's holiday and family obligations had nearly put an end to my well-laid plans. It was only after considerable cajoling and wheedling on my part that I was able to cobble the band together. Angela stayed home, flatly refusing to go along. Gibbard and Kraus had only been able to join us by claiming they were doing charity work for their church. (Which, in a way, they were.) K.C., of course, was always at my beck and call. Being as he was my identical twin and the younger of us, I held some sort of psychic thrall over him. And Caleb, my idiot stepbrother, was easily influenced.

But Renee, the most important and the most necessary of the Colorado Boulevard Irregulars, was the most difficult to recruit for the occasion. The reasons for this difficulty were twofold. First, she had been selected as the Rose Queen. This was part of a primitive midwinter festival of harvest and rebirth known as the Tournament of Roses Parade in Pasadena. Every year, a beautiful, nubile young virgin (it was hoped) was selected from the residents of Pasadena to be a sacrifice to the floral gods. Not an actual sacrifice, you understand, at least not normally. No blood is shed; no organs are removed. America has grown too sophisticated for such aboriginal practices. It is more of a ceremonial sacrifice. Renee would ride on a structure made of dying flowers and offer herself to the crowds and the television cameras and the Goodyear blimp and the Blue Angels as they jetted high above. She would be an offering to the New Year in the hopes that it would be a propitious one and that all would have good luck in 2001. From the viewpoint of the future, one can only say that it did not turn out that way. Not at all.

Renee viewed her position as Rose Queen from a sardonic outlook at best. Her mother, a transplant from Europe, had wanted the honor for her daughter far more than Renee ever did. Renee had seen it more as a social experiment. She wondered: Could a liberal, atheist, communist anarchist really obtain this most Republican of honorifics? If she did her hair and her lips and her nails just so, would the powers-that-be not see past her perfect, smiling exterior and into the dank darkness of her decadent soul? As she waved to the crowds on Colorado Boulevard, she would think of it as a practical joke on the whole of America.

But that wasn't the reason it was hard to get her down in the Devil's Dam. There was a more mysterious reason. Renee's research. She was mum about it and shared few details with even her most intimate friends, of which I was surely one. All she would say was that her investigations involved tracing her own genealogy back to France, back to Germany, back to the Gauls, back to the Romans and beyond. She said there were dark secrets there. Secrets that would make the blood of even the strongest man run cold. Secrets that would make those hidden in the Devil's Gate seem like mere child's play. Secrets that were among the darkest and most horrible the world has ever known. Secrets that had recently led her father to take his own life, during the celebration of the Tournament of Roses.

After that, the black cloud that had always hung over my cousin Renee seemed to descend upon her and swallow her whole. Her father consummated the true meaning of the Tournament by taking his life during the parade. Still, I persuaded her to take time away from her grief to join me in my investigations into the nature of reality and unreality. To join me in delving into the cryptic mysteries of the Devil's Gate Dam.

We stood atop the soaring arches of the Devil's Gate Dam just as the sun was disappearing in the west. In the fast-fading twilight we descended the impossibly narrow concrete steps from the top of the levee down into the depths of the Arroyo. It is the nature of Southern California that the land is bone-dry 364 days out of the year, so the dam that was built to hold back flooding waters stood on a dusty, parched riverbed for most of the year. Therefore, as we walked single file down the precarious staircase into the dark ravine, we arrived on land that was as arid as the surface of the moon.

We brought some equipment with us. Flashlights to illuminate our way. Cell phones to communicate with each other. Candles, matches, ropes, and chalk for other purposes. K.C. had even brought a first-aid kit, in case of unforeseen accidents. He was so responsible.

We stood on the floor of the ravine and gazed up. A gorge of problematical depth rose above us on all sides and, as we approached the Devil's Gate, the beams from our flashlights played eerily on the rugged granite cliffs and crossed each other like the arms of an iridescent octopus swimming in the depths of a murky ocean.

As we crept across the Arroyo, a wild screaming suddenly filled the air, like the crazed laughter of a thousand maniacal children.

Gibbard yelped like a little kitten and nearly dropped his light. Renee snorted derisively. "Calm down," she said. "It's just the feral parrots of Pasadena. You've heard them before." The tropical birds had supposedly escaped from a private aviary in the 1930s and found the warm climate of the Southland perfectly hospitable for them and their descendants.

"Yes," Gibbard said. "But not at night. And not sounding like that."

"Perhaps they're imitating some sound they've heard in the area," Renee said. "Parroting the Demon's laugh."

"That's not funny," Gibbard said.

"The Demon thinks it's funny," said Kraus. "Listen to him." And the parrots kept up their loud, incessant gibbering from above.

"Don't make fun, Kraus," I said. "He's right to be afraid. You don't understand what the parrots are saying. They are imitating an ancient language known only to a few expert scholars of archaic lore."

"You're so full of shit. What are they saying, then?"

"That they are psychopomps."

"You're making that up."

"Not at all. A psychopomp is a spirit who escorts newly deceased souls from this world to the next. Like whippoorwills or ravens. Or the Grim Reaper, if you insist on being obvious."

Gibbard covered his ears. "I wish they'd shut up!"

"Oh, no you don't," I said. "As long as they're still calling out, that means they're waiting for a soul to be delivered to them. But once they're silent, once they fly away, that means they have one in their clutches. That someone has died and they're carrying his soul to Hades."

Kendrick gasped, but when I looked over at him I saw that his ejaculation was not caused by what we were saying. Rather it was occasioned by what K.C. saw in the beam of his flashlight. There rising before him like a cyclopean monstrosity was the Devil's Gate itself. It looked far grander and more horrendous than I had anticipated. The twisted, gnarled expression seemed to burst forth from the granite and cry out either in anguish or ecstasy or both. The jagged horns on the monster's forehead seemed to stab at the stars like daggers of stone.

"Is that it?" asked Caleb in his halting, lumbering tone.

"Yes, that's it, Caleb. We can set up the ceremonial circle now."

I used the rope to fashion a crude ring, and with chalk I drew the hoary symbols I had learned from an ancient book of proscribed and unnamable lore. I won't tell you the incantations and rituals we performed; it wouldn't be wise. I can say only that it took some time and that while we held hands and chanted, a wind commenced to blow. The gust, trapped in the wind tunnel of the Arroyo, began to spiral and twist into a sandstorm, what we call in the terminology of the region, a "dust devil." Appropriate, no? The parrots cried out in a deafening cacophony, all but drowning out our intonations.

What was the purpose of our incantations? To open the gate to the other world. To communicate with whatever lay beyond. I should have suspected, but didn't know, that Renee had a more specific goal in mind.

The moment we finished with our ululations, the winds ceased too, but the birds continued with their harsh cries so that we did not realize it at first. And the moment we knew that the miniature twister had ended, our attention was drawn to yet another sound. A low moan that came from the bottom of the Devil's Gate. A bass vibration that rumbled in my rib cage and made my teeth rattle. I looked to the others and saw that they could hear it, too. Or rather they could feel it, in their bones.

Kraus and Gibbard took off for the stairs, climbing and stumbling for the safety of the outside world. I let them go. This was no place for dilettantes. Renee turned her flashlight toward the source of the sonorousness. There was an old, rusted gate set into the granite wall of the gorge and, beyond that, there was a dark and ominous tunnel leading off into the unknown. The sound boomed out of that tunnel, as if it were a speaker in the stage equipment of some cosmic rock band.

She approached the gate and reached out so that her fingertips brushed the bars. They vibrated to her touch. "It's behind here," she said.

"What's behind there?" Caleb intoned.

"The psychopomp," Renee said. "Or whatever we summoned."

K.C. heard that and fainted dead away. "For God's sake, brother," I said, shaking his shoulder. "It's only the wind."

Renee shook her head. "I don't think so," she said. Then she made her move. Renee, it should be understood, was small but very athletic. She had been a gymnast in her younger days. So when she climbed up the gate and slipped between two broken bars, then dropped down onto the other side, I wasn't surprised. I was appalled, not surprised.

"Renee," I said, supplicating. "What are you doing?"

"Exploring the unknown," she said. And then she was gone, running off into the darkness. The parrots screamed louder as I tried to climb the gate and follow her, but to no avail. I wasn't the gymnast that Renee was, and I slipped back down the bars, tearing my palms and skinning my knees. I pulled my cell phone from my pocket and dialed Renee. She answered, her voice sounding distorted due to the echoing from the tunnel walls. "Hello, Renee here! What's up?"

"Come back! You don't know what you're doing!"

"I know exactly what I'm doing! I'm going to see my father!"

"Don't! Don't open that door, Renee!"

"It's already open!"

"Come back here this instant!" I cried.

Caleb lumbered up beside me and grasped the bars in his big, beefy hands. At first I didn't know what he was doing, then I began to hear grunting noises coming from low in his chest and I understood. The big man had sensed my distress and was trying to bend the bars so I could pass through. A loyal creature, always.

I heard Renee gasp over the phone. "What?" I asked her.

"My God, Noel! If you could only see what I'm seeing!"

Was she teasing me? I cursed the bars that were keeping me from her and yelled over the shrieking parrots. "What? What do you see?"

"It's terrible, Noel! Monstrous! Unbelievable!"

Caleb grunted more loudly and strained at the bars, the veins in his arms bulging with the effort. "What is it, Renee?" I shouted into the phone.

"God! I never dreamed of this!" she said, her voice trembling.

"What?"

Through the phone, there was a sound of shuffling feet. Of quick steps. Of running. Then Renee's voice came through. Panicked. Unnerved. Terror-stricken. "Noel! Oh God, I should never have come! Leave! Get out! Run! It's your only chance!"

"What..."

"Don't ask me to explain! Beat it! Go!"

My mind whirled. Caleb grunted, braced himself, put all his strength into his arms while I screamed into the phone and the parrots squawked ever louder and louder. The phone signal began to cut out. I could only hear fragments of what she was saying. "...hellish things...curse...legions..."

"Renee, are you there?" Then, all at once, silence. Silence more deafening than the loudest noise. The parrots suddenly and without warning ceased their chatter and took wing, flying en masse over the face of the moon, so that their bat-like shadows flittered over the mouth of the tunnel. And the low, rumbling sound was gone too. So was any audible trace of Renee from my phone. "Renee!" I shouted. "Are you there?"

From the phone I heard a rasping sound as if someone were dragging it over the rough surface of the tunnel wall. And then there was a voice. A voice the likes of which I had never heard before and never wish to hear again. A deep, gelatinous, hollow, unearthly voice that sounded like, and yet didn't sound like, Renee's father!

And this was what it said: "You fool, Renee is gone!"

Then the rain came. With terrible and horrendous force, it burst forth from the heavens as if summoned to wash away this evil blight that had been awakened. It seemed to give Caleb the strength he needed. With a great wrenching sound, the gentle giant ripped one of the bars out of the gate. As he pulled it free, I squeezed through the opening and went running down the tunnel. But as far as I ran and as much as I called out and as far as I shone the flashlight beam, I could find no sign of Renee Zerbe.

I reached the other end of the tunnel. There was only the broad expanse of the Hahamongna Watershed and the 210 Freeway off in the distance. K.C. regained consciousness and called the police. The authorities searched the area for a week.

No trace of Renee Zerbe was ever found.

CHAPTER THIRTEEN

Noel closed the notebook and looked up. "That was the first indication I ever had that I was a Targeted Individual. It's been a long journey. Thank you."

As Will crossed to give Noel a hug and everyone applauded, Crush felt like he was going to crawl out of his skin. The clapping for Noel was a bit longer and louder than the applause for the others had been. They knew a good story when they heard one.

Crush turned to Gail, "Now?" he whispered.

Gail gestured to him to wait. Crush ground his teeth.

"Is that how it happened?" Gail whispered to him.

"No," Crush said. "And yes."

The man next to Gail crossed his legs again. The meeting progressed. No doubt about it, this man was definitely as annoyed as Crush was. Crush took a longer look at him. It was Evan Gibbard.

Christ, Crush thought, *this really is old home week*.

The meeting was over. Crush leapt to his feet and grabbed Noel by the arm. He tried to hurry him out, but Will came over to them. "We're pleased you could join us," Will said, offering his hand. Crush ignored him and hurried out.

Gail gave Will a regretful smile. "He doesn't believe in

shaking hands. The Overlords can take control of your mind that way."

Will nodded. "A lot of people believe that."

"But not you?"

Will shot back his shirtsleeve and exposed a bracelet. "I wear copper to protect me."

"Good idea." Gail moved on.

When Gail got outside she found Crush leading Noel to the Buick. Before he could get him there, the man in the surgical mask came up to Noel and grabbed his arm. The man was so upset that he even lowered his mask.

"Why?" Evan Gibbard asked. "Why do you insist on reading that crap to us every month?"

Gail hurried to join them as Crush said, "Sorry, we're in a hurry," and tried to brush by Evan.

But Noel stood his ground. "Why do you object, Evan? Because you don't like hearing the truth?"

"That's not the fucking truth and you know it. It's a fucking fabrication."

"You're in denial, friend. Either that or you're in league with them."

"Shut up!" Evan said. "You know I'm not in league with anybody. You're the one who's in denial. You could have saved her and you know it."

"I'm not listening to this. You're just channeling the enemy."

"Channeling the enemy? You're the one who's channeling H.P. fucking Lovecraft. Don't you think anybody in the group has ever read a book?"

"The group supports me," Noel said. "You're the only one with a problem."

"My problem is I know what really happened. I'm the only one who was there."

"You think so? You think you're the only one?" Noel

turned to Crush. "Caleb. You remember Evan?"

Crush nodded. "I remember him. How have you been?"

"Caleb?" Evan said, amazed. "I thought you'd be dead by now."

"I've tried, but it doesn't stick," Crush said. Evan didn't look like quite as much of an asshole as he had at seventeen. The years had either been kind to him or cruel. Either way, he seemed to have mellowed.

"Caleb," Noel said, "you were there that night. What I said was the truth, wasn't it?"

"It was *your* truth. That's the important thing," Crush said.

"Yes, it was my truth because it was *the* truth," Noel insisted. "Right?"

"Well, to be honest," Crush said, "I remember a few things a little differently."

"Like what?"

"Like...just about everything," Crush said. "Except the parrots. You got the parrots right."

Noel stared at him with the look of a man betrayed. "I thought you were on my side, Caleb. I thought you were *with* me. But now I see you're with them."

"I'm not with anybody, Noel," Crush said. "I'm with me. Come on."

"Do you refuse to corroborate my story, Caleb? Is that what you're saying?"

Crush rolled his eyes. "Look, I corroborate the broad outline. Just not the details."

Noel looked hurt. "The only reason I shared that story was that I thought you'd back me up, Caleb. That you'd make Evan see that he's been wrong for saying I was lying."

"I never said you were lying," Evan told him. "I said you were conflating."

"It's the same thing."

"No, it's not. Lying is telling a falsehood. Conflating is combining two different things until they make something new."

"You're playing the psychiatrist game now," Noel said. "Trying to make people think I'm crazy."

"I don't really have to try very hard," Evan said.

Noel ignored him and turned to Crush. "Have you heard from my brother?"

"No. That's why we have to go."

"K.C.?" Evan asked. "Has something happened to him?"

"He's been kidnapped," Noel said, as if he was letting Evan know his brother had been suffering from a little head cold. "He'll be all right." Noel turned back to address Crush. "What did my father say after he heard the message?"

"He said to fuck off," Crush replied.

Noel nodded. "That sounds like my father. So that's what he told them? The ones who have my brother?"

"He hasn't told them anything," Crush went on. "They haven't called again. Your sister's trying to talk your father into being more cooperative."

"That sounds like my sister. When are they going to call?"

"We don't know," Crush said. "That's why we have to go."

Evan looked at Crush, alarmed. "His brother's been kidnapped?"

"Yes," Crush said, because he couldn't think of anything else to say. "We have to go."

Then Will, the friendly group leader, approached Noel and took his hand. "Noel, do you have a minute?"

Crush tried to object, but Evan was still talking to him. "The Overlords are getting bolder and bolder. The End Times approach." Evan smiled. "It's good to see you again.

We should talk."

"Sure," Crush said, watching Noel and Will talk on the sidewalk. "About what?"

"Iraq."

"Were you there?"

Evan nodded gravely. "I was."

"In the Marines?" Crush asked, surprised.

"No. Blackwater," he said. Blackwater was the infamous private military company now renamed Academi, to distance itself from the unfortunate massacre at Nisour Square. "Sonny and I joined in '06."

"Sonny Kraus. How is he?"

Evan made a face. "They say he had PTSD. But we know what that really means. The Overlords were trying to discredit him. In the end, they made it look like he killed himself. Typical."

"I'm sorry." What else could Crush say to that?

"Maybe we could talk sometime? About the truth," Evan said.

"Great. I'll call you. What's your cell number?"

"I don't have a cell phone," Evan said. "They listen to all wireless communication. Why don't we meet at the Devil's Gate Dam?"

"Really?" Crush couldn't help but ask.

"Not down at the Gate. On top of the dam. The microwaves can't read you there, because it's on a ley line. How about six tomorrow night? I'll be there. You will be, too. And remember to come alone. You can't trust anyone." He nodded significantly, pulled his surgical mask back over his face, and walked off.

"Why do you want to talk to him?" Gail asked.

"I want to find out what happened that night. Hear his version."

"His version will probably be crazier than Noel's version. Besides, weren't you there? Don't you know what happened?"

"I was there," Crush grumbled, "but I don't know what happened. Come on."

Crush started to walk toward Noel when a truck drove up and bounced over the curb, screeching to a halt in front of Will and Noel. The two of them looked up, startled and afraid. But they weren't nearly afraid enough, Crush thought.

He recognized the truck. It was the decoy UPS truck that had delivered the bomb to the Zerbe mansion.

Crush took off running as the truck's doors flew open and two men in ski masks jumped out, pushed Will to the ground, and grabbed Noel. They threw him into the truck and slammed the door just as Crush ran up to it. He hammered on the window as the truck pulled out and drove down El Centro.

Not even stopping to think, Crush ran to his Buick. Gail was almost as fast, jumping into the passenger seat just as Crush started the car and pulled out.

The truck passed the post office, driving straight through a stop sign and heading toward the library. Down the street toward Orange Grove Boulevard and the freeway entrance.

Crush tore away from the curb and flew down the tree-lined street. He blew through the stop sign at Fremont. Passing cars hit their brakes and honked their horns.

"You were supposed to stop at that," Gail said.

"I know," Crush said.

They drove on. They could see the truck tearing past the library and turning right on Meridian. It went out of sight.

"Fuck," Crush said and drove faster, taking the turn at Meridian with a squealing of brakes. The back end of the

Buick fishtailed, but Crush was able to keep it under control and he barreled down Meridian toward Mission Street and the freeway entrance.

At the last moment, Crush slammed on the brakes and the car squealed to a halt just inches from the back of the UPS truck, which was stopped dead still. In front of it, the crossing gates were lowered and signal lights were flashing. The Metro Gold Line would be here any second.

Crush leaned forward, grabbed a heavy flashlight from the glove compartment, and leapt out of the Buick. Running up to the passenger window of the truck, just as the Gold Line sped past them, Crush slammed the butt of the flashlight into the glass, smashing it to bits. He reached in and grabbed the first person he could grab and hauled him out through the window.

It was one of the men in the ski masks, and Crush drove his elbow down on the man's head and threw him aside. The passenger door flew open and crashed into Crush's side, knocking him over. Another man in a ski mask jumped out, with a jack handle in his fist.

He moved in on Crush while he was down, ready to brain him with the weapon. But Gail was behind the man. She smacked him in the back of the head with a spinning roundhouse kick that sent him crashing into the hood of the truck. Crush sprang to his feet and slammed the man's head into the windshield. The window cracked but it didn't break. The same couldn't be said for the man.

Crush rushed around to the driver's door just as it swung open. He kicked it shut and smashed the door against the driver as he was climbing out. The driver was pinned halfway out the door. He was holding a gun in his right hand. Crush pushed on the door and at the same time slammed his forehead against the man's face with a vicious head butt, crushing his nose with a loud crunch.

But then Crush's head began to spin. The world twirled around him as he stumbled and fell on one knee to the pavement. He toppled over like a toddler who was just learning to walk. *I forgot about my concussion*, he thought, as the bright day started to go dark.

The driver pushed the door off him with a groan and looked down at Crush, lying stunned on the pavement. He leaned against the truck, breathing heavily. Then he raised the gun that was still in his right hand and pointed it at Crush's head.

From behind him, Gail came at the driver with a left hook straight to his head, instinctively turning her foot and popping her elbow out to give it more force, twisting her hip to put her whole body weight behind it. Her fist hit the back of the driver's head with the force of a hammer. He staggered and she grabbed his right hand and twisted it around his back until she heard a satisfying crack and the gun fell to the curb.

The driver dropped into the cab of the truck, clutching his arm, and Noel came clambering over him. Gail was already kneeling over Crush to see if he was all right, so when Noel climbed out of the truck, he fell right on top of her. Gail scrambled to get out from under Noel when the crossing gate began to rise.

The driver and the two henchmen struggled back into the truck and it pulled out, turning to the left and disappearing down the road.

"They're getting away," Crush said. He sat up, shaking his head, then holding it steady with his right hand. "Remind me not to shake my head again," he said.

"Or give somebody an Irish kiss," she said, using the politically incorrect slang term for a head butt. "At least, until you're healed."

"My head used to be my strongest weapon," Crush said.

"Used to be," she said.

Noel staggered to his feet and looked down the road. "They tried to kidnap me," he said.

"That's right," Gail said.

"Why would they do that? They already have K.C.," he said, as if he were arguing about a referee's bad call.

"Maybe they think your father needs more pressure," Crush said. "To stop the bullet train."

"Is that what this is about?" Noel asked.

"Apparently," Crush said.

Noel shook his head. "Then they don't understand my father very well."

"What do you mean?" Gail asked.

"That high-speed rail means more to him than any of his children do."

"That's a pretty harsh thing to say," Gail admonished.

Noel looked at her in blank surprise. "Why would you say that? Children live and die. The high-speed rail will be forever."

Gail didn't know what to say to that. "Won't it break down eventually?"

"Of course," Noel said. "And then it will be replaced with an even better one. Can you say that for children?"

Gail didn't know what to say to that either.

Crush made it to his feet, feeling pretty steady actually.

"We should get you to the hospital," Gail said.

"I'll go," Crush conceded. "After."

"After what?" Gail asked.

"After we get Zerbe back." He took Noel by the arm and started leading him back to the Buick. "I need to ask you some questions."

"Oh, right," Noel said. "You want me to take *your* car, so they can listen to everything we say?"

"The Overlords, you mean?"

"Yes. They're everywhere. I'm taking a random Uber. They aren't prepared for that."

"An *Uber*?" Crush said. "You know who runs Uber, don't you? The *Masons*, that's who. And you know if the Masons are involved, the Trilateral Commission can't be far behind!"

Noel's expression grew more confused. "Well, what do we do?"

"It's only about two miles," Gail said. "We could walk." They both looked at her as if she were insane; she had suggested the craziest thing they'd heard all day: walking in LA.

"We can take my car," Crush said. "It's safe. I had it modified with special spinel ceramics so the delta rays can't penetrate it."

This seemed to convince Noel. Crush led him to the Buick, opened the rear door, and got in. Noel joined him, and Gail got in the front seat and started the car. There was no argument about her driving this time. Crush grabbed the seat in front of him to keep his balance as the car pulled away from the curb. He shut his eyes and winced.

"Are you okay?" Noel asked.

"I'm fine," Crush said.

"He should be in the hospital," Gail said. "He has a concussion."

"We don't know that," Crush said.

"We don't know that 'cause you won't get an MRI," Gail said.

"Well, I don't blame you," Noel said. "Those MRIs can read your mind."

Crush shook his head and tried to clear his double vision. It didn't work. Never mind. It was time to ask his question.

"Did you tell anybody else about your plan? To kidnap K.C. and get him arrested?"

"No," Noel said. "Well, the group, of course."

"You told the group?" Crush asked in disbelief. "The Targeted Individual group?"

"Yeah, I shared about it. But that's okay," Noel reassured him. "It's a safe place. And it's anonymous."

Crush rubbed his temples. "So you only told fifteen people about your plan?"

"Fifteen *anonymous* people. And actually, I think there were more there that day."

"Was Evan Gibbard there?" Gail asked.

"Let me think," Noel said with a frown. "Yes, I guess he was. Why?"

"Well, think about it, Noel," Crush said. "The person who really kidnapped K.C. had to know he'd be at the warehouse, right?"

Noel smiled at Crush as if he were a simpleton. "You're forgetting about their time-traveling abilities. They could've asked anybody, at any time, where K.C. was that night and then gone back in time to kidnap him. Understand?"

Crush stared at him. Maybe it was the concussion, but that almost made sense.

CHAPTER FOURTEEN

It was the boredom more than anything else that made him do it. Zerbe would have thought, if he'd heard about someone who had done this thing, that they would have done it out of desperation or terror. But the terror he'd felt earlier had exhausted him, and he'd lapsed into a state of dull anxiety. So he did it, really, just because there was nothing else for him to do. The darkness and the silence were so all-encompassing that the only thing he had to think about was the plastic strap that tied his wrists together behind the metal chair and how to get out of it.

At first he just tried to slide it down his wrists, but his hands, of course, stopped it from going any farther. Then he tried to pull his hands apart to snap it. When that didn't work, he tried to twist his hands in such a way as to break it. When that didn't work either, he tried to pull his right hand out. Then his left.

It occurred to him that he could have gotten it off if it weren't for his thumb. His right thumb or his left thumb. If either one hadn't been there, bulging out the way it did, he felt sure he could have slipped the damn plastic zip tie off and freed his hands.

And then what could he do? He could scratch his nose,

for one thing. That would be great. And he could reach the table in front of him. See if that cell phone was still there. If it was, then he could call for help. But he'd have to lean awfully far forward to get it. Maybe he couldn't reach it after all.

But wait! What an idiot! If he reached down with his freed hands and worked on the straps that tied his legs to the chair, he could get them free, too. And then? Then he could stand up and walk to the table. Hell, he could walk to the door and get out of this damn van. He could dance all the way home.

If it weren't for his fucking thumbs. But what could he do about them? He couldn't cut them off. No...but he could dislocate them. Or just one, anyway. It would only take one, right? But which one? Well, he was right-handed, so the left one would make the most sense, right? He tried to think what he used his left thumb for and couldn't come up with much. So he decided to try it.

Using the slats of the chair, he tried to push his left thumb out of its socket. It hurt so much that he stopped after only a few seconds. But then the boredom got too much for him and there was nothing else to do. He might as well try it again. It still hurt, but somehow it didn't feel as bad as it had the first time. And he kept working it and working it. It took a long time, but what else did he have to do?

He thought he'd hear a sound when his thumb popped loose, but instead it just got limp and sore and very swollen. At first he was afraid that it was so swollen that the plastic strap would be harder to slide off, not easier. But he went on trying to pull his wrist free. He tried for what seemed like hours and hours. After all, how else could he pass the time?

The rhythmic moving of his wrist was hypnotizing to him, and he'd almost fallen asleep when...*what was that feeling?* That feeling of the strap slipping off him? That feeling of...freedom? He'd done it! He'd gotten loose from the zip tie! He gasped.

Now what the hell was he supposed to do?

He tried to move his arms from around the back of the chair but found that they were only so much dead weight. He realized that the smartest thing about his recent maneuvering wasn't that it would help him escape; it was that it kept the blood flowing to his arms and hands. Otherwise, he might have lost them. He had a mental image of his hands growing green and black and having to be amputated. Could that happen? He didn't want to find out.

Concentrating hard on his right arm, he hoisted it over the top rail of the chair. Then he brought his left arm around to join it. He rubbed his hands together and enjoyed the tingling feeling of the blood rushing back to his fingers.

His dislocated thumb started hurting more. In fact, it was throbbing with a blinding pain. To distract himself from the agony, he bent over and reached down to examine his legs. His ankles were securely zip-tied to the legs of the chair. He tugged at the plastic bonds but knew he couldn't break them. He gave up and thought he'd try to stand.

He lifted his butt from the chair. It felt good to stretch his legs, to flex his buttocks, to slowly stand upright. But before he could straighten up all the way, he bumped his head with a crack on the ceiling of the van. He stood there, bent over, stretching his legs and tightening his glutes. It felt good, but not good enough. He had to get his ankles free. He had to get out of this fucking van.

He tried to think of what his heroes would do in this situation. James Bond would cut the strap with a laser beam hidden in his watch. Maxwell Smart would have a small bomb in his boot heel. Jack Bauer would probably tear his own feet off and run away on the stumps.

Get a little closer to home, he told himself. *What would Crush do?*

Crush would think.

So Zerbe thought.

⌘

When Crush and Gail and Noel got to the Zerbe mansion, Donleavy greeted them at the door. They went into the ornate dining room, where Angela and Emil were sitting at opposite ends of a long table, looking like the protagonists of a gothic novel.

Emil, eating calmly from a bowl of soup, looked up and said, "That will be all, Ms. Donleavy. We have private matters to discuss."

Donleavy cast a disapproving eye at Crush and went out, shutting the door behind her. Crush knew Donleavy's Rules for a Bodyguard, and for once he was thankful for them. Rule No. Two: Do Whatever the Principal Says. The Principal in this case was Emil Zerbe. Of course, Rule No. One was: Don't Let the Principal Get Himself Killed. The two rules often conflicted with each other.

Emil glanced at Gail. "And who's this?"

"My sensei," Crush said.

Emil gave Gail a one-sided leer. "I approve," he said, returning to slurping his soup.

Angela turned to them in exasperation. "What's the point in talking to him? He gives me nothing! He hasn't even told me what that weird message meant. He won't agree to give the kidnappers whatever it is they want."

"They're bluffing," Emil said, sipping from his spoon. He looked up with that stroke-twisted face of his. "They're too cowardly to hurt my son."

"They just tried to kidnap your other son," Gail said. "If it hadn't been for Crush and me, they'd have gotten him, too." She recounted the story as succinctly as she could. After she was done, Emil sat in silence for a moment.

He shrugged it off. "If the two of you could stop them, they couldn't have been very vicious," he said. "Why didn't they just shoot him in the truck? And shoot you afterward? No, they're bluffing. I can feel it."

Angela pushed away from the table. "It's the stroke. It's made him crazy. He's not thinking clearly."

Crush pulled out a chair and sat at the table facing Emil. "No, the stroke hasn't changed you, has it? You've always been a stubborn asshole, haven't you?"

"An asshole, perhaps," Emil said. "But stubborn? I prefer decisive."

"Right. I guess you still have those Bob Dole campaign buttons?"

"Dole would have made a fine president, mark my words."

"And you still think Nixon was railroaded out of office?"

"He should have held out a little longer."

"And you think the wrong side won World War II?"

Emil's good eye slid over to stare at Crush. "Hitler was bad. Stalin was worse. Are you going to argue with that?"

"I'm not going to pick one genocidal maniac over another."

"Roosevelt and Churchill did," Emil said.

Crush had a feeling he was getting out of his depth. Before he had to reply, they were interrupted by the loud ringing of a telephone. Crush, Angela, and Gail pulled out their phones. Nobody's phone was ringing. They were puzzled for a second. Then Angela spoke up. "It must be the landline."

"Well, answer it, why don't you?" Emil said, not realizing

how rare it was to get an actual call on that piece of antique technology.

"It's just a sales call, Dad," Angela said.

Crush spotted the telephone on a side table. It was an old black rotary thing, so he had to answer it blindly, without knowing who was on the other end. Just like the old days. Plucking the receiver from its cradle, Crush held it to his ear. "Hello."

"Will you accept a collect call from Kendrick Zerbe?" an operator said.

"Yes," he said quickly. "Of course." When was the last time he'd spoken with an operator?

Another voice now. A familiar voice. "Um, is Emil Zerbe there? This is his son. Would you tell him to send somebody to come pick me up? I've escaped."

"Are you okay, Zerbe?"

"Yeah," Zerbe said, in a faltering tone, "No. I don't know."

"Where are you, Zerbe?"

"I don't know that either." Then there was only silence on the line.

⌘

"Hello!" Crush's voice came from the dangling receiver. "Zerbe, are you there?"

Zerbe was sitting in a crumpled heap at the bottom of a phone booth, watching the phone as it swung back and forth, like the blade in "The Pit and the Pendulum."

Clearly he was hallucinating. He was still, he assumed, back in that white van, tied to that metal chair, imagining this daring escape. And Crush's voice, yelling at him from the tinny speaker, was just wish fulfillment. Oh well, at least this illusion was a way to pass the time.

He remembered his dream of escape pretty lucidly. He remembered how, with his legs still zip-tied to the chair, he'd been clever enough to reach up and explore the ceiling of the van. He remembered the cracking sound his head had made when he stood up. How it hadn't sounded solid. It had sounded crinkly. Like plastic. Crush would investigate, and so Zerbe would, too.

He felt around up there until he found it. The ceiling light. With a plastic lens covering it. And he had an idea. Not exactly a *MacGyver* idea, but an idea nonetheless. He tried to crack the light fixture with his elbow. When he couldn't strike it with enough force, he used the top of his skull, slamming it repeatedly against the lamp until it cracked. He sat back down after that, his head throbbing and spinning from the impact. Once his brain had cleared, he stood back up and reached for the light fixture, feeling the broken shards of plastic with his fingers, trying to pry one loose. One he could use as a tool.

Once he had it in his hands, he brought it down to his lap. He examined it with his fingers in the darkness. It was sharp enough. But it was sharp on every side, and he had nothing to protect his fingers. Well, if he was going to do it, he'd better do it soon. He wrapped the fingers of his right hand around the broken piece of plastic and bent over to saw at the zip tie that held his right leg in place. He sawed at it for a long time, the shard cutting into his fingers faster than it cut into the strap.

The blood from his fingers made them slick, and the plastic slipped from his grasp and fell to the floor. He searched for it in the dark but couldn't find it, so he had to reach back up to the lamp for another.

It took him a long time to cut through the strap on his right leg and even longer to cut through the one on his left.

By the time he was finished, both of his hands were useless: strained, dislocated, and bleeding. He sat with them cupped in his lap and wanted a long rest.

But no. He was free from the zip ties and he needed to make his move before his kidnapper returned. Then he realized he had no plan. No strategy. No blueprint for escape.

Well, he could sneak out of the van. Open the doors and creep out. But what would be waiting for him outside? He might find an army of kidnappers waiting for him. There had to be another way. He could stay right where he was until his kidnapper came back in. He could feign being tied up and when his abductor came close enough, he could...he could what?

He tried to picture himself struggling with a live human being, wrapping his useless fingers around a throat of flesh and blood and choking it until...until what? No, he couldn't do it. He doubted that he could do it physically and he knew he couldn't do it emotionally. He would have to sneak out now, regardless of what dangers he might walk into.

Lifting himself to his unsteady legs, he moved slowly across the floor of the van, bracing himself against the table. He explored its surface with his hands, hoping against hope that the cell phone had been left there, that he could make a call for help. But no. The table was bare.

Making his way to the doors of the van he felt for the handle with his mangled fingers, took a deep breath, and pulled it. The door swung open. He poked his head out.

The van was parked inside a Quonset hut with a dirt floor. Sunlight streamed through gaps in the corrugated metal walls. He could see that, except for the van, the building was empty. No squads of kidnappers were waiting to leap on him. They were probably right outside the hut. Waiting to leap on him.

Climbing out of the van, he stumbled and fell in a heap in the dirt. His head throbbed and his hands burned with a searing pain. Using the bumper, he pulled himself to his feet and limped around the inside of the hut. He was looking for a hiding place, but realized that that would just be delaying the inevitable. It occurred to him that he might have been better off staying tied up in the van and being a good hostage. After all, his kidnapper hadn't actually *said* he was going to kill him. Well, it was too late to go back to that now. Better to just go outside and face the music.

Walking over to the door, he swung it open. Outside he saw nothing but scrubby hills and a two-lane road snaking off into the distance. He waited by the door for a few minutes, not knowing what to do, then made a circuit around the outside of the hut. He found himself oddly disappointed to find no one. Unable to think of anything else to do, he started walking down the narrow road. The temperature was comfortable, in the mid-seventies, but the sun beat down on him and he squinted and sweated. He wasn't used to being outside.

He didn't know which direction was north, south, east, or west. He just walked forward. His hands hurt, and he couldn't put them in his pockets, so he held them out in front of him like Frankenstein. That made him laugh so hard that he tripped and nearly fell down. He sat by the side of the road and laughed and laughed until he started crying.

He wiped off his tears, got up, and kept on going. After about fifteen minutes it occurred to him that he shouldn't be walking along this road in broad daylight. The kidnapper could drive past him, stop, and load him right back into the van. But no matter. He was too tired to walk off-road. He trudged on.

A few cars sped toward him, and though he tried to stick

out his swollen thumb to hitch a ride, they just drove on. He thought he should have checked to see if there were keys in the white van before he left it. He could be driving down the road, listening to music, singing along, instead of walking drearily on. *Oh well*, he thought, *I'll remember that next time. The next time I'm kidnapped.*

As he walked, he began to sing, just to pass the time. *"To the dump, to the dump, to the dump, dump, dump,"* he sang. *"To the dump, to the dump, to the dump, dump, dump. To the dump! To the dump, dump, dump."*

Then he saw it. Like the monolith from *2001*, it stood there in the lonely desert, a beacon for wandering travelers.

A phone booth.

It was then that he thought he must be experiencing delirium. What the hell was a phone booth doing out in the middle of nowhere, in the early years of the twenty-first century? He slowly approached it, expecting it to fade into the horizon like a mirage. But it remained solid and substantial, right until he reached out with his bloody fingers and touched the door.

It was real.

Either that or his hallucination was very concrete. He pushed the folding door open and stepped inside. The phone was there. The cord was attached. He lifted the receiver and heard the dial tone. It worked! He could call Crush. He could go home! Back to his beloved loft. He could leave the real world behind!

Then he realized—he didn't have any change. Change! When do you ever need change nowadays? Never! He never did until this instant, when his life depended on it! He felt like Burgess Meredith breaking his glasses at the end of that *Twilight Zone* episode. He would be perfectly happy if he had that one thing! A fucking quarter! Without it, he was as good as dead.

He looked at the receiver. Maybe if he explained, it would let him place a call. But explain to what? It was just a machine. It couldn't understand how desperate his situation was. He thought of all those old songs where people sang to operators and explained their sorrows. But did they still even *have* operators?

He pressed the "0" repeatedly. A voice came over the line. "What number do you wish to call?"

"Operator! Thank God. I don't have any change. What can I do?"

"Would you like to place a collect call?"

Of course, a collect call! Zerbe remembered collect calls. Collect calls didn't require change! He was saved!

"Yes, yes! A collect call. I'd like to place a collect call."

"And what number would you like to call?"

His face fell. What number? He didn't know any phone numbers. Who knew anyone's number anymore, with the memory on your cell phone? Who used their real memory for anything?

"What number would you like to call?" the operator repeated.

Think, Zerbe! You must know a phone number. Any phone number. Think. Think of a goddamned phone number. But the only number he could recall was the one he'd memorized in childhood. His old home number. His father's number. He didn't really want to talk to his father now, but what choice did he have?

He gave the number and waited.

It was when he heard Crush's voice on the end of the line that he really started thinking this was only a dream. What would Crush be doing at his house? Crush wouldn't be caught dead there. No, this was all just an illusion. Before long, his kidnapper would come back in the van, wake him up, and start beating on him again.

"Zerbe, are you there?" Crush's dream voice was saying to him through the phone.

"I am, but you're not," Zerbe said.

"Zerbe. Is that you?"

"Sure, it's me."

"Where are you?"

"I'm locked in a van somewhere."

"Where are you calling from?"

"I'm not calling you. You're just a dream. Shut up and let me sleep."

"Zerbe! Where are you? Listen to me."

"To the dump, to the dump, to the dump, dump, dump," Zerbe sang, to the tune of the *William Tell Overture*.

"Stop singing and tell me where you are," Crush said.

Zerbe sighed. "First of all, I don't know. Second of all, you're not really there. This is just a dream."

"It's not a dream, Zerbe."

"Well, you'd say that, 'cause you don't know it's a dream 'cause you're *in* my dream."

"Why do you think it's a dream?" Crush asked.

"Because I'm in a phone booth and there aren't any phone booths. Because you're there. And because I heard the road sing."

"You heard what?" Crush asked.

"I heard the road singing. When we were driving over it. Just before we stopped."

"What did it sing?"

"To the dump, to the dump, to the dump, dump, dump."

"Stay where you are. Stay right there. We're coming to get you."

"What are you talking about?" Zerbe was getting very

annoyed by this hallucination.

"I know where you are," Crush said. "I'm going to give the phone to your sister."

"Oh, my sister now," Zerbe said, grabbing the dangling receiver.

"Yes. Whatever you do, don't hang up," Crush said.

"Of course not," Zerbe said. Then he hung up. This dream was getting really obnoxious. He wished he could wake up.

⌘

Crush told Gail about the phone call as they rushed out to the Buick. He got behind the wheel. Gail laid her hand on his arm. "You cannot drive, Crush."

"We're in a hurry," he explained. "I drive faster than you."

"You have to listen...."

Crush looked her dead in the eye. "Not this time."

She gave up and got in the passenger seat. "So where are we going?"

"Lancaster." Lancaster was a little desert community out near Palmdale.

"Why Lancaster?" Gail asked.

"Did you ever hear of the Musical Road?"

"Is that a fairy tale?"

"No, it's a road. I heard about it at the Glendale Car Rally. It was made for some car commercial. A two-lane road with specially designed grooves in it. When you drive over it, it plays the theme from *The Lone Ranger.*"

"Why would they build that?"

"Hell if I know. They do that in some places. There's a road in New Mexico that plays 'America the Beautiful.' I hear there's one in France that does 'La Marseillaise' and one in Korea that plays 'Mary Had a Little Lamb' for some reason. I guess people have a lot of time on their hands."

"So Zerbe's not crazy?"

"I'm not saying that. But the road is real."

"And he's there?"

"He's close to there."

"How long is the trip?"

"The way I drive? A little under an hour."

A phone rang loudly. It was Crush's cell, in the back pocket of his jeans. He shifted a little. "Could you get that? What does it say?" Gail reached into Crush's back pocket and pulled out his phone. "It says, 'Unknown Caller.' "

"Answer it. Put it on speaker," Crush told her.

She did so and a voice came from the phone. "Would you accept a collect call from..."

"Yes," Crush said without waiting for the operator to finish.

Zerbe's voice came over the line. "Crush! Is that you?"

"Yes, we're..."

Zerbe cut him off, exultantly. "I remembered your number! I actually remembered your number!"

"Yes, that's right."

"I dreamed you were at my house."

"I *was* at your house. We're coming to get you. Just hold tight."

"How do you know where I am? I don't even know where I am."

"It's okay. I know."

"How do you know?"

"On account of the Musical Road."

There was silence on the line. Then Zerbe said, "Oh shit. I'm still dreaming."

"This isn't a dream, Zerbe. I'm really here," Crush said. "Stay on the line. I'll find you, I swear."

Crush glanced over to Gail as he drove. Over her shoulder, through the passenger window, he saw it. The Devil's Gate Dam. They were driving right by it, and it didn't look ominous at all. It looked like an ordinary Army Corps of Engineers project, circa 1920.

Nothing at all like the entrance to Hell.

CHAPTER FIFTEEN

I t was January 21st, 2001.

Crush was walking down the narrow concrete steps from the top of the Devil's Gate Dam to the bottom of the Arroyo Seco, all the while wondering why in the world he was doing this. For the other kids, he knew this was an adventure, something to break the dull monotony of their lives. Crush's life had had little monotony, and the adventures he'd taken part in would put their little nocturnal camping trip to shame.

But who was he kidding? He knew why he was there. She was walking down the steps in front of him. His flashlight was playing on her raven-black hair, dipping down occasionally to illuminate her distractingly beautiful rump. Renee Zerbe was the reason he'd let himself get talked into the excursion. She was the reason they were all going on this adventure. To get her mind off her recent tragedy.

Since her father's suicide, they hadn't seen her much. She'd come over to the Zerbe mansion last night, but nobody knew what to say to her or how to make her feel better. Oddly, it was Noel who seemed to comfort her most, or at least to distract her from her grief. Perhaps it was because he was the least tactful of the bunch.

While everyone else was tiptoeing around her tragedy, he just came out and asked, "Why do you think your father shot himself in the middle of the parade?"

She said she didn't know. Then Noel just changed the subject and started talking about his latest obsession: local hauntings and spooky places. He spent a lot of time talking about the Devil's Gate—he'd been going on about its history for the last few months. This time Renee said, "Why don't we explore it? Tomorrow night?"

Since this seemed to be the only thing Renee was interested in doing other than drinking and staring at the wall, they all agreed to make the trip. So here they were.

In the months that Crush had been living in the Zerbe mansion, he had gradually, in spite of his best efforts, become entwined in the household. The Zerbe children had become a part of his world, or he had become a part of theirs. They were not his siblings exactly. Certainly not his friends. What then? His extended family? Like cousins you visited on tedious holiday vacations, put up with, and eventually kind of enjoyed?

He went to school with them, for one thing. Crush had gone to school as little as possible. Blaz Kusinko didn't believe his sons should waste time in classes when they could be out learning things like how to break bones and sell drugs. Crush found that he liked school. He liked the regularity of classes and homework. He didn't do well on tests, but he didn't care. He wasn't going to be there long enough to worry about his GPA anyway.

K.C. Zerbe had told Crush that he didn't like school. He did well in classes and got along well with the teachers, but he was picked on by his asshole classmates. The bullies. Crush had little patience for bullies. He knew that anyone who bothered to tease and belittle smaller kids or outsiders was just too much of a dick to be tolerated. When he caught them beating on K.C. in the gym one day, he put a stop to it then and there.

That got Crush in trouble at school, but it made K.C. his friend for life. Really. And though this gratitude made him a little uncomfortable at first, he had to admit that he enjoyed K.C.'s company. He taught Crush the pleasures of comic books and grade-Z movies and classic rock 'n' roll, all things that Crush hadn't had the time to enjoy.

He also invited Crush into the inner circle of his siblings' friends. That, he didn't enjoy as much. Angela was like a self-centered five-year-old in a grown woman's body. Noel was a thinking machine with no empathy for his fellow humans. Evan Gibbard and Sonny Kraus and the other hangers-on were just predators who hadn't found their prey yet.

And then there was Renee Zerbe. Crush knew she was damaged far beyond her years. He knew that after what had happened to her, she couldn't ever be normal and whole again. She laughed a lot and sang a lot, but through it all there was a sadness that cut right into his soul and made him want to try to protect her.

Years later, when Crush discussed this with his AA sponsor, Bill Ingol, while going through the endless fourth step, Bill brought up the obvious. "She reminded you of your mother."

That had never occurred to Crush, and the fact that it was so clearly true made him angry. "You're saying I wanted to fuck my mother?"

"You said that, I didn't." Bill was endlessly, infuriatingly calm. "I said you wanted to protect your mother."

"Sure," Crush had said bitterly, "I wanted to protect my mother. I wanted to protect Renee. I didn't do either of them a damn bit of good."

"Is that why you became a soldier? And a bodyguard? To protect people? To make up for what you couldn't do when you were a kid?"

"No," Crush said. "That's why I became an alcoholic." And to prove his point, he went on a bender that lasted three weeks and ended up in a whorehouse in Ensenada.

But that was years later. At the time, all he knew was that he couldn't stop thinking about Renee. He even thought, sometimes on warm winter nights, that he might actually be in love with her. That is, if love was a real thing that someone could be in.

And even if he was in that thing-people-called-love, there wasn't anything he could do about it. For a lot of reasons. For one, she didn't love him, she loved Evan Gibbard. The fact that Evan Gibbard treated her like crap didn't make a difference. The fact that she threw herself at Sonny Kraus to make Evan jealous, and Sonny took joyful advantage of that, didn't make a difference either.

There was also the fact that Crush didn't know how to put himself out there, to express his feelings in a non-sleazy way. Oh sure, he knew how to hook up with a girl. He'd hooked up with plenty of them in Kusinko's bratva. But to tell a girl that he really cared about her? He didn't even know what that meant. To "have feelings" for someone? That was just TV-show talk. Stuff they said on *Melrose Place* and *Dawson's Creek*. Nothing to do with real life.

And then there was K.C. Zerbe.

K.C. had come to mean something to Crush. Not as a friend exactly. Both from his mother and father, Crush had learned to mistrust friends. Friends were liable to betray you, and to use your weaknesses against you. If they were stronger than you, they'd try to beat you. If they were weaker, they'd resent you.

But K.C. was different. He didn't seem to want anything from

Crush. He just liked to be around him. Even the protection Crush provided was just a bonus, not expected. He seemed to actually like Crush. Go figure.

Crush knew that K.C. was in love with Renee. In Love with a capital I and a capital L. In love without any of the complicated reservations that plagued Crush. He knew this was a taboo love, one that broke any number of state and ethical laws. K.C. knew that, too. He just couldn't help himself.

So Crush couldn't help but think that K.C. had "been there first," and that it would be breaking some kind of bratva friend-bro code if he moved in. Or maybe he was just using that as an excuse to not do anything about his feelings for Renee.

But as he followed Renee down into the Arroyo Seco, he knew he was at the end of his "doing-nothing" rope. Tonight he'd make his move. Whether he was rejected or accepted didn't really matter. He'd already been defeated. He was caught up in this family and its circle. He'd always told himself he could hit the road whenever he wanted. Now he knew he couldn't pick up and leave without leaving a little piece of himself behind.

He cursed his mother for bringing him into this house. Then he cursed himself for cursing his mother. It had been so easy for so many years. Just the two of them, Toni and Caleb, against the world. Now these others had been brought into it. Could you really care about more than one person? Wouldn't you eventually have to choose between them?

By the time he reached the bottom of the stairway, he was in a foul mood and wasn't talking to anybody. The others didn't notice, because he didn't talk too much when he was in the best of moods. Angela called him "the stupid silent type." He didn't mind. He supposed he was stupid in some ways. He knew he was smart in others.

They gathered in a circle, smoked some weed, and talked some shit about school while Noel gathered some dry brush and started a little campfire. They didn't perform any ritual and they didn't summon any demons. They just complained about school until the conversation lagged. Then Noel and Evan closed their eyes and fell asleep.

No one knew quite what to say to Renee. Did she want to talk about her father? Or did she want to talk about anything but her father? During the awkward silence, Angela, who'd had a little too much gin and a little too much pot, peeled off and started to make out with Sonny, which Crush thought was kind of crass. After all, Sonny had just dumped Renee rather rudely two months earlier. And that was a month after Evan had dumped her and handed her off to Sonny, like a regifted Christmas present.

A little over a year ago, Crush had been a part of the Russian Mafia: collecting gambling money, selling drugs, and worrying about being whacked by rival gangs. He found himself missing that comparatively peaceful life. Pasadena Prep was a serialized drama that made *The Sopranos* seem tame.

Crush slid over to talk to Renee. He didn't know what to say, but he felt like he should say something. "How are you?" As soon as the words left his lips, he was appalled by them.

She turned and gave him a withering gaze. "Did you really ask me that?"

"I couldn't think of anything else to say."

"Then don't say anything." She glanced over at Angela and Sonny embracing in the dirt. She looked back at Crush. "Do you want to kiss me?" she asked.

Crush did. But from the corner of his eye he could see K.C. sitting quietly, watching them. He couldn't move. When he hesitated,

Renee got up and walked away into the darkness. Crush started to go after her, but K.C. moved more quickly.

Crush stayed where he was.

"Why don't you go after her?" Angela asked. He hadn't noticed Angela come up next to him. That bothered him. He usually had a sixth sense about people coming on him from behind. He must have been distracted.

"He can handle it," he said, nodding toward the darkness.

"K.C.?" Angela asked with a drunken laugh. "You know what they say. 'Vice is nice, but incest is best.' "

"Shut up. What happened to Sonny? I thought you were getting busy with him."

She just smiled a wicked smile. "I like to keep him guessing. I know you've been mooning after Renee for months. Why don't you make your move?"

"I can't."

"Why not?"

"She just lost her father."

"Exactly. What better time?"

"I see," Crush said. " 'Sorry your father killed himself. Want to fuck?' Like that?"

"You could just offer her some support. A kind word. A shoulder to cry on," Angela said. "Sometimes people need a little physical comfort, you know."

Crush felt a little ashamed of himself. "Okay."

"Then ask her if she wants to fuck," Angela added with a laugh.

Crush laughed too, although he felt sure he shouldn't. She moved uncomfortably close to him. "Where's Sonny?" he asked.

"Oh, he's smoking dope and nodding off. Can you believe it?" Angela was very close to him, and the night air was filled with her jasmine fragrance and her warm breath. Maybe it was because he was tormented by his feelings for Renee, maybe it was because he was seventeen, but for whatever reason, he kissed her. Or she kissed him. He was never sure which.

They were both teenagers, which doesn't excuse what came next, but it does partly explain the fumbling of hands, the rustling of clothes, the mad unbuttoning and unfastening and unzipping. The rush of skin on skin and the not-caring-what-part-of-the-body one was touching for the sheer glory of touching it.

Whether it went on for five minutes or a half-hour, Crush couldn't say, but they hadn't gotten very far through the labyrinth of clothes and limbs and hair when K.C. came up to them.

"She's gone," he said.

It took a while for the words to register. It took longer than that for Crush and Angela to untangle themselves from each other and ask what he meant.

"She went down the tunnel," Zerbe said.

The tunnel was set into the wall of the Arroyo below the rock formation that everybody said looked like the Devil but that, to Crush, looked more like one of the jagged cliffs Wile E. Coyote used to stand on and push huge boulders onto the speeding Road Runner.

And, in fact, the tunnel itself looked like one of those illustrations of tunnels Coyote used to paint on cliff faces, in order to lure the Road Runner to a particular X-marked spot. A big arch going off into nothingness with an iron fence across it. A disaster just waiting to happen.

"I was talking to her and she just ran away." Zerbe pointed frantically down the tunnel. "We have to find her. She was upset. She might do something." He didn't have to say what he was afraid she would do. They all knew.

"The gate is closed," Crush said. "Are you sure she went down there?"

"Yes!" Zerbe shouted. "She climbed up the gate and jumped over it. Then she ran down the tunnel. We have to stop her!"

By now Zerbe's yelling had awakened Sonny from his nap by the campfire. Noel and Evan woke up and rushed over to ask what was going on. When they were told, they all hollered for Renee as loudly as they could. They must have awakened a flock of parrots, because the birds started screeching and squawking so loudly it almost drowned out the human cries.

Crush tried to pry one of the bars off the gate. Noel and K.C. made an effort to hoist each other up the fence. None of this worked. Angela called 911, but she couldn't get a signal down in the depths of the Arroyo. Then Evan and Sonny got spooked by all this, but mostly by the parrots' almost-human screams. They ran away, up the stairs to the top of the dam—to get help, they said. They never came back.

For the next thirty minutes or so Crush strained his muscles on the gate while the Zerbe brothers tried to find a way around it and Angela kept trying to find a spot with cell phone reception. Finally, Crush pried the gate open just enough to squeeze his bulky frame through the gap. He ran down the tunnel. It was dark, and he collided with the walls a few times, but kept on running till he reached the other side.

It opened onto a flat, marshy plain. He ran on, calling Renee's name for what seemed like hours, with no answer, until he collapsed, winded and sweating. Since he was a kid he had relied on his strength to defeat whatever problem might confront him, but his muscles couldn't solve anything this time. He clutched his aching side and gasped.

It started to rain then. Really pouring, as if the sky had been waiting for months to let loose. Raindrops thudded down on his back, and he shut his eyes and sank into the mud.

And that was how the police found him.

A couple of cops shined a flashlight on him and yelled at him to get up. When he didn't, they pointed their pistols at him and told him to keep his hands where they could see them. They grabbed him by the shoulders and hauled him to his feet.

"Where is she?" a cop hollered at him. "What have you done with her?"

⌘

"Why were the cops ganging up on you?" Gail asked.

Crush shrugged. "Because I was there. Because I was big. Because they'd just found her shirt with blood on it."

"Where?"

"A few yards away from me."

"But Renee? They never found her?"

"They never did. They took me downtown and questioned me. With their fists. Everything they learned about me made them more sure I was the one who'd grabbed her. They searched that rain-swept field for days. Went over every inch of it. Again and again. They couldn't find a thing. Not a trace of her. So they had to get me to confess."

"Is that why you don't trust the police?" she asked.

"Oh God, no. I stopped trusting them long before that." Crush blinked his eyes to keep them focused on the road. "Anyway, there I was. A drifter. The son of a whore. No known father. When they traced me back to Brighton Beach and the Russian mob, I was like their wet dream of a suspect. They didn't need to look any further.

"There was only one problem. They never found Renee. They couldn't find a body or any evidence, other than that shirt. And it's pretty hard to charge somebody with murder when you can't find the body."

"It's been done," Gail said.

"Sure. But there was no evidence either. No blood on my hands or clothes. No hair. No DNA. They couldn't pin it on me. No matter how hard they tried.

"Of course, it ruined my mom's marriage. She demanded that Emil hire the best lawyer to get them to release me. Emil dragged his feet. Renee was his niece, and it didn't look good for his own stepson to be suspected in her murder. It drove a wedge between them.

"Even after I was released, she wanted to sue the police department for false arrest. I told her they'd never actually arrested me, and she wanted to sue them for that, too. But Emil wouldn't do it. He wanted to forget all about it. He even wanted to forget about her.

"One day, we went to see a lawyer on our own. When we came back to the house, the locks had been changed, and our belongings were out on the front lawn. There wasn't very much, of course. Some dresses and jewelry for my mother. A couple of books for me. Including the *Tacitus*."

"The what?"

"Never mind. Samantha came out and offered to drive us to a hotel. She'd never liked Toni, but I think she liked me and she felt bad about the way things had turned out. My mother had signed a prenup, so she wouldn't get much out of the divorce. But even that didn't come through, because he had the marriage annulled, claiming that my mother had conned him into marrying her and that she was still married to my father. Well, we didn't want to bring my father into it. Blaz would kill us if he found out where we were. So she just let it go. Within a few months, we were living pretty much as we'd been before. Easy come, easy go."

Gail let loose a long breath. "I want to say I'm sorry all that happened to you, but I know you don't want to hear it."

Crush shrugged. "It's what happened. No use whining about it."

"That's my Crush," she said with a wry smile. "But how did little Caleb feel about it?"

"Little Caleb? He wasn't so little."

"He was little on the inside. How did he feel?"

"He felt fine. What do you want me to say?" He thought it over. "I didn't miss that house. I missed Zerbe a little."

"And?"

Crush looked over at her. "Renee? That was unfinished business. Everyone thought she was dead. Some people thought she'd killed herself. A few people thought that I'd raped and killed her. I almost convinced myself she'd run off somewhere. Started a new life. A better life. Almost...."

"I wish I could have known you then," she said. "I would have comforted you."

"I wouldn't have wanted it. Besides, if I'd met you then, I'd have just tried to...steal from you."

"Thanks for clearing that up."

"Don't mention it." Crush wanted to change the subject. He addressed the speakerphone. "How are you, Zerbe? Is that how it went down?"

"What?" Zerbe said through the phone.

"The night at the Devil's Gate Dam. What do you think?"

"I wasn't really listening. I fell asleep. And I really have to pee."

"We're almost there, Zerbe. Don't hang up."

Zerbe hung up.

"Goddamn it," Crush muttered. He was getting closer to

Lancaster. Taking the Avenue G exit, he drove for about ten minutes until he passed the sign that read "Musical Road." He steered the car into the left lane and slowed down to fifty miles per hour.

The vibrations on the road played the familiar tune. Sort of.

"Wow," Gail said.

"Wow," Crush said. "But didn't that sound a little off to you?"

"It *was* kind of sour," Gail said. "But I guess it must be hard to tune road surfaces just right. You can't tighten the strings." Gail was always charitable.

They drove on for a few more miles, keeping their eyes peeled for phone booths or Quonset huts. After about fifteen minutes, they saw it by the side of the road, just standing in the dust like a relic from some forgotten time. An old-fashioned phone booth. The kind Superman used to change clothes in. Crush saw a truck parked next to it.

A poorly painted UPS truck.

"Shit," Crush said.

Then he noticed the broken window on the phone booth. And the twisted pair of human legs sticking out of it.

The UPS truck roared to life and took off down the road. Crush had a second to decide what to do. Follow the truck or check on the person who was in the booth.

He stopped the car and opened the door. "Stay here," he said to Gail. Whoever was in the booth, he wasn't moving.

CHAPTER SIXTEEN

Zerbe hung up the pay phone and looked around for a place to go to the bathroom. If he'd only had to pee, like he'd told Crush, it wouldn't have been much of a problem, but his situation was a bit more complicated than that. He opened the door of the phone booth and looked around for a secluded place to do his business. There was nothing but flat, featureless desert as far as he could see. A few outcroppings of succulents were scattered here and there, but they afforded no protection from the blazing sun and little shelter from passing cars.

Now that he thought about it, there hadn't been any passing cars for ages, but one was about to pass by. A brown UPS truck was kicking up a lot of dust as it drove slowly toward him. Very slowly. In fact, it was pulling over on the shoulder, just a few yards ahead of him.

Why? Did the driver need to use the phone? Had his cell phone died? Did he want to ask Zerbe for directions? He'd get a laugh out of that.

The driver's door opened and a man got out. Instead of the familiar brown uniform, he wore khaki pants and a blue chambray shirt. As he walked over to the phone booth with a cheery smile, Zerbe noted that he appeared to be a very friendly African-American man...who was holding a gun in his right hand.

Zerbe froze. What now? There was nothing he could do; nowhere he could run. Nothing but open space all around him. He backed into the phone booth, knowing that it was a dead end. That it was nothing but a glass trap. With his bloody hands, he closed the folding door of the phone booth, then opened it again, wincing with pain from his dislocated thumb. The door afforded him no protection. He was at the mercy of this man.

The man stopped just outside the phone booth and smiled at Zerbe. "Hey! You escaped!" he said by way of greeting.

Zerbe's brain whirled. He knew Zerbe had escaped. That meant he was the kidnapper. Or one of the kidnappers. This was it. Zerbe had escaped, only to be caught again.

"Did you kidnap me?" Zerbe asked.

"No," the man replied. "I just helped. I told him he shouldn't have left you there. You look dumb, but that may just be an act." He laughed as if he'd made a good-natured joke, but the pistol in his hand belied his real intentions.

"What are you going to do to me?" Zerbe asked.

"Come on." The man thrust the gun forward. "The Overlords can't help you now."

"The Overlords?" Zerbe asked. "What are you talking about? Who the hell are the Overlords?" Where had he heard that term before?

"I don't want to have to do this," the man said, looking distressed. "You're not giving me a choice."

Zerbe looked down at the gun and knew the man was going to shoot him. He decided to act. Well, he didn't actually decide. If he'd had to decide he would probably have chickened out. He just did it.

He slammed the door shut on the man's wrist. Hard. The

man was thrown off balance and the gun dropped from his hand. It clattered on the floor of the phone booth. The door didn't close all the way, so Zerbe pressed his body against the fold in the door to try to keep the man's hand trapped while he bent down to pick up the gun.

The man threw his own weight against the door and sent Zerbe crashing into the back wall of the booth. Zerbe snatched up the gun and raised it at the man, who was coming toward him.

He didn't even mean to pull the trigger.

The gun's report was deafening. The man looked down at his chest in surprise. The splotch of blood that had suddenly appeared on his chest spread and grew. He dropped, falling onto Zerbe.

Zerbe screamed and clawed his way out from under the man. He dropped the gun, scrambled out of the phone booth, and sprawled on the ground. Still screaming.

Slowly, he came to his senses. Or some of them. This man was dead, but there was at least one more still out there. And then there were the Overlords.

But wait. Weren't the Overlords trying to help him? Isn't that what the dead guy had said? It didn't matter. The thing was, he wasn't safe. He went back to the phone booth and retrieved the gun. He looked over at the UPS truck. He went back to the phone booth and searched the man's pockets until he found some car keys.

Just as he pulled the keys free, the man's eyes opened and his hand grabbed Zerbe's wrist. Zerbe pulled away and stared down at him.

"Help me," the man said.

Zerbe thought about shooting him again. Finishing him off. But he couldn't do it. He hurried to the truck and started it. Just in time, too. A red muscle car pulled up to the booth.

"He" must have arrived.

Zerbe floored the UPS truck and tore out of there.

⌘

The man in the booth wasn't dead. Not yet. Blood was gurgling from his lips as Crush looked down at him. Gail pushed him aside and bent over the wounded man.

"Call 911," she said to Crush as she pressed down on the man's wounded chest. "You're going to be all right," she lied.

"He shot me," the man wheezed.

"Don't think about that," said Gail. "Think about why you want to live."

He shook his head. "They'll win. They always win."

Crush was on the phone with the 911 dispatcher, giving them as little information as he could. He glanced back at the dying man and recognized him. When he got off the phone he went back to the booth and spoke to him. "Will? Is that you?"

The man turned his head to look at Crush. "Yes, I'm Will," he said. "And I'm a Targeted Individual." Those were the same words he'd used when he'd led the Targeted Individual support group in South Pasadena. "Do you have anything you'd like to share?"

"Who sent you? Why did you come here?"

"Crush!" Gail said, reprovingly. "You don't have to answer Will. Just rest."

"I have to fight them," Will gasped. "The Overlords. Emil. The Zerbes. They've killed so many. They'll kill more."

"Who did they kill?" Crush asked.

"Victor," Will said. "And Renee. And the seventy-six thousand. Who knows how many more...and me. They killed me."

"Who killed you?"

"K.C. Zerbe. It runs in the blood. From the Templars through the Masons to the Nazis. They are the Overlords."

Crush watched him for a few moments. Then he took Gail by the arm. "Come on." She yanked her arm away and kept applying pressure to the wound. "Look, we have to go," Crush said.

"We can't leave him."

"The paramedics are on their way. He'll be taken care of. We have to catch up with Zerbe. He's in that truck."

"You go then."

"Gail, he's dead."

Gail lifted her hands from his chest and looked at his staring eyes. "The poor man."

"If Zerbe killed him, it must have been in self-defense. This is one of the kidnappers. Did you see that truck? Did you notice the cracked windshield? That's the truck they were driving when they tried to nab Noel. That's the same truck that delivered the bomb. They are crazy people. Some kind of cult."

"The poor man," Gail repeated.

"Come on." Crush pulled Gail's arm, and this time she let him lead her away. They got in the Buick, and Crush tore down the road.

"What was Will's last name?" Gail asked.

"I don't know."

"We were the last people he saw on earth and we don't even know his last name."

"Yeah, well, if it makes you feel any better, I don't think he even knew we were there," Crush said. "He probably thought he was talking to his crazy friends. His last words were about Nazis, remember. Renee talked about Nazis, too. Why does everybody get all 'Nazi' when they go crazy?"

"What a horrible way to die. A person's last moments

should be peaceful."

"They rarely are, Catherine."

Gail looked over at him. He didn't use her first name often. Just like she didn't use his. "That's very sad, Caleb."

"Take it up with God. That's the way he made the world."

Then they saw it. Parked by the side of a Dairy Queen. The UPS truck. Crush pulled up next to it.

"What are you going to do?" Gail asked.

"I'm gonna go in and get a Blizzard. What do you want?"

"What if the bad guys are in there?"

"Then I'll get two Blizzards."

They walked into the air-conditioned climate of a fast-food paradise. They saw him at a table in the back, in his Captain America T-shirt and sweatpants, dabbing his bloody fingers with napkins.

Zerbe looked up at them in surprise. "Crush. Gail. So it *was* you in the Buick. I thought about that after I pulled out. Listen, do you have any money? For a burger or something? I'm starving."

Gail sat down in the plastic chair next to him. "Are you all right?"

"I don't know," Zerbe said, thinking it over. "I don't think so. But I'm better than I could be."

"What do you want to eat?" Crush asked.

"One of everything. No, two. Two of everything. And some ketchup."

So Crush got him a bacon-cheeseburger and a chocolate shake, and Zerbe ate it without pausing to take a breath. When he was finished he held his head in his hands, belched, and said, "I think I'm gonna be sick."

"You want another round?" Crush asked.

"Yes."

"Shouldn't we be going?" Gail asked. "Won't they be

looking for you?"

"Who?" Zerbe asked.

"The police. Didn't you just shoot a man?"

"Oh, yeah. I did do that," Zerbe said, wiping his mouth with a napkin. "But I didn't mean to. It just sort of happened. You know how things happen."

"I know," said Crush. "I'll get you another burger and we'll go. You can tell me what happened on the way."

"Are we going back to the loft?"

"We'll see," Crush said.

"Do you want to go back there?" Gail asked him.

"I do," Zerbe said. "Very much." He closed his eyes and started to cry.

A few minutes later, Crush was driving the Buick back toward Pasadena, while Gail sat in back with Zerbe and put bandages on his damaged hands, using a little first-aid kit Crush kept in the glove compartment. Crush was on the phone with Angela, telling her that they'd found Zerbe.

"Is he all right?" Angela asked.

"He's fine. A little shook up is all." He didn't tell her about the guy Zerbe had shot. What she didn't know.... "I'm bringing him back to the loft."

"Fine," she said. "I'll let everyone know. They'll be so relieved."

"Some of them will be," Crush said, ending the call, tossing his phone into the passenger seat, and rubbing his head.

When she saw him do that, Gail remembered she really shouldn't have let him drive. "How's your head, Crush?"

"Fine," he said. "How's yours?"

"Did you hurt your head?" Zerbe asked.

"A little."

"How?"

"In a car accident," Gail said. "He was chasing that truck.

The one you stole back there. After it delivered a bomb to your house."

"A bomb?" Zerbe asked.

"But it was only a fake bomb," Crush said, brushing it off. "A reminder. To goose your father into doing what they want."

"Right," said Zerbe.

"Do you know what they want him to do?" Crush asked.

Zerbe nodded. "The kidnapper talked to me for a little while. I didn't want him to. I couldn't see his face and he used that stupid voice distorter. He said they want my father to stop building the train."

"Who are 'they'?" Crush asked. "A group? An organization?"

"I don't know. He didn't say."

Crush shook his head. That was not a good idea; his world started to spin around him. He gripped the wheel to stop from seeing double and got back to the point. "I don't get it," he said. "All this just to stop the construction of a damn train? Why?"

"He talked to me," Zerbe continued. "I tried not to listen, but he kept talking. He said Victor knew. And Renee found out after that."

Crush drove in silence for a moment. "Is that why they killed her?"

"*They* didn't kill her," Zerbe said. "*They* want to avenge her. And Victor."

"So Victor was murdered, too?" Crush asked.

"Yes. At least that's what he said."

"Then who killed them?" Crush asked.

Zerbe hesitated. "He said it was my father. I didn't believe him."

"Of course," Gail said. "Your father would never do

anything like that."

"No, I could totally see him doing it. It was just the reason he gave. My father's motivation."

"Let me guess," Crush said. "Nazis."

"How did you know?"

"It's been going around."

"He said my father doesn't want it to come out that he worked for the Nazis. That doesn't make any sense. My father was born in 1947. Germany surrendered in 1945. Unless he was a time traveler, my father couldn't have been a Nazi."

Unless he was a time traveler, Crush thought. *Unless....*

⌘

"We have to go to Irwindale," Noel said, standing in the front parlor of the Zerbe mansion.

"Why?" Donleavy wanted to know.

"We have to go to Irwindale," Noel repeated. "To ride in the float. In the Rose Parade tomorrow."

Emil, who was sitting by the fireplace in his wheelchair doing a jigsaw puzzle with Angela and Samantha, growled, "Your float is magnificent, but I'm not climbing onto it and waving at the crowd like a king or a goddamned queen. I'm not going to let people see me like this."

"But it's your triumph, Dad," Noel said. "You finally succeeded in pushing the bullet train through. Revel in it."

"Zerbes don't revel," Emil grumbled.

"Well, I have to go anyway. To put the finishing touches on the float. I'll be driving it tomorrow."

"No, you won't," Donleavy said. "Have somebody else drive it. Your father's perfectly right to stay off it. It's not secure. Have Kagan here drive it." She pointed to one of her men. Kagan looked startled.

Noel made a sour face. "You can't just put anyone behind the wheel of a float. It's not like a Honda. It requires experience. I know that float. I designed it. I built it."

"It's not secure," Donleavy reiterated. "Cancel it if you have to. It's only a float in a parade."

Noel stared at Donleavy as if she had just said there was no Santa Claus. Noel turned to his father. "Did you hear what this woman said?"

"I heard," Emil said. "And you're going. The float is too important. I'm not going to let these pranks scare us."

Donleavy grimaced in frustration. "Pranks? Then what did you hire me for?"

"As a bodyguard," Emil said. "To guard our bodies. Not to keep us locked away in the house. I could have done that. Do your damn job, Donleavy."

"All right," Donleavy said, "but we're going in my car."

"That hearse?" Noel objected.

"It's a Chevy Suburban with protective armor and bullet-proof glass. The kind they use in presidential motorcades."

"It still looks like a hearse," Noel said, sulking. "I want to take my Tesla."

"You'll go in the Suburban and you'll like it," Emil said.

Noel grumbled but agreed. Then Samantha spoke up. She didn't often speak, but when she did, the family listened. "Angela, why don't you go with him?"

"Why?" she asked.

"To make your brother listen to Ms. Donleavy. And not do anything foolish."

Angela sighed. "Maybe I can make him listen to Donleavy. But I don't know if I can stop him from being a fool. It's in his DNA."

"We share the same genetic makeup," Noel said. "So if you're calling me a fool, you're calling yourself one, too."

"I believe the phrase is, 'I'm rubber; you're glue.'" Angela said.

Emil Zerbe shook his gray head and muttered, "What did I do to deserve this?"

Samantha stared at him. "You tell me."

⌘

The sun was setting as Crush drove down Lake Avenue through Pasadena. They were taking a detour on their way home, because Zerbe asked to stop at Pie 'n Burger. It wasn't that he was particularly hungry, not after that orgy of food at the Dairy Queen. It was just that he realized he was going back to be trapped in his loft-prison and he hadn't been able to enjoy his involuntary freedom. He thought he owed himself at least one carefree excursion while he was in the outside world.

Crush parked on California Boulevard, and they walked up to the tiny hamburger joint. He could smell grease from the griddle that had been there since the place opened in 1963.

"Take a breath!" Zerbe said, loving it. "Can't you just feel your arteries hardening?"

"I'll have a salad," said Gail, not sharing his enthusiasm for the joint.

"You're really not entering into the spirit of this place," Zerbe said, sliding into a greasy booth. "I'll have the pie. With extra ice cream."

"Do you know what all that sugar does to your body?" Gail asked, wiping the table clean with a threadbare napkin.

"Hey, I just had a gun pointed at me," Zerbe said. "I was kidnapped and tied up in a van, and I killed a guy. I can take whatever sugar can throw at me."

They ate. Crush had a burger, fries, and an iced tea. Zerbe had peach pie with vanilla ice cream and also a piece of chocolate cake. Gail had a tossed green salad. She tried not to feel superior, but it wasn't easy.

While they ate, Crush kept flipping through his phone. This wasn't like him at all. He used his phone only when absolutely necessary.

"Whatcha looking for?" asked Zerbe.

"An address. I'm trying to find somebody." He put the phone away. "I found her."

"I'll bite," Zerbe said. "Who are you looking for?"

"Renee's mother," Crush said.

Zerbe paused, a spoonful of ice cream just inches from his mouth. "Why?"

Crush dipped a french fry into the pool of ketchup on his plate. "This whole thing goes back to New Year's Day, 2001. The day your uncle committed suicide in that damn parade."

"And you think she'll be able to tell you...what?" Gail asked.

"Why he did it. Or *if* he did it," Crush said.

"I don't think..." Zerbe tried to think of a tactful way of saying it. "I don't think she'd want to talk to you."

"Why not?" Crush asked.

"She might still blame you. For..." Zerbe left the rest unsaid.

Crush thought this over. "Okay. But she'll talk to you. You're family. She lives in San Marino. Just about a mile from here. We have to go."

"Now?" Zerbe asked.

"Yes. I don't think this thing is over. I think your kidnapping was just the beginning. I think you were supposed to be killed. I think others are going to die."

"My family?"

"I don't know. But I'll tell you this much...the Targeted Individuals are fighting back."

CHAPTER SEVENTEEN

On the last day of January 2001, not long after Renee's disappearance, Crush waited in a bookstore for Angela Zerbe to meet him. The place stank of incense. The rainbows from a hundred dangling crystals danced over the spines of books about yoga, alien abduction, Bigfoot, the secrets of the Knights Templar, and the lost cities of Lemuria, Ur, and Atlantis.

Crush had called Angela and asked to see her, but why she had suggested that they meet here, at Alexandria II, the New Age shop on Lake Avenue in Pasadena, he couldn't imagine. It had been weeks since they'd seen each other. Since he and his mother had found themselves locked out of the house on San Rafael and had to start their lives over again. Although those weeks had been long ones for Crush and, he supposed, for Angela, he couldn't imagine that they had been long enough for her to find religion. To go from ridiculing her brother Noel's mystic faith in demons and witchcraft to embracing it.

Still, Crush had learned the hard way in his seventeen years that you could never tell what people would do. The most abstinent people would turn into drunks. The most peaceful would turn violent. The most well balanced would go howling-at-the-moon insane. The most sensible would look for a faith. Crush had even found himself in churches occasionally this month. He couldn't explain it. It just happened.

"Hello, big guy," a voice said from behind the Cryptozoology section. He turned around and was surprised to see Evan Gibbard standing there.

Angela came out from behind him. "Hi, Caleb."

"Hey," he said. Crush had not expected Evan to be with her. He hadn't liked Evan before he ran out on them that night at the dam, and he had absolutely no use for him now. "What's he doing here?" he asked Angela.

"Well, you wanted to meet me," Angela said. "I haven't got a driver's license yet and I needed a ride. So take it or leave it."

Crush decided he'd take it. "You going to drive us there?" he asked Evan.

"Sure," Evan said. "Anything for Angie."

Crush knew that Angela hated being called Angie. Evan had a way of doing the things you hated.

They went out and got into Evan's new BMW and drove into San Marino. To Renee Zerbe's house.

Crush had never been there. He had never seen Renee's mother, except for one glimpse when she picked Renee up at school for a doctor's appointment. The world of teenagers was surprisingly parent-free.

He hadn't even known her name. He'd had to look it up to learn that it was Valerie. Crush thought it was a nice name. Valerie had no other children and, of course, no husband now. She was alone in the world.

Crush wanted her to know that he was not the reason.

His mother tried to talk him out of going there. She said it would do no earthly good for her to see him. It would only cause her pain, and it wouldn't give Crush what he was seeking. And what was he seeking anyway? Absolution? Forgiveness? That implied a sense of guilt. No, Crush wanted to be seen as innocent in the eyes of at least this one person. This one person for whom Renee's death mattered most.

So he called up Angela and K.C. Zerbe and asked them to go with him to Valerie's house. K.C. said he was crazy to want to go. He wanted no part of it. Angela said sure, she'd go. Angela was always good for an adventure.

Only she hadn't said she'd bring Evan. Crush didn't like having him with them. They should have left Evan at the bookstore and gone to see Valerie together in Crush's "new" (stolen) Mustang. But when Crush suggested that, the two of them just laughed as if he were joking and got in the Beemer. Okay, Crush could be flexible. It wasn't as if this was a date with Angela.

As Evan drove them into San Marino, land of large estates and open, manicured lawns, Crush rehearsed what he would say to Valerie Zerbe. He hadn't gotten much past "Mrs. Zerbe, I'm so sorry and I didn't kill your daughter" when they pulled up in front of the massive Craftsman-style "bungalow" that was Victor and Valerie Zerbe's home.

An elegant Greene & Greene creation, the house was a stop on many architectural tours of the city, but Crush didn't know that at the time. He just walked up to the front door, dreading this encounter more with each step.

Angela had called to say that she was coming, but she hadn't mentioned whom she'd be bringing along. "It's not too late to back out," she said to Crush, sensing his dismay. "You can go off with Evan, and I'll pay my visit."

Crush shook his head. He had to do this. And he just now realized why. He did have to ask Renee's mother for forgiveness. Not for killing her, but for not saving her. For not finding her that night in the rain. For letting her go into the darkness and disappear.

Angela walked up to the broad, carved wooden door and pressed the doorbell, which chimed majestically throughout the house. They waited a few minutes.

"I hope she answers soon," Evan said. "I gotta take a whiz like a racehorse, you know what I mean?"

"I know what you mean," Angela said. "You just said what you mean."

Still there was no answer. Evan knocked, and when he did, the door swung open.

The three of them peered into the dark house. It was dark, even though it was midday, because Craftsman-style houses had been designed to keep the inhabitants in the comfortable dimness of midnight at all hours.

Angela called out. "Aunt Valerie?"

There was no answer.

The three of them exchanged a look. "You called, right?" Crush asked. "You said you were coming over?"

Angela nodded. Then she said. "We should go."

"Fuck that," Evan said. "I have to pee. Where's the bathroom?" He walked into the foyer and started opening doors until he found the guest bathroom. While he went in to do his business, Angela and Crush walked to the bottom of the broad staircase, uneasy at trespassing in this house of mourning.

Angela cocked her head "Do you hear that? It sounds like running water."

Crush shrugged. "Well, Evan said...."

"No. It's coming from upstairs." She walked up the steps to the second floor. "Aunt Valerie? Are you there? I just came in because the front door was open...."

The door to the master bedroom was open, and Angela poked her head in. The master-bathroom door was ajar as well. The sound of running water was coming from in there. Crush joined Angela in the doorway.

"Aunt Valerie?" she called out.

The only answer was that rush of water. Crush craned his neck to look inside. He grabbed Angela's arm. There was a pool of water spreading on the bedroom floor.

Angela was about to ask what to do when Crush sprinted for the bathroom. Angela hurried to catch up, and by the time she made it to the door, he was already hauling Aunt Valerie out of the water. The tub was littered with empty prescription bottles that bobbed about like lanterns in a Chinese New Year celebration. Valerie's head was limp. Her eyes were open but drifting vaguely.

Crush carried Valerie's naked, dripping body from the tub and across the room. "Call the paramedics." He sat her down on the toilet and started slapping her face. "Valerie! Wake up!"

Valerie smiled at him and laughed, mumbled something in French, and slipped off the toilet and onto the floor.

"What's going on?" Evan asked from the doorway.

"She tried to kill herself," Angela said. "Call 911."

"No shit?"

"Yes, shit," Crush said. "Do it. Now."

"All right, I'm doing it, you don't have to yell," Evan said, pulling his cell phone out of his pocket and stepping out into the bedroom.

Crush sat Valerie up against the clothes hamper. She seemed awake but not conscious of what was going on around her.

"Caleb," Angela said. "You have to go."

"What?"

"It won't seem right. You being here. It'll seem suspicious."

Crush thought for moment. "No. I have to see if she's all right."

"She's all right. They'll be here in a minute. Go."

Crush stood up, uncertain.

Evan walked back in. "Okay. I called. You happy?"

"Not even a little bit," Crush said.

In the end, Crush left the house but he stayed across the street, watching to make sure Valerie was alive when she was taken out to the ambulance. Then he sighed with relief and started the long walk back to Lake Avenue.

As he was walking, he tried to make himself think about why Marcus Aurelius would let his obviously corrupt son Commodus take over the Roman Empire, but it was no use. He was only able to replay the events of the past two months in an endless loop.

A horn honked behind him and he jerked around. Evan's BMW cruised up, and Angela opened the rear door. "Want a lift?" she asked.

He got in and Evan took him to Alexandria II. Evan was surprised when Angela wanted to be dropped off with Crush. He drove off in a huff.

Angela and Crush had lunch at Burger Continental and talked over the events of the day. Then they went back to the apartment Crush shared with his mother in Glendale. His mother was out looking for work, so they had the place to themselves.

They made out. Then they did more than make out. Then Crush drove Angela home, and he didn't see her again until Zerbe's trial three years ago.

Hence that elephant in that particular room.

⌘

Creedence Clearwater Revival's "Bad Moon Rising" was booming through the speakers in Donleavy's Suburban. "Could you turn the radio to another station?" Angela asked.

"It's not the radio," Donleavy said. "It's my playlist. On my phone."

"Could you switch to another playlist?"

"It's only got one playlist. CCR. All day, all the time."

"Could we turn it off?"

Donleavy gave Angela a sidelong glace. "You ride in my car, you listen to John Fogerty."

"I thought this was the kind of car they used in presidential motorcades? If I was the president, you'd turn it off for me."

"If you were the president, you'd know that this music is a national treasure."

"Stop arguing," Noel said from the back seat. "You're interfering with my train of thought."

"What are you thinking about?" Donleavy asked.

"Those pits," Noel said, looking out the window of the moving car. In the dwindling twilight, the massive, empty gravel pits of Irwindale loomed around them, a hundred feet deep in places, looking like craters on the moon. "They're reminders of what it takes to build a city," Noel said. "Sand and gravel from those pits is what built the roads and freeways throughout LA. Every street and subdivision in Los Angeles County has a little bit of Irwindale in it."

"On second thought," Angela said, "turn the volume up so I can't hear Noel's inner monologue."

Instead of laughing at this quip, Donleavy took a quick breath and swung the steering wheel far to the right, but not quickly enough to avoid the impact from the SUV that came upon them suddenly, going the wrong way down the 605.

The crash sent the Suburban spinning, but Donleavy was a good wheelman and just about had things under control when another car hit them from behind, sending them off the road and careening into the depths of one of Irwindale's craters.

⌘

The paint on the Greene & Greene house was peeling. Ivy was growing over it, and one of the windows was boarded up. It looked like it was decorated for Halloween, but it was late December, and the neighboring houses still had their Christmas lights up.

"It doesn't look very inviting," Zerbe said.

"When was the last time you saw your Aunt Valerie?" Crush asked.

"I haven't been to many Thanksgiving dinners for the past few years, what with the prison sentence and all," Zerbe said. "I think I saw her about ten years ago."

"How did she seem?"

"Who's that crazy lady from that Charles Dickens book? Miss Havisham?"

"I never read it," Crush said.

"She was like that," Zerbe said.

Gail pressed the doorbell, and the same majestic chime sounded. Crush felt déjà vu, but this time the door opened and a careworn face greeted them with a wary stare. "Yes?"

Crush pushed Zerbe to the front of their little group and nudged him. "Hello, Aunt Valerie," Zerbe said, with a stupid grin.

Her face relaxed and she grinned. Her grin was prettier. "Noel, how are you?" she said, in a slight and very lovely French accent.

Zerbe's grin turned into a grimace as he thought this

through. On the one hand, he never liked to be mistaken for his twin brother. On the other hand, he was supposed to be in a loft on Wilshire Boulevard, and if anybody knew he was out wandering around on his own, he might get sent back to prison. "I'm fine," he said, deciding to go with it. "I just wanted to wish you a happy holiday."

"Well, that's very nice. Who are your friends?"

"This is Catherine Gail and Caleb Rush."

Valerie didn't seem to be listening, but she invited them in anyway. She said she didn't have much to offer them but coffee and a little Bundt cake. They said that would be just fine.

They sat in the front parlor. The curtains were drawn, so the room was dark and felt oddly moist. The furniture was musty, and Crush could see actual cobwebs in the ceiling corners. Valerie was dressed in a bathrobe and slippers, despite the fact that it was 6 p.m.

"I can't remember the last time I had visitors," she said with a laugh. It was a surprisingly cheerful laugh considering the circumstances. Valerie finished pouring them all coffee in Fiestaware mugs and sat down on the edge of the sofa. The group fell into awkward silence.

Gail raised her mug in a toast. "Well, happy New Year." When she saw Valerie's face fall, Gail realized she'd committed a terrible faux pas.

"Yes," Valerie said, with a catch in her throat. "Happy New Year."

"I'm sorry, Aunt Valerie," Zerbe said. "She didn't know."

Valerie waved her hand. "It's all right. I forget that not everyone knows. I forget that it was so long ago." She choked back a sob.

"I'm sorry," Gail said, stricken.

"My husband died on New Year's, you see. Was it really so long ago? What year are we getting to?"

"I remember," Crush said. "I was there."

Valerie looked at Crush, trying to place him. "You were the boy. The one in the float."

"Yes," Crush said.

"And the one they arrested for killing my daughter."

"Yes. But I didn't do that."

She smiled a little. "I know." Then she looked at him more closely. "And the one who found me. In the tub. Was that you, too?"

"Yes."

She sat back on the sofa. "You do get around."

"I'm sorry."

"What for?"

"For not...finding her."

Valerie shook her head. "She didn't want to be found." Then she sipped her coffee. "I suppose I should thank you for saving my life." She glanced away, thoughtfully. "I suppose...."

Crush didn't want to push her, but he had to. "Do you know why he did it?"

She looked back at him. "Why Victor killed himself? Yes, I know. It was the same reason Renee ran away."

Gail spoke up. "Do you think Renee is still alive?"

"After all these years?" Valerie asked. "I don't know. I hope so."

"But you haven't heard from her?" Gail asked.

"No," Valerie said. "Not one word."

"Why?" Crush asked. "Why did they do it? Why did Victor kill himself? Why did Renee disappear?"

She shut her eyes. "It's the damn bullet train. Victor was researching the SGCF. You know, the Société Générale des Chemins de Fer Français. The French railroad. We were key shareholders, and he was hoping to bolster the company's reputation and help us get the high-speed rail through."

She paused and opened her eyes. "Do you believe that the sins of the father can be visited upon his children?"

Crush thought of his own father and of Brighton Beach. "I hope not."

"That's not an answer." She shut her eyes again and leaned back. "Victor and Emil's father was Anton Zerbe. He ran the French railroad system during the war. You know which war is the war, don't you?"

"World War II?" offered Zerbe.

"I only heard stories about it, of course. How the Germans came and everything changed. How our family had to...get along. How the Vichy government was formed. To hear it now, you'd think everyone was in the resistance. That everyone wore berets and planted bombs and waited for de Gaulle to come in and save the day. But it wasn't that way. They had to...compromise.

"Victor had known that, of course. He'd known his father wasn't a hero. He knew that the railroad was seized by the Nazis and put to use to transport Jews throughout France to the concentration camps. Seventy-six thousand French Jews. In stifling cattle cars with little food or water. All but two thousand were killed.

"Victor had known that, as I said, and it had always troubled him. That his father had been so weak, so terrified of the Germans, that he allowed that to be done on his watch, as it were."

She swallowed. "But in his research, he found documents that proved that his father...that Anton Zerbe had not been an unwilling accomplice in genocide. He discovered that Anton was in charge of the evacuations. That he'd been an eager engineer in this massive commute of innocent men, women, and children to the death camps. That he'd been well paid for it. In the beginning of the war he had been well off; by the time it was over, he was a rich man.

"Their family...my family...all our wealth had been built on the corpses of fellow Frenchmen. Victor couldn't handle it. He told me. He told Renee. He wanted everyone to know, and he couldn't bear the thought of people finding out. He went to his brother, Emil." She looked toward Zerbe. "Your father. He told him. He asked him what they should do. They couldn't keep the money, he said. It was blood money. It stank of death.

"Do you know what Emil said? He said, *'Pecunia non olet.'* That's Latin. It's a quote from Emperor Vespasian. When his son complained that taxing urine was unseemly, he said, 'Money doesn't stink.' That's what Emil said. 'Money doesn't stink.' "

She shut her eyes again. "So my husband took a gun with him and blew his brains out in the middle of the Rose Parade. I suppose he thought he was making a statement. Then my daughter ran away one rainy night and started her life over again with a new name and a new history. I hope."

Opening her eyes, she sat forward and stared at Crush. "And I tried to kill myself, but a big man pulled me out of the water, slapped my face, and told me to live. So I've lived."

They sat in silence for a while.

"Do you want more coffee?" she asked.

They said they didn't, and got up to leave. She led them to the door and as he was walking out, Crush turned to her. "That day, when I pulled you out of the tub, you said something to me. In French. I've always wondered what you said."

Valerie gave him a sad smile. "I called you my *ange gardien*. My guardian angel," she said as she shut the door.

⌘

Gail drove them back to LA. Crush was too tired to argue when Gail insisted that she take the wheel.

"How 'bout that," Zerbe said. "It *was* about the Nazis."

"And how do you feel about that?" Gail asked.

"What do you mean? How do I feel about the fact that my grandfather was a Nazi collaborator? Well, I don't feel great. But I never knew him, and the family disinherited me years ago. So I guess I'm clean. I guess."

"It still doesn't tell us who's behind this," Crush said.

"In books and movies," Zerbe said, "it's always the person you least suspect."

They drove in silence for a while.

"Renee." Gail said her name.

"Renee?" Crush asked.

"Well, we're all thinking it, aren't we?" Gail said. "She has a motive. And it would explain why she disguised her voice for Zerbe and all of you. She knew you'd recognize it the moment you heard it."

Crush's head really hurt. "But why now? Why wait till now to...take her revenge. And what does she have to do with the Targeted Individuals?"

Gail pressed on. "She's got reason to be paranoid, doesn't she? The Nazis were actual, real Overlords trying to take over the fucking world. And as far as 'Why now?' Well, I don't have an answer for that one. Except...why not now?"

Crush's phone rang. He was thankful for the interruption, and pulled his iPhone from his pocket. The readout said, "Unknown."

"Fuck," said Crush. He answered.

"Hello, Caleb," said the Miley Cyrus voice. "Recognize them?"

On the screen he saw three figures tied to chairs in a dark room, gagged with duct tape. Noel, Angela, and Donleavy.

"We need to talk," the Miley voice said.

CHAPTER EIGHTEEN

Mick Kagan, Donleavy's right-hand man, stood at attention on the front steps of the Zerbe castle and watched as the Buick came to a halt and Crush got out. Crush had always liked Kagan. He was a fellow Marine, a few years younger than Crush and with a full head of blond hair. Crush didn't hold either of those things against him.

Zerbe, Gail, and Crush came running up the steps. Kagan stopped Zerbe. "Noel," he said. "I thought you were going to Irwindale. Where's Donleavy?"

"That isn't Noel," Crush said. "There's no time to explain. We have to see Emil."

Mick led them to Emil's bedroom, where they found him sitting up in bed watching *Jeopardy* with Samantha. "What is it now?" he snarled.

"Hi, Dad," Zerbe said.

Emil looked at his son with his one good eye. He was a good enough father that he could tell his twins apart. "K.C. I thought you were being held prisoner."

"I escaped."

"See?" Emil said. "I told you they were bluffing."

"I had to kill somebody," Zerbe said. "It was pretty awful."

"Still, you're okay. End of story."

"Not quite," Crush said. He looked over at Kagan. He thought of telling him to leave but figured, the hell with it. "They have Noel and Angela."

Emil looked stricken. "Angela? What do you mean?"

"They have them Dad. It's not good," Zerbe said.

"Donleavy, too," Crush added, because he thought it should be said.

"I don't believe it," Emil said.

Crush showed him the picture on his phone. The three of them tied up in a dark, cavernous place.

"Let me see that," Kagan said, reaching for the phone.

"The kidnapper made new demands," Crush said. "That you should discontinue the bullet train or he'll kill them all."

"Oh, please," Emil scoffed. "He didn't kill Kendrick, did he?"

"I had to kill somebody to escape," Zerbe said. "Did I mention that?"

"He also said that he'll release the facts, Emil," Crush went on. "You know what facts he means, don't you?"

Emil glared at him with his one glittering eye. "Ancient history. No one cares about that."

"Someone does," Crush said. "Someone wants to destroy you."

"Let them try."

Zerbe sat on the edge of the bed. "Dad, look at my face. They beat me up. They beat me so you could see that they were serious. They are serious."

Emil looked at his son's battered face. His twisted face seemed to soften. "How many of them are there?"

"We don't know," Crush said. "Enough."

Emil touched Zerbe's swollen eye. "I'm sorry, son. But you do know this isn't my fault. I had nothing to do with it. I shouldn't have to pay."

"I know that, Dad," Zerbe said. "But they don't. They have Angela and Noel. And they're crazy, Dad. Flat-out crazy."

Emil looked away. "I've been trying to get the HSR built for thirty years. It is my life's work. I can't just let it go!"

"You shouldn't," Kagan spoke up. "You shouldn't negotiate."

"Then what should he do?" Crush asked.

"Go to the authorities. Let them handle it."

"The minute you do that, they'll kill the hostages," Crush said.

"Then what do you suggest I do?" Emil asked.

"Give in," Crush said. "Give them what they want. It's the only way."

Emil looked blankly ahead of him. "I wish I'd died when I had that stroke. Then I wouldn't have had to live to see this day." He gathered himself up. "All right. They win. How do I give them the message?"

Crush glanced at Zerbe. "That's the hard part."

⌘

They spent the rest of the night preparing. The next morning, at 7:48 a.m. on January 1st, Emil and Samantha Zerbe sat in the high throne on the very top of the massive floral train that was the California High-Speed Rail—The Future Is Now—Zerbe Enterprises float. Far below, Crush and Zerbe sat inside the massive float, encased in polyurethane and hundreds of flowers, staring down at the pink line on the pavement at their feet. In twelve minutes six F-16s would soar overhead, signaling the start of this year's Tournament of Roses Parade.

Getting Crush behind the wheel—well, behind the

driving levers, to be exact—hadn't been the plan. Noel was supposed to do the driving, but Zerbe was posing as Noel now, and he didn't know the first thing about driving a float. So Kagan informed the White Suits in charge that Tigon Security was putting a man inside the float with Noel. To ride shotgun, as it were. When the hatch was closed, Crush and Zerbe performed the difficult maneuver of switching places so Crush could get his hands on the controls.

Actually, Crush had no experience driving a float either, but he'd at least ridden in one. What's more, he'd driven most every kind of vehicle known to man. He felt sure he could handle it. With a little practice anyway.

It had taken hours to get the huge float towed into position. Now it stood in line, its streamlined Art Deco locomotive seeming to fly off into the air, with all the other floats and marching bands and equestrian groups waiting on Orange Grove Boulevard for the parade to begin.

Emil Zerbe, in position on top of the float with Samantha by his side, twenty feet in the air, looked like the engineer of a fantastic, futuristic, organic train. He seemed as glum and grim as ever. They were just behind the Lakers float and just in front of the Singapore Airlines one. Emil had hoped for a better position.

The instructions from the kidnapper were simple. Emil and Samantha were to ride on the float. They were to follow the parade to the intersection of Colorado Boulevard and Fair Oaks. Then the float was to make an unscheduled stop. To freeze the parade in place, for all the world to see. To make the entire nation see that the float representing the high-speed rail from Los Angeles to San Francisco was stopping dead in its tracks. To announce to the world that the bullet train was dead.

While they were stopped, Emil was supposed to take the

microphone and speak to the crowd. To tell them that the HSR was dead and buried. And to tell them why. To tell them about his father's Nazi collaboration. To tell them about his blood money. Only then would Angela, Noel, and Donleavy be released.

Or so "Miley Cyrus" had said. It seemed to Crush like kind of a theatrical way of doing things, but then this whole business hadn't been exactly subtle from the get-go.

A roar and a sonic boom from above told Crush that the flyby was happening and the parade was about to begin. He adjusted his earpiece and peered through the tiny peephole that provided his only view of the outside world. He waited for the cue to start rolling.

"Do you think she'll keep her word?" Zerbe asked.

"She?" Crush asked.

"Renee."

"You really think it's her?"

"If it isn't, it's somebody doing it in her name," Zerbe said.

Crush was about to respond when Gail's voice came over his earbud. "I think it's time." She was posted on the top floor of the Wood & Jones building on Colorado, with a somewhat obstructed view of the first third of the parade route, from the Norton Simon Museum to Fair Oaks and beyond.

Through the peephole, he saw the Lakers float begin to move. Zerbe turned a switch and some inspirational, quasi-classical music came blaring out of massive speakers that were hidden in the float's framework. At the same time, Crush put the engine in gear and pressed the lever that made it go forward. It was a fairly simple mechanism. Forward with the right hand. Brake with the left. There was no reverse. Floats didn't go backward in the Rose Parade.

He crept up Orange Grove and made the turn onto

Colorado, using the pink line in the road as a guide to keep himself in the middle of the broad boulevard.

Colorado was the main thoroughfare in Old Pasadena. A four-lane street of storefronts from the turn of the last century, it looked just like it did in photographs and postcards from the 1910s. The buildings were two or three stories high, with shops on the street and offices on the upper levels. The best people lined the windows of those upper stories, so they could watch the parade without having to mix with the hoi polloi who lined the streets in sleeping bags and tents, eager to watch the passing spectacle.

"Who else could be behind this?" Zerbe asked. "Aunt Valerie?"

Crush grunted. "She doesn't seem the type."

"Who else?" Zerbe insisted on drawing Crush into the conversation. "Could it be an inside job?"

"Who are you thinking about?" Crush said. "Noel? Angela? Samantha? Why? Evan Gibbard? He hardly seems like an avenging angel. Personally, I think the Targeted Individuals group finally found a real enemy."

"How about my father?" Zerbe suggested.

"Your father?"

"Think about it. Maybe Emil's doing it all to himself. Maybe the stroke drove him crazy and his guilt is making him do it."

Crush shook his head. "Emil doesn't feel guilt. And that only leaves you and me. And I'm pretty sure we didn't do it."

Zerbe looked over at Crush. "I don't think you did it. You're too levelheaded. I wouldn't put anything past me though."

They rode without speaking after that. The cheers of the crowd and the syrupy faux-Puccini were all they could hear. Through the peephole Crush kept his eye on the distance between his float and the Lakers float. All he could see was that giant basketball bobbing in front of him. It was as if he were in a spaceship, orbiting around an orange moon.

Gail's voice spoke up in his ear. "You're at the intersection, Crush."

He eased the float to a stop, giving the Singapore Airlines float behind them time to catch on and not cause a ten-float pileup.

On top of the suddenly motionless float, Emil took the microphone and threw the PA switch to another setting, turning off the music. He cleared his throat and struggled to his feet, holding himself up by gripping the railing, crushing the floral decorations with his twisted hands. He stood there and looked out at the crowd.

"Hello," he said. "Sorry to interrupt the festivities, but I have an announcement to make. The California high-speed rail, which we were planning to make a reality, shall unfortunately not come to fruition. The bullet train, in other words, will not be built."

Crush opened the hatch to look up at Emil as he spoke. He was doing an admirable job of killing his life's work.

"You may be wondering why. It has recently come to my attention...." Well, that was a lie, Crush knew. Unless recently meant sometime in this century. But Crush let him have that saving grace.

Letting his eyes sweep the crowd, Crush felt his bodyguard instincts take over. This parade was a soft target if there ever was one. Cops were everywhere, of course, and the street and the floats had been swept for bombs. This year there was even a metal detector that the crowds had to pass through. But there was no way to keep danger totally at bay.

Emil went on. "It has recently come to my attention that the SGCF—the French railroad conglomerate of which I am a major shareholder..." There was a blur and a whistling sound. Emil noticed it but soldiered on. "...was involved in some less-than-savory dealings with the Third Reich during the Second World War."

Another whistling sound. This time Emil looked down at his arm and saw a long wooden stick embedded in it. He stared at it, puzzled. Another one shot through the air and stuck in his leg. He screamed.

Arrows. Someone was shooting arrows at the old man! Crush leapt out of the hatch and climbed up the float. Another arrow flew through the air and struck near Crush's leg, missing him by inches. Samantha, sitting next to Emil, screamed as an arrow pierced her shoulder. She fell over, twisted around, and tried to clamber down from the top of the float. Crush climbed up to her and dragged her down into the relative protection of the hills and valleys of the float's landscape art.

By now, the crowd had figured out what was going on and was yelling and screaming and running. Crush tried to scale back up the float to Emil.

The old man, rather than hiding or protecting himself, was shouting in the direction of the arrows. "Where are you? Show yourself, you coward!" The arrows flew past all around him, barely missing him. Emil must have thought he was invincible.

Then an arrow struck Emil in the chest. He fell back against the railing just as Crush reached him. The railing gave way, and he would have fallen to the street if Crush hadn't grabbed him by the arm. Crush pulled him back up and hoisted him onto the throne again. Crush threw himself on top of him, shielding Emil from any further shots. An arrow hit him on the left forearm as it protected Emil's head. He pushed the pain away and concentrated on his job. Protection.

Crush heard the sound of rushing feet and the panicked crowd. But there were no more arrows. He lifted his bloody arm and looked at Emil. The old man was glaring at him with undiminished anger.

"Fuck it!" he yelled. "I'm gonna build that damn bullet train if it's the last thing I do!"

⌘

They rode the elevator in silence. Zerbe was beat. Crush rested his aching head on Gail's shoulder, his left arm wrapped in stiff bandages. He told Gail he was going to the hospital as soon as he delivered Zerbe back home to the loft. Gail didn't believe him.

Angela and Noel and Donleavy were still missing. The man who'd shot the arrows was apprehended, but his name meant nothing to Crush or Zerbe. Emil was in surgery, but the prognosis was hopeful. Samantha was also hospitalized but was just under observation, having suffered the proverbial flesh wound. The Tournament of Roses Parade had never gotten such high television ratings. So there was a silver lining to this, after all.

Opening the loft's door, they were greeted by Frida Morales, who leapt up from the kitchen table, ran to Zerbe, and threw her arms around him. "Thank God, you're all right! I saw what happened on TV! They said it was Noel, but I knew it was you! How did you escape?"

Gail maneuvered around Frida and Zerbe to slump on the sofa. Crush headed straight to the fridge.

"It's a long story," Zerbe said. He glanced at her wrist. She was wearing his ankle monitor like a bracelet. "What's this?"

"Gail called me yesterday and said she had to leave," Frida said. "I came over to walk the monitor. I didn't want you to get caught."

"Thanks. But didn't you have to go to work?"

"I quit my job," she said. "It feels great. That job wasn't right for me."

Zerbe looked at her blankly for a moment, thinking it over. "That means you're not my parole officer anymore."

Frida stepped away from him. "That's right, K.C. We'll have to come up with another reason to see each other twice a month."

Zerbe's mouth opened and closed a couple of times.

Crush, rummaging through the refrigerator, said, "Don't we have any bacon? I wanted to make BLTs. We all need BLTs."

In the end, they borrowed some bacon from a neighbor and Crush made lunch for everyone. They sat around the kitchen table, munching in silence.

"The arrows were wooden," Crush said after he swallowed. "So they could pass through any metal detector. That's clever. And I don't think they even intended to kill Emil. They just wanted to make a statement."

"But if the whole idea was to get the information out there," Zerbe said, "about my grandfather and the Nazis, why shoot him before he said it?"

"I don't know," Crush said. "And why didn't they release Angela and Noel and Donleavy when they said they would? And then not make any more demands? It doesn't make sense."

"Didn't they find out anything from the guy who shot the arrows?" Frida asked. "The archer?"

Crush looked up at that. "Archer. What was that group you used to play bow and arrows with in prep school? The archery group."

"The Roving Archers of Pasadena," Zerbe said. "They were a bunch of real geeks. And, remember, this is *me* talking. I'm telling you, they were Society-for-Creative-Anachronism-style geeks. Real Renaissance Faire geeks."

"Which one of you practiced with them the most?"

"Noel. And Renee, she was pretty good with a bow." Zerbe stopped. "You don't think..."

"I don't know. But everybody who had something to do with Renee's disappearance—you, Noel, Angela—you've all been targeted."

"And you, Crush," Zerbe said pointing to his arm. "Maybe those arrows were only shot at my father to bring you out into the open. Maybe they were really aiming for you."

"But there were other people there," Gail said, "that night at the Devil's Gate Dam?"

"Yes," Crush said. "Sonny Kraus. He killed himself. PTSD. And Evan Gibbard."

"Is he okay?" Gail asked.

"I don't know."

"Can you call him?"

"He doesn't believe in cell phones." Crush checked the Felix the Cat clock over the stove. It was almost five o'clock. "But I have an appointment with him. In an hour."

CHAPTER NINETEEN

It had started to rain. A light, misty shower that the rest of the country wouldn't even notice but Angelenos call a downpour. It had just started to fall when Crush walked the long, narrow wooden pedestrian bridge on Flint Canyon Trail and turned onto Oak Grove Drive, where it ran over the top of Devil's Gate Dam.

The dam curved slightly to the right. It was dark this time of year at six o'clock. A few streetlamps threw pools of light along the path, with splashes of darkness between them. The only other light came from passing headlights from the 210 Freeway, which ran parallel to the dam.

Evan Gibbard sat on the sidewalk in one of the dark patches between streetlights. As the headlights washed over him, he turned to look at Crush, and when the lights moved on, he seemed to vanish. When the next headlights hit him Evan was standing up, leaning against the concrete railing. The illusion that he had suddenly popped into another place, without even moving, gave Crush a chill. He brushed it aside. Evan wasn't a ghost. That much he knew.

Crush walked into the light of a streetlamp and stopped. He let the light work for him.

"Did you come here alone?" Evan asked, though he could

clearly see the empty road stretching off behind Crush.

"You said to."

Evan stayed in the darkness. He was invisible one moment, and the next, the headlights showed that he had moved three steps closer.

"Well," Crush said, "where are they?"

Evan stopped. "Who do you mean?"

"Angela. Noel. Donleavy. You know."

Evan stepped into the edge of the light cast by Crush's streetlamp. "What are you talking about?"

"I thought we came here for the truth?" Crush asked. "What's the truth, Evan?"

Evan looked down at the rain falling on the curb. "It's complicated."

"This isn't a Facebook status page. This is real life. This is as real as it gets."

Evan opened his mouth as if to speak. Then shut it again.

"You can talk, Evan. Remember the ley lines. The Overlords can't hear us."

"I know that," Evan snapped. "I'm not afraid of that."

"What are you afraid of?"

Evan looked ahead. "You."

Crush thought that he should be. But he gestured to his bandaged arm. "Why? Look at me."

"Because you were there. You know."

"Because I was where?" Crush spoke softly. So softly that Evan had to take another step toward him.

"Noel doesn't remember," Evan said. "Not really. He's built himself new memories he likes better. K.C. was too afraid to remember anything. And Angela was too drunk. But you...you remember."

Crush shook his head. "I don't remember much."

Evan leveled his eyes at Crush. "I'm glad you lied to me. It makes it easier."

Crush did his best to look confused. "Okay. But really, where are they? Just tell me."

"They're safe," Evan said.

Until that moment, Crush held out hope that Evan was just harmlessly crazy. Now he knew. He was anything but harmless. "Safe?"

"As long as the bullet train doesn't go through."

"But Emil said...."

Evan cut him off. "I don't trust Emil Zerbe. As long as he's alive he might make it happen."

"And after he's dead? Don't you think other people will pick it up?"

Evan smiled. "Maybe. But they'll have their own plans. Their own routes. It'll be all right."

Crush had so many questions running through his head. "So you're going to keep holding them until Emil dies?"

"Which would have been much sooner if you hadn't messed things up," Evan snapped.

"I'm sorry," Crush said. "How did you get the Targeted Individuals to work with you? Why did they do it?"

Evan looked impatient with Crush, as if he was a dull student in an advanced class. "Why did they do it? Because they had to. Emil Zerbe is one of the Overlords. We had to stop him. We had to make a statement."

Crush lost his patience. "Are you really crazy? Or are you just pretending to be crazy so you can use them?"

Evan laughed. "You might ask the same thing about Sonny Kraus. Was he really crazy, or did he just kill himself to make us think he was crazy?"

Crush didn't want to let himself be distracted. "Tell me why you're doing this. Why do you care whether the bullet train is built or not? Is that part of the Overlords' take-over-the-world plan?" He looked out into the darkness. He could feel the soft rain blowing over the Hahamongna Watershed and onto his face. Then it came to him.

"*'The GV is dead. The SG is out of the HSR,'* " Crush said. "The GV stands for the Grapevine. This route. The one that goes up the Grapevine along the 210. *That's* what you want to stop, isn't it?" Evan stepped back into the darkness, and Crush knew he'd struck a nerve. "But why?" Crush went on. "Do you really care about that Least Bell's bird?"

"Do you want to know the truth?" Evan asked, half in light, half in shadow.

"That's why I came here."

"But do you *really* want to know the truth? I could tell you, but then I'd have to kill you." Evan stepped into the light and Crush saw that he was holding a pistol. A Glock 9mm from the look of it. "Seriously."

"Well, you have to kill me anyway, am I right?"

Evan grinned. "You're right. Move." He gestured with the gun.

"Where?"

He pulled a flashlight from his pocket and shone it down the steep staircase that led to the Devil's Gate. "There."

"Oh, sure," Crush said. "Can I have the flashlight, though? I might break my neck."

Evan considered this. "I'll chance that," he said and gestured for him to move.

Crush walked to the end of the bridge, with Evan moving behind him, training the flashlight on the path. They climbed over the concrete railing and clambered down to the steep staircase that led to the bottom of the Arroyo Seco.

Treading carefully on the cement stairs, hoping the rain didn't get worse, Crush said, "Say, why not tell me now," as if to pass the time. "You can pretend you're at a meeting."

"A meeting?"

"You know," said Crush, "a Targeted Individual meeting. Say it. My name is Evan and I'm...."

"A Targeted Individual," Evan said completing the mantra. "Okay. I want to talk about it, actually. I've kept it in so long. And I know it will be safe to tell you."

Why would it be safe? Crush wondered. "Because we're at a meeting."

"Sure," Evan said, noncommittally. "You see, she wanted to run away. She wanted to start a new life."

"Renee?" Crush asked.

But he just went on as if Crush hadn't said a thing. "She came to us. To Sonny and me. We were good with fake IDs and all that stuff. She thought we could make her a new identity. Like a witness-protection program or something. Well, we didn't know where to start, but we said 'sure.' We thought we'd make some shit up. The first step was to put her in a safe place. A motel room somewhere. Where we'd have her all to ourselves."

Have her all to ourselves. Crush felt his stomach churn with rage. But he just said, "Uh-huh. Then what?"

"Well, that was when they were searching everywhere for her. When they arrested you even. It was kind of funny when you think about it, because all this shit was going down and she was safe in a motel room in Alhambra. You know?"

"Sure," Crush said. He remembered that time well. He didn't think it was funny.

"But then...Sonny, he got a little rough with her, I guess. You know how he is. Or was. He got tired of waiting for her to stop crying about her father and the Nazis and show him some appreciation for...you know, for all we were doing for her. She started to chicken out. And when she heard about the trouble you were in, on account of her, she decided she wanted to go home. Sonny got mad. He said she'd better not tell that we were involved. She said she'd tell anybody anything she wanted to. Sonny told her to quiet down. He smacked her. He started to...take advantage of her. She fought him off. She scratched his face. He hit her. Hard. I tried to break them up. To calm her down. I tried, but...."

"But you killed her," Crush said.

"I didn't! It wasn't me! It was...." He stopped himself and took a breath. "It wasn't *either* of us. It was an accident. It just happened. Something got into our brains. You know? You believe that, don't you?"

Crush could see it all. How they had taken advantage of Renee's mental state to keep her prisoner. To do God-knows-what to her and then to kill her when she got unruly. He felt anger flood every muscle in his body. He wanted to twist around and throw Evan off this steep, treacherous staircase onto the hard dirt below. To rip the bandage from his arm and feel Evan's flesh and bone collapse under his fists.

But not now. He had to know where Evan was leading him. He had to find out where the others were.

"Sure," was all he said.

"After that, what could we do? Really, what could we do? We had to get rid of her. You can see that? We had to get rid of her body."

"And what better place than the place they'd just searched."

"That's right! And where they'd found nothing. The watershed. That's what *I* said. It was the perfect place to hide her. Nobody will *ever* look there."

"Unless they dig it up to build a railroad."

Evan's voice dropped. "Yes. Well, we did it. We hid the

body. We buried her."

Crush thought of Renee decaying and turning to dust, forgotten and alone, buried somewhere in that windswept plain. His hot anger turned ice cold. And determined.

"Well, after that things started to go wrong with our lives," Evan said.

"After that, huh?"

"Yeah. We went to college but we just couldn't find anything to focus on. We graduated. We joined Blackwater. Sonny did well for them, but he got lost I think.... He liked it too much. You know?"

"I think I know." A killer like Sonny would be right at home with Blackwater.

"And when we got back, he just couldn't fit in, you know? Started doing drugs and shit. I mean, *more* drugs. It got out of control. He started going to that Targeted Individual group, which I thought was pretty crazy at first. I mean, at first I just went along to take care of *him*. And to make sure he didn't say too much. But after a while, it started to make all the sense in the world. There *were* evil forces in the world. We'd seen them."

Yes, you certainly have, thought Crush as he descended the rain-splattered stairs.

Evan kept on. "Then we heard about the bullet train. How Emil Zerbe was going to build it. And where. Sonny started to lose it. He got obsessed with the idea that the body would be discovered. He said we should go and find it. Move it to some other place. He went to look for it. But the only thing is, there are no landmarks on that goddamned watershed. Every place looks the same. *So he couldn't find it*. And he kept going back, again and again. Digging up the whole damn place. In broad daylight even. He was going to give us *away*. So I had to..."

"Yeah," Crush agreed, "you had to."

"I made it look like he killed himself. Which wasn't hard. He'd been acting pretty crazy for years. After that, I thought things would calm down. I thought I could take a breath. But then I read that the damn train was definitely going through. It was in the papers, on the news, in the news-feed on my phone. They were going to start digging the place up *next month*. Well, I had to do *something*. I gathered the Irregulars—that's what I called my Targeted Individual friends—and explained to them that Emil Zerbe was one of the Overlords and that his damn bullet train was really a mind-control project. It had to be stopped at all costs."

Crush reached the bottom of the stairs and turned to face Evan. "So this isn't even about the Nazis," Crush said. "Or the Overlords. It's about covering up for a murder." He tried to control his fury, to make his voice sound calm. He didn't do a very good job.

Evan looked offended. "This most certainly *is* about the Overlords. And the Nazis."

"Then why did you make that guy start shooting at Emil before he finished his confession? Because you were more concerned with killing him than exposing the truth."

"No. That's not true. The murder is a part of it, I admit, but only a part of it. That was just the starting point. That was the way they tried to control us. To control our minds."

"By getting you to kill Renee?"

"Exactly. They got into our heads. But we outsmarted them. We have them on the run now."

"I can see that."

"Where was I? Oh, yes. Next I talked Noel into leading his brother into my trap—to protect K.C. from the Overlords, of course. I thought Emil would agree to stop the train to save K.C. Shows what I know. When that didn't work, I decided to grab Angela and Noel."

"And Donleavy?"

"She was just collateral damage."

"And how did you find the archer?"

"The Targeted Individual Group is full of people with special talents," Evan said. Then he looked at Crush as if he were considering something. "Turn around."

"Why?"

"Just turn around."

"I need to know why. Because, if you're going to shoot me, fine, but if you're going to hit me with that gun butt and try to knock me out, I have to ask you not to. My head just won't take it. I have a concussion."

Evan looked a little uncertain.

"Look," Crush said, "wherever you want to take me, I'll just go there. I'll close my eyes if you don't want to me to see. It's just that if you hit me again, you might kill me, and if you want to kill me you might as well shoot me, you know? It's quicker."

Evan looked frustrated. "I don't want to kill you. Yet."

"Then come on, do me this solid. Let's just pretend you knocked me out and I'll walk where you want. That way you won't have to carry me. I weigh a lot. You wouldn't like it."

Evan gestured with the gun and led them across the floor of the dry riverbed to the Devil's Gate itself. The gate stood open and the dark tunnel was quiet and ominous, just the way Crush remembered it.

"What happened with Will?"

"Oh, that," Evan sounded annoyed. "I told him to go and kill K.C. if he could find him. I never thought K.C. would kill *him*. Just goes to show you, you never know what will happen." Evan walked up to the iron gate and swung it open.

"Anyway, the important thing is, I needed to stop that train, once and for all. And I did."

"Once," Crush said. "Not for all. Emil will change his mind."

"I know," Evan said. "That's why we have to prove to him that we mean business." He waved his gun toward the tunnel. "This way."

Crush entered the darkness, feeling a sense of dread and nausea, not only for what he feared he was going to find but for what he had not found so many years before.

Only this time there was a light at the end of tunnel. Or halfway down the tunnel, anyway. A Coleman fluorescent lantern sat on a cardboard table in the middle of the path. It illuminated the bricks of the tunnel and a lone woman standing at attention, holding a pistol awkwardly in her hand. Against the wall were three figures tied to chairs, with bags over their heads.

"What are you doing?" asked the woman. "I thought you were going to—I didn't think you were going to knock him out, but I thought you were going to knock him out?" Crush recognized her at once as Amy from the Targeted Individuals group. The first one he heard testify. Her speech patterns were unmistakable. She waved her gun around like it was a toy. It looked like a Korriphila from Germany. A mean gun.

"It's fine," Evan said. "He came along willingly."

One of the hooded figures sat up. Amy swatted it with her hand. "Down when I say down!" She looked at Evan. "What are we supposed to do with them?"

"Don't worry. I have a plan. Just keep an eye on them. Especially that one." He pointed to the figure that Crush guessed was Donleavy. At least it looked the most like her. The figure reached its hands out in front and Crush could see they were zip-tied together. "I told you to put their hands behind their backs!" Evan snapped.

Amy looked like she was about to lose it. "Hey, I'm only one person! You have me guarding these three Overlords and I have my hands literally full here! Not just full but full! Excuse me if I don't get every little detail right!"

Evan sighed. "I'm sorry. I didn't mean to micromanage. Now bring that chair over here."

Amy brought the lone empty chair over and sat Crush down on it. Out of the corner of his eye, Crush saw that, with her guard distracted, Donleavy was getting to work. She was bent over and had started to untie her shoelaces. Good. Now if Crush could just keep Evan's and Amy's attention focused on *him*, Donleavy might have the chance she needed.

"Do you have any water?" Crush asked. "I could use a drink of water."

"No, we don't have water," Evan said. "What do you think this is, a five-star...." Amy picked up a bottle of Arrowhead from the table. Then she put it back down. Evan saw her and said, exasperated, "Well, give him the water. He sees it now. If it's here, give it to him."

Crush watched while Donleavy skootched the hood off her face and used her teeth to thread the shoelace through the zip tie that bound her hands. She knew how to get out of zip-tie handcuffs, given enough time. Time was what they all needed.

"Cover me," Evan said to Amy as he crossed to the table and picked up the voice modifier. "Now we're going to make a call. Give me your phone."

"Okay," Crush said, reaching into his back pocket with his bandaged arm, making it look as difficult as possible. "I'm just getting my phone. Nothing else. You hear that?" he said pointedly at Amy and her gun. "Don't shoot me. Not yet, anyway."

He tried not to look at Donleavy as she bent over and tied

the lace she had threaded through the zip tie to the lace that was still in her other shoe.

Crush handed his phone to Evan. Evan told Crush, "Now you're going to call Emil Zerbe. You're going to tell him that his children will be held prisoner until the day he dies."

"What?" Amy asked. "We can't keep them until he dies. Until he *dies* dies?"

"Shut up," Evan said. He turned his attention back to Crush. "That is what you'll say. Tell him he cannot change his mind about the bullet train."

"I can't," Crush said.

"You can and you will."

Still leaning over, Donleavy grabbed her other shoelace and tied the two of them together.

"No, I really can't, he's in surgery," Crush explained. "You had him shot with arrows, remember?"

Evan swallowed. "When will he be out?"

Crush shrugged. "Not for hours, I don't think. Maybe tomorrow?"

"Well, what do we do now?" Amy asked. "I can't live like this. This is a stupid way to live!"

"Be quiet!" Evan said. "All right, then you'll call K.C. He'll have to deliver the message to his father. We have to prove to Emil that we mean business!"

"You keep saying that, but this isn't really business, is it?" Crush was trying to annoy Evan, to keep him engaged and looking at Crush and not at Donleavy. "It's more like a crusade, wouldn't you say?"

Donleavy had the shoelaces tied to the zip tie in the shape of a T. She lifted her legs and bent her knees. And waited.

"Shut up," Evan said. "Do what I say!"

"I can do that," Crush said, agreeably. "I can call Zerbe

and tell him that. Exactly that."

Satisfied, Evan examined Crush's phone. "He's under my favorites," offered Crush, helpfully. "Under Z. For Zerbe."

"I can see that," Evan said. He took the voice modifier and held it to his mouth. "Don't speak until I tell you to."

"Right," Crush said. Evan pressed the speed-dial number, held the phone up to Crush's face, and listened to it ring.

The screen flickered to life. Zerbe's face filled the monitor. "Crush! You're using FaceTime! I don't believe it. What's up?"

Evan spoke through the voice modifier. "Hello, K.C. Zerbe. Do you recognize this voice?"

"Fuck," Zerbe said. "It's the goddamned kidnapper." Gail's and Frida's faces filled the screen, and there was a commotion on the other end of the line. Donleavy used that distraction to begin. She kicked her legs from side to side, trying to saw the shoelace against the zip ties and break the plastic. She didn't have quite enough time. The hum of conversation on the phone ended with Zerbe coming back into view, and Donleavy had to stop.

"What the hell do you want?" Zerbe asked.

"Crush has something to say to you," Evan said in his best pop-star voice. He gestured to Crush to begin.

"Hey Zerbe?" Crush said with a smile.

"How are you, Crush?"

"You know. Been better."

"What happened?"

"I ran into a bit of a snag here."

"Was it Evan?"

Evan shook his head off-screen at Crush.

"No, it's not Evan. Definitely not Evan. Anybody but Evan. The thing is...they, whoever 'they' are, have your brother and your sister. And Donleavy, too, although nobody seems to care much about her. He wants you to tell your father that he's going to keep them, as a guarantee that Emil never builds the bullet train."

With the conversation occupying everyone's attention, Donleavy started sawing on the zip tie again.

"What does that mean?" Zerbe asked. "Is he going to keep them prisoner?"

"Yes, I think that's what it means."

"What? He's going to keep them forever?"

"Apparently. Or at least until your father dies."

"I don't think he can do that," Zerbe said. "Can he do that? Won't somebody track them down? He can't be serious."

Evan spoke up. "I am serious. I'll show you how serious this is." With that, Evan raised his pistol up to Crush's head and pulled the trigger.

CHAPTER TWENTY

One second before, Donleavy had snapped the zip tie and leapt out of her chair, diving for Evan and his gun. She struck his arm just as Evan pulled the trigger. The barrel skidded against Crush's head as the gun fired. The report boomed like thunder in the close confines of the tunnel. Crush fell to the ground, limp.

Amy was taken by surprise by all of this, but she came up guns literally blazing at Donleavy. What she lacked in precision, she made up for in sheer volume. Donleavy was struck in the side, but spun around and rushed on Amy, pushing the gun to the side and pulling her down to the ground. Frightened, Amy struggled free and raced off.

Lying on the floor, blood pooling from the wound to her side, Donleavy thought she was pretty much done for the day. Crush lay motionless at the foot of the chair. Amy was gone. Angela and Noel were still tied up. Only Evan was still in motion, standing up stunned and shaking his head. The Glock was still in his hand.

There wasn't much that Donleavy could do other than push over the card table with the lantern on it and hope that darkness would help even the score. So she reached up and flipped the table. The lantern clattered to the floor and went rolling off. The scene was thrown, if not into blackness, at least into twilight.

Evan took a blind step. Crush pushed himself up and blinked, wondering if he had a bullet hole in his skull. The report of the gun had caused a tinny ringing in his ears that continued to chime. He was blinded, both from the dimness of the light and the blood streaming down into his eyes. He felt effectively helpless.

But as Evan moved, he tripped over Crush's legs and fell to the ground. Crush threw himself forward onto Evan's body and felt blindly for his arm. And the gun. He gripped the cold metal of the Glock, twisted it, and threw it away. It clattered off into the darkness.

Crush grabbed for Evan's throat, but Evan scuttled out of his grasp. He scrambled away, and Crush crawled off in pursuit. Evan made it to his feet and ran, stumbling through the tunnel. Crush clawed up the wall, wiped the blood from his eyes, and felt for his brain oozing out of his head. His skull seemed to be in one piece. The bullet had merely grazed him.

He took off in a shuffling run after Evan. Every footstep was a jarring earthquake in Crush's brain. His skull could barely contain the throbbing pain.

Rain started pelting his face. He ran out of the tunnel and onto the broad expanse of the Hahamongna Watershed. The rain was falling hard now. The ringing in his ears diminished, and he heard the sound of the raindrops hitting the grass. Then the sound of Evan's running feet, just ahead of him. Crush strained to catch up, but he was too exhausted. Digging down for some last vestige of strength, the most he could do was try to keep pace with him.

Evan was getting away. The man who killed Renee Zerbe and buried her like so much garbage somewhere in this field was getting away. Crush felt a raging fury rise in his chest.

This man who had caused all this madness to fall upon them was getting away. And there was nothing he could do about it.

He heard a crazy cacophony of chittering cries and screams coming from above them. Evan heard it, too. He looked up at the night sky. An undulating black mass hovered above. Like a cloud, or a haze of smoke, that seemed to be coming down on them. Evan looked up in terror and stumbled, falling to the ground.

Crush saw his final chance. He ran forward and threw himself on top of Evan. The two of them struggled in the mud, Evan trying to push his fingers into Crush's eye sockets, Crush grabbing for Evan's throat. Crush missed and his fingers dug into the mud. They felt the hard roughness of a stone. He grasped the rock and raised it above his head....

⌘

Crush limped back into the tunnel. He picked up the fallen lantern and looked for his cell phone. Once he found it, he called 911, praying that there were more signal towers now than there had been in 2001 and that the call would go through.

The call went through. Crush told them where he was. He told them there were at least two injured people. Maybe three. Then he ended the call and sat down next to Donleavy.

"How are you doing?" Crush asked.

"I got shot," Donleavy said. "That's never good. But I stopped the bleeding."

"Help will be here soon," Crush said. "You'll be okay."

Donleavy grunted. She looked around. "Where's that crazy girl with the gun?"

"She took off, I guess."

"Good riddance. Let me see your head."

Crush lowered his head and let Donleavy see. "How does it look?" he asked.

"You don't want to know," she said. "How are Noel and Angela?"

Crush looked to the rear of the tunnel. They were still sitting with their hoods on. "They look fine."

"You oughta go check on them, you know."

"All right." Crush sighed and got weakly to his feet. His head felt like it had been run over by a steamroller and then flattened by an anvil. "You know, Donleavy, when this thing is over, I think I'm going to get an MRI."

"You do that," Donleavy said. "Grab my pocketknife from the table—the bitch found it in my boot when she tied me up."

Crush got the knife and stumbled over to Angela and Noel and pulled off their hoods. They'd been gagged with duct tape, which explained the blessed silence. He pulled the tape off Angela.

"What the hell is happening?" she asked, terrified.

"It's okay," Crush said. "We're safe."

He yanked the tape off Noel. Noel got more to the point. "That was Evan, wasn't it?"

"Evan?" Angela said. "Why did he do all of this?"

Crush was too tired to explain it. "Because of Renee. And because of the train."

Using Donleavy's knife, Crush cut them free from their zip ties. Noel got up stiffly and walked toward the back of the tunnel. He asked, "Which way did he go?"

"That way. Out to the watershed," Crush said.

Noel started walking that way.

"Don't, Noel," Angela said, alarmed. "He might come back."

Crush put his hand on Angela's arm. "He won't come back," he said.

She looked at him. Grabbing his hand, she said. "Thank you, Caleb."

He leaned down and kissed her fingers. Softly. In memory of another time. The elephant in the room always remembers.

⌘

Noel stood on the rain-swept watershed looking down at the inert body of Evan Gibbard. Crush hobbled up to join him.

"What happened?" Noel asked.

"He was running," Crush said. "Something must have startled him. He stumbled. And fell."

"What happened to his head?"

"He hit it on that rock."

"And it killed him?"

"Yes."

Noel looked at Crush, the rain washing over his face. "Convenient."

"It was."

"What startled him?"

"Oh," Crush said, looking up at the sky. "That was the parrots. They flew right over us. Didn't you hear them squawking?"

Noel nodded gravely. "I heard them. But I didn't recognize them. The psychopomps. The ones who escort the dead to the afterlife."

"If you say so," Crush said. "Anyway, they were screaming bloody murder."

"Yes, they were," Noel agreed.

CHAPTER TWENTY-ONE

Zerbe watched Renee's funeral from the loft on Wilshire, via live-streaming. He thought 'live-streaming' was a rather questionable term for the occasion, but since under the terms of his parole he couldn't attend the service in person, he took what he could get. Frida bought him a dark suit from the local Goodwill and the two of them watched the service on his laptop, sitting on the sofa holding hands.

The service was held in the Wee Kirk o' the Heather at Forest Lawn, Glendale, a perfect replica of a quaint Scottish church. Ronald Reagan was married there, for the first time anyway. Jean Harlow and Carole Lombard had their funerals there. So did Walt Disney, Errol Flynn, and George Burns. More Hollywood royalty had passed through that nondenominational church than through Grauman's Chinese Theatre.

Zerbe could see pictures of Renee as Rose Queen, displayed around the urn that contained her ashes. It was all very tasteful.

Back in January, the police had spent a week searching through Hahamongna, looking for some trace of her body. They were about to give up when they brought in cadaver dogs, which sniffed something and started digging. That seemed appropriate. Renee had always liked dogs.

It took about six weeks to get a positive DNA identification and another month to discover how she died and yet another month to decide that there was nothing to be done about it, so it was nearly May before Renee Zerbe was finally laid to her eternal rest.

Zerbe could see that the funeral was well attended, despite being about seventeen years overdue. Quite a few of her high school friends had come to bid her a last farewell and, of course, all the Zerbes were there. Renee's mother sat in the front row, weeping, finally able to achieve some closure, if only of the bitterest kind. Samantha, Angela, and Noel sat with her, offering her what comfort they could. Emil sat off to the side in his wheelchair, alone and stone-faced. Zerbe couldn't see Crush or Gail, but he knew they were there, probably standing in the back, ready to make a quick exit. Crush didn't like funerals.

When the funeral ended, the screen went blank. Zerbe shut his laptop, put Jackie Wilson on the stereo, and made a couple of fried-egg sandwiches for himself and Frida. Then they talked about life. About Zerbe's new parole officer and what a dick he was. About how Zerbe was going to be finished with his sentence by the end of the year and how the first thing he was going to do when he was free was get a chili dog at Pink's on La Brea, then go to Disneyland and go on the Haunted Mansion and the Pirates of the Caribbean rides. They talked about Frida's new job as a teacher at an inner-city grade school and how much she loved it. When they were done talking, they went into Crush's bedroom and shut the door. Crush's bed was more comfortable than Zerbe's.

Two hours later Crush and Gail walked in. "Where's Zerbe?" Gail asked.

Crush pointed to his bedroom door.

"Again?" Gail asked, rolling her eyes.

"Give 'em a break," he said. "It's been a while. For both of them."

Gail wanted to say it had been a while for her, too, but she thought better of it. Instead she asked. "How's your head?"

Crush looked out the window over MacArthur Park. "May Gray" was settling in, and the city looked like it was in perpetual twilight. "My head's fine. It's tired of you asking about it."

"It's just that you didn't talk all the way home."

"All the way home from a funeral," he said. "Don't forget the funeral part."

Gail pressed her lips together. "Do you want to talk about it?"

Crush pressed his forehead against the windowpane. "I really don't."

He set the urn down on the pool table. "Why the hell did she give it to me?"

"I don't know, Crush," she said. "Maybe she trusts you." In the parking lot at Forest Lawn, Valerie Zerbe had stopped and handed Crush the urn. All she said was, "You take care of her, Caleb," before she walked off.

"What does she want me to do with it?" Crush asked.

"She wants you to take care of her."

"Stop calling it 'her,' " Crush snapped. "I don't even think it's legal for me to have this. Don't I have to file some kind of papers?"

"You're not adopting her. You're just making room for her on your bookshelf."

Crush looked at the smooth metal urn. "I didn't take care of her. Not when it mattered."

Gail put her hand on his shoulder. "You tried. You saved

her on the bridge. You chased after her. And in the end, you found her."

"I didn't find her. A dog found her."

"You told them where to look."

"I wasn't her guardian angel."

"No," Gail said. "You were just the best friend she had."

Crush shut his eyes. "A pretty lousy best."

"Sometimes that's all you can hope for."

She bent down and kissed Crush on his scarred bald head. "You want me to stay?" She had moved into a new apartment in Boyle Heights, and she was teaching at a dojo near Hazard Park. Things were looking up for her.

"No, I'm fine," he said. "You go along home."

When she'd left, Crush got up and went over to the bookshelf. He grabbed some of Zerbe's polyhedral dice from his old Dungeons & Dragons set, rattled them in their cup, and tossed them across the pool table in front of Renee's urn.

He looked at the scattered numbers and weird symbols on the dice. "I have no idea how to play this damn game." He sighed. "But I guess I'm going to have to learn, huh?"

The urn sat on the pool table and did not respond.

ACKNOWLEDGMENTS

Robert Petersen, whose "The Hidden History of Los Angeles" podcast is a constant delight and who kindly helped me trace the histories of the Devil's Gate Dam and the Irwindale craters.

Beverly Stansbury and Fiesta Parade Floats, who assisted me with the details of the Tournament of Roses Parade and the building of parade floats.

Roseschel Sinio of Li'l Book Bug Bookstore in Lancaster, California, who helped me with the Musical Road.

Colleen Dunn Bates, my beloved publisher and editor, who gave me more time than she should have and whose fine eye made this a better book. Assistant editor Dorie Bailey's fine eye helped, too.

Ronnie Wise, who helped me understand Dungeons & Dragons.

Chris Lackey and Chad Fifer, whose "H.P. Lovecraft Literary Podcast" provided inspiration and psychopomps.

Mark Jordan Legan, who contributed friendship, movie nights, and help with Targeted Individuals.

W.L. Ripley, who read this book and offered much needed advice.

My writing group: Naomi Hirahara, Gar Anthony Williams,

Miriam Trogdon, Gracie Charters, and Sharon Calkin.

Lee Goldberg, for inspiring me constantly.

Pat Lenz, for her help and guidance.

And finally, my dear wife, Dawn Bodnar-Sutton, who read this book more often than is humanly possible and who helped me shape it. I couldn't have done it without her.

ABOUT THE AUTHOR

Phoef Sutton is a novelist, television writer, and playwright whose work has won two Emmys, a Peabody, a Writers Guild Award, a GLAAD Award, and a Television Academy Honors Award. The first novel in his Crush mystery series, *Crush*, was a *Kirkus* Best Mystery of 2015 and a *Los Angeles Times* "Summer Reading Page-Turner." The second in the series, *Heart Attack and Vine*, was named one of *Milwaukee Journal- Sentinel*'s "Best Books of 2016" and a *Kirkus* Best Mystery of 2016.

Sutton has been an executive producer of *Cheers*, a writer/ producer for such shows as *Boston Legal* and *NewsRadio*, a writer for *Terriers*, and the creator of several TV shows, including the cult hit *Thanks*. He is also the co-author, with Janet Evanovich, of *Curious Minds* and *Wicked Charms*, both *New York Times* bestsellers. His other novels include the romantic thriller *15 Minutes to Live;* coming in 2018 is the novel *From Away*. Sutton lives with his family in South Pasadena, California.